Lady (Sydney) Morgan

Lady Morgan's memoirs: autobiography, diaries, and

correspondence

Lady (Sydney) Morgan

Lady Morgan's memoirs: autobiography, diaries, and correspondence

ISBN/EAN: 9783742832375

Manufactured in Europe, USA, Canada, Australia, Japa

Cover: Foto ©Raphael Reischuk / pixelio.de

Manufactured and distributed by brebook publishing software
(www.brebook.com)

Lady (Sydney) Morgan

Lady Morgan's memoirs: autobiography, diaries, and

correspondence

COLLECTION

OF

BRITISH AUTHORS

TAUCHNITZ EDITION.

.

VOL. 639.

LADY MORGAN'S MEMOIRS.

IN THREE VOLUMES.

VOL. 3.

LEIPZIG: BERNHARD TAUCHNITZ.

PARIS: LIBRAIRIE C. REINWALD, 15, RUE DES SAINTS-PÈRES.
PARIS: THE GALIGNANI LIBRARY, 224, RUE DE RIVOLI,
AND AT NICE, 48, QUAI ST. JEAN BAPTISTE.

COLLECTION

OF

BRITISH AUTHORS.

VOL. 639.

LADY MORGAN'S MEMOIRS.

IN THREE VOLUMES.

VOL. III.

LADY MORGAN'S MEMOIRS:

AUTOBIOGRAPHY,

DIARIES AND CORRESPONDENCE.

COPYRIGHT EDITION.

IN THREE VOLUMES.

VOL. III.

LEIPZIG

BERNHARD TAUCHNITZ

1863.

CONTENTS

OF VOLUME III

———

LADY MORGAN'S MEMOIRS.

CHAPTER I.

THE YEAR 1825.

In the year 1825, Lady Morgan, for the first time, began to keep a diary, and from this date the account of her life will be chiefly drawn from the entries in her diaries. For a year or more, these entries are somewhat barren of incident; they are occupied with mere reflections, and with the rough draft of an autobiography afterwards more fully developed, and given in the first volume. A brief extract from the diaries 1825, 1826, will suffice for the general reader — the paragraphs, like so many others of Lady Morgan's papers, have no date. The first would appear to have been written in April, or early in May, of the year 1825.

Letters from Italy state that the tribunals of Austria have just condemned to death Count Confalonieri, the Marquis Pallavicini, M. Castiglioni, Colonel Moretti, and three young students. The crimes imputed to these individuals, who are held in the highest estimation in Italy, are not even looked on as faults there, as, according to the letters alluded to, they consist only in the explicit manifestation on their part of the aversion

which all Italians entertain for the domination of
Austria as their country. My poor Confalonieri! how
little, when I knew him bright and brilliant in Italy,
did he dream of this day of darkness in store for him!
Even if his doom be commuted into *carcere duro*, it
will be almost worse than death.

May 4.— Received the affecting news of Dénon's
death, he was only ill fifteen hours. He was nearly
eighty.

Lord Archibald Hamilton is dead. I first met him
chez the Duchess of Sussex, 1811. He was then rather
a *ci-devant*, but an epitome of rank and fashion. He
was much in love with the sister of the Duchess of
Sussex. His mind was enlightened, his spirit independent, and he was full of integrity. He was a man
of kindly temperament, and he will be much missed,
especially in Scotland.

Journey to London. — Struck by the changed phy-
siognomies of the population — more intelligent-look-
ing and less well fed. Blessings of science and all-
pervading illumination staring one in the face at every
mile through the Welsh mountains — their romanticism
disappearing — their civilization increasing.

St. Albans and its delicious abbey!

London. — Curious visitors — General Pepe, the
Neapolitan chief, and all the young revolutionary
leaders of Piedmont and Lombardy, — the eldest but
twenty-nine, — with me every day, and talking of
erecting a statue to me when Italy shall be free —
hélas! Sir Robert Wilson called on me; mild and inter-
esting-looking; speaking well, but with gravity; must
have been, and indeed is still, very handsome. General
Pepe most affected of all the Italians I have seen by

the disasters of Naples. Lady Caroline Lamb called,
— quite comical, talking religion, and offering me
half-a-dozen of her Pages. Went to Miss White's assembly; found her in the midst of a brilliant crowd,
dying of the dropsy. Many persons presented to me
of notoriety, Washington Irving, author of *The Sketch
Book;* the Magnus Apollo of the *bas bleus* — Hallam,
author of *The Middle Ages.* Moore (Anacreon) called
to-day; said "Murray raves of you, not as an author
only, *entendez vous*, but as a woman." When I told
this to Colburn, he looked aghast. I said to him,
"Colburn, I observed to Mr. Moore, that I hoped my
conquest would get me a good price for my next book."
"Did you say that?" exclaimed Colburn, in a pathetic
tone. His fear of *his* author, is like the Irish Quaker's
complaint, of "somebody having taken his drumstick
from him."

Went to St. James's Palace to see Mrs. Boscawen,
the Queen's maid-of-honour. [The Mrs. Boscawen
referred to was Anne, daughter of General the Honourable George Boscawen, and grand-daughter of Hugh,
first Viscount Falmouth. She was born in 1744, and
died in 1831.] Found her niched in the old court
garret with a most fantastical little balcony, and terrace
full of plants, flowers, and foreign birds. She was delighted to see me; talked of my books, and offered me
a bouquet in return for all the charming things she
had read of mine; — full of old court news, and of the
King's going to throw down her apartments; — could
talk of nothing else, and of her waylaying the King on
his departure for Ireland. Spoke of nursing him in
his youth; — knew Mrs. Delany: — told me she had
a great desire to go to Lady Pepy's blue-stocking

parties. Her companion is Miss Tickell, descendant of the poet. Collation at St. James's with Mrs. Boscawent; — went through the palace. I met Mrs. Boscawen a fortnight after; — took up the account of the rooms; she called Lady Cork "her fellow-servant." Miss Porter, mild and unaffected; Mr. Place, the Templar, worth all the rest; — Holland House, the school of political corruption, spoilt all the young men; — Miss Benger, tall, thin.

At Miss White's dinner; — Porson (not the author of the *Parody*) and Milman were there; — W. Spencer reminded me he knew me at Lisburne; — Mrs. Somerville, a celebrated mathematician, young and prettyish; — Mrs. Marcett, the political economist, getting hold of W. Spencer and preaching Christianity to him, wishing him to go to church at Geneva, that he might be converted through the pretty women; — General Church there, it is well I had not Pepe with me!

Ugo Foscolo dined with us at Mrs. Brown's; — full of paradoxes, — hated Italian music, — cried over my Irish song; — his account of his novel *Jacopo Ortis*, all true; — was six times more in love than he described; — defended England's conduct to Italy; — cried down the Whigs for originating the present system. He despised the society *du bon ton* of London; — it only gave him the trouble of writing apologies.

Went with Lady Caroline to Miss White's.

London, Bury Street, St. James. — *June* 15. — Yesterday's campaign we had thousands of Italians who came to pay their *devoirs*, amongst others, Castiglione, as handsome as ever; — the Marquis de Prie, a very elegant young man. At seven o'clock we set off to our dinner-party at the Macneil's. The company were, the Hon. Charles Brownlow, M. P., who made the famous Protestant speech a little while ago; Mr. and Mrs. Horace Twiss, the nephew to John Kemble; Mr. Douglas Kinnaird, brother to Lord Dunsany; Mr. Edwards, son of Kensington, and Mrs. Alexander, daughter of the Bishop of Meath. A few people came in the evening; we left at past eleven o'clock, and set off for Lord Listowel's Kensington Gore, which we did not reach till near twelve. Their company had left, and they were all dressed themselves to go to a ball; we staid a little time, and then went on to Lydia White's, and although it was long past twelve, we found the invalid lying on her couch in the midst of her party; Sidney Smith, of the *Edinburgh*, and *the* wit, *par excellence*. What a difference in the political thermometer? our dinner redhot orange, and our *soirée* of the coolest *green*, where it was not *blue!*

June 17. — To-day, dinner at Lady Cork's; there never was anything to equal the splendour of her entertainments and her rooms. In the evening we went on to Lydia White's, thence to Mrs. Burton's.

Carlton House was on fire the other night; there was one roomed burned, but they succeeded in extinguishing it before it did any more mischief.

The King was in the house at the time, and he held a levee the next morning.

I saw a warming pan at Strawberry Hill, the other day, which had belonged to Charles II.; there is on it the following motto, "Sarve God and live for ever;" the date 1660 — the period when his love for Barbara Palmer, afterwards Duchess of Cleveland, was in its first bloom.

This is all of the diary 1825, which the general reader will perhaps care to have. The following letters from Colonel Webster, son of Lady Holland, and aid-de-camp to Lord Wellesley, the other from the ever attractive Madame Jerome Bonaparte, continue the amusing gossip of the day.

The chief event in her affairs of this year was, that in August 22, 1825, *Salvator Rosa* came to a second edition; but Lady Morgan and Colburn had many squabbles together — she complaining of his shabbiness, and he complaining that she was "very hard upon him;" but neither of them wished to separate in their business transactions. He was looking anxiously forwards to a new Irish novel from her, and she was meditating how to make him pay the interest on her increased popularity. She and Sir Charles were, at this period, regular contributors to the *New Monthly* and the *Metropolitan.*

Captain Webster to Lady Morgan.

PARK, AMPTHILL,
September 11, 1825.

MY DEAR LADY MORGAN,

It is an age since I have heard of you, and I really was in hopes when you arrived safe and sound on the other side of the water, that you would have sent me some news of you and yours.

Colonel and Mrs. Dawson are on their way to Buxton to visit Mrs. Fitzherbert, who would not be present at the marriage, but sent her a thousand guineas; the morning after the event, Miss Seymour received a packet from the King, enclosing a charming letter, begging her to be kind to her best friend, Mrs. Fitzherbert, and enclosing a draft for two thousand pounds; after Buxton they go to the Continent. I fear that Uxbridge and his wife will be separated — his temper is too violent, and she does too little to please him; they say that Uxbridge intends to keep the pretty little children, of which he will be heartily tired in six weeks.

I shall hope to hear of you, if you send your letter to Castle it will be forwarded to me; let me know what is going on among you all. I hope you are in your own house again, and that it is done to your satisfaction.

Adieu, pray make my remembrances acceptable to Sir Charles, and believe me

Very sincerely yours,

HENRY W.

Madame Patterson Bonaparte to Lady Morgan.

PARIS,
November 18.

MY DEAR LADY MORGAN,

Mrs. Evans has given me your welcome letter; I cannot express to you how much I was delighted at hearing that you had not forgotten me. I passed only a few months in Italy, where I saw the most beautiful woman in the world, who since died in her *husband's* palace at Florence, surrounded by friends, and conjugally regretted by Prince Borghese! He buried her in the handsomest chapel in Europe. She left a legacy to my son of twenty thousand francs. Voila en peu de mots ci que j'ai a dire de la Princesse Pauline. I have been *pour mes pechés*, a great deal in Geneva — that centre of prudery, heartlessness, and illiberal feelings.

I left it with pleasure, and hope that I never shall return to it. I have paid a short visit to America. "Aux cœurs bien nés la patrie est *chere*," which does not mean that one should not prefer the *séjour* of Paris to that of the dullest place on earth. Lafayette was caressed, adored, and substantially rewarded. I saw him in Baltimore, and talked to him of you, whom he loves and admires, *malgré le temps et l'absence*; Miss Wright was with him, or near him, all the time he was in America. She intends writing *something* of which he is to be the *hero*. Why did Moore destroy Lord Byron's memoirs? It was a breach of confidence — they were intended for publication.

You are very kind in inquiring after my father and my son. The former is living, the latter has grown up handsome — a classical profile, and *un esprit juste*. He is in America. My health is, as usual, neither good nor bad — nerves very tormenting, mind, as formerly, discontented, although I flatter myself that I am growing more patient of injustice and egotism. What do you say of De Genlis? Her memoirs are said to be *peu véridiques*. People seem to be disappointed that she does not relate her gallantries; but of course she thinks, *que cela va sans dire*. One of her *truisms* is, that Madame de Villette was convinced of the truth of the Christian religion — a conviction that our poor dear friend certainly imparted to none of those who lived with her. Genlis has pleased no one by the publication of this work of imagination — the drippings and last squeezings of her brain. She lives at Mantes with Casimir, the boy whom *elle avait ramassé en Alle-magne*. He is infected with her *devotion*, or her hypocrisy, or both.

Poor Dénon is dead; Madame D'Houchin is, I hear, dreadfully grieved at her deplorable *veuvage du cœur*. Nothing can, I think, console for the loss of a person whom one has loved and been loved by. Madame Capodoce is here, regretting poor M. de Brito, who died some time since; she looks dreadfully ill — her husband now lives with her after an absence of thirty years. "Un mari suffit rarement pour remplir le cœur" was said to you by Madame Suard — this *agreeable* person is still living, and *folle comme autrefois*. Do you know a dull writer called Julien, who publishes a periodical paper. I thank Sir Charles for his kisses, which I reciprocate at the same time; but I send my love to him. I hope the gloves fitted — wedding gloves, sent by the Lord-Lieutenant of the Marchioness of Wellesley!!! Was the Duke, Great Bolingbroke, at the wedding? Do contrive to get a letter to me by *une occasion particulière*. I do not like the idea of the police, your readers, receiving what was intended for me. Pray let me know what you are doing, &c., &c. Be assured I shall not slip through your fingers through my negligence. Adieu,

Believe me,

Ever most affectionately, yours,

E. PATTERSON.

PS. — Warden is as usual; he never leaves the Faubourg St. Germain. I have no doubt that he has *un sentiment* — nothing else could keep any one there. What do you think of Miss Harriet Wilson's life, written by herself? Every one reads it. She is living in Paris, which seems to be the favourite residence of all naughty English women. Miss Harriet is mar-

ried to a very handsome man, who was willing to make
an honest woman of her. I have fifty scandalous
things to tell you; but I write in haste that I may
send my letter to England by a friend. I have been
in Paris only a few days; I have seen no one. All
the people whom I knew are dead or absent.

CHAPTER II.

THE YEAR 1826.

DURING this year, Lady Morgan's chief employment
was upon the Irish story which Colburn had been looking for so long, *The O'Briens and the O'Flaherties*.

A great Protestant petition to Parliament for the
repeal of the political and religious disabilities which
in Ireland pressed so heavily on the Roman Catholics,
was got up in the early part of this year. It was in-
trusted to the hands of Sir Charles Morgan to receive
the signatures, and most of the leading nobility of Ireland came forward to the appeal, and signed it. That
petition was a great incident in the battle for Catholic
Emancipation — a battle which is still faintly echoed
in the periodical squabbles about the Maynooth grant.
It cost more moral courage to be a liberal in those
days, or rather to have the courage to be *just*, especially in Ireland, than can now be understood; to be
liberal then, needed a very earnest conviction. We
return to the diaries: —

March 13. — My novel of *The O'Briens and the
O'Flaherties*, is announced as much nearer finished than
it really is.

I was last night at a private party at the Castle. I was (as of late I have constantly been) the centre of a circle. It changed its character very often, at first; the courtiers, chamberlains, and aides-de-camps, all waiting near the door for the Vice-Regal entry, and as the circle widened, I found I was the nucleus of the falling set; on one side O'Connell, Lord Killeen (the Catholic chief), and my ultra-liberal husband — on the other side, stood North, whose gentle, temporising, Whig-Toryism, places him with the Doctrinaires of our country; Dogherty, the ministerial *enfant trouvé*; Col. Blacker, Grand Master of the Orange Lodge, commonly called "the roaring lion;" and Joy, the Solicitor-General, the *oriflamme* of every species of intolerance and illiberalism, all standing amicably side by side, like the statues in the "Groves of Blarney," though *not* "naked in the open air"! Thirty years ago the roof would not have been deemed safe which afforded O'Connell, and such as he, a shelter.

That —

First flower of the earth,
First gem of the sea,

O'Connell, wants back the days of Brian Borru, himself to be the king, with a crown of emerald shamrocks, a train of yellow velvet, and a mantle of Irish tabinet, a sceptre in one hand and a cross in the other, and the people crying "Long live King O'Connell!" This is the object of his views and his ambition. Should he ever be king of Ireland, he should take Charley Phillips for his prime minister, Tom Moore for chief bard, J. O'Meara for attorney-general, and Counsellor Bethel for his chief-justice. O'Connell is not a man of genius; he has a sort of conventional talent applicable

to his purpose as it exists in Ireland — a *nisi prius*
talent which has won much local popularity.

November 27. — Darby O'Grady, the Chief Baron's
brother, is *impayable*; he walks about the street in tight
yellow buckskins and a dandy hat.

Here is a picture of O'Connell "in his habit as he
lived," or rather as he lives, which almost realises my
fancy portrait! It came to-day in a letter from William
Curran.

"The only country news I have is that some rain
has fallen, and the fields are beginning to look almost
as green as O'Connell, for he walks the streets here in
the full dress of a verdant liberator — green in all
that may and may not be expressed, even to a green
cravat, green watch-ribbon, and a slashing shining
green hatband, and he has a confident hope that 'the
tears of Ireland will prevent the colours from ever
fading.'"

Sir Charles Morgan's daughter by his first marriage,
Annie, was about to be married, and Sir Charles came
to England to arrange preliminary business with her
mother's family. By the marriage settlements, his own
fortune was to revert to her on his death.

It was the first time Sir Charles and Lady Morgan
had been separated since their marriage, as on this occasion Lady Morgan did not accompany him. The
following letter gives Sir Charles's account of his doings
in London.

Sir Charles Morgan to Lady Morgan.

FLADONG'S HOTEL, LONDON,
May 29, 1826.

DEAREST SYD.,

I have this moment received your two letters and enclosures. The latter I will get set up in type, and correct before I leave town. *I* think it good and amusing; but I fancy Colburn will be frightened to death at its boldness.

I have written to Count Porro. Ugo Foscolo is in *quod*, cut by his friends and countrymen, after diddling Lord John Russell out of a thousand pounds. I dined yesterday with Harry Storks; he was talking of some reprobate Roman Catholic who would eat a horse on Ash-Wednesday, upon which, says I, "not unless it was a *fast horse!*" "Ah, ah, ah." (This is for Livy's tender ear) there never was Clarke's equal on the floor of creation; it is a great misfortune he has never turned his mind to the philosopher's stone, I am sure his perseverance would discover whether such a thing is catalogued on the book of nature or no. The children shall have new silver nothings of some sort.

Oh this London! this London!! here have I been on my legs all day, like a penny-postman. I went to Lydia White's last night, who was lying on the same sofa, in the same drawing-room, with the same blue furniture and blue hangings as usual — she was precisely what you know her. I only spoke to her and Moore, and went away in half-an-hour, in the *blue* devils. Moore is rapidly undergoing that transformation which will qualify him for a place in Hallam's book. He is not going to Ireland. On Saturday, I

dined at home, and went to the Opera. I have just
opened a new mine for magazine writing; but this is a
secret. Colburn wants me to write a *political* novel —
for God's sake make me out a *canévas*, and I shall try
my hand at it. I have just got a kind note from
Madame Patt., wanting me to fix a day for dining with
her; but I do not think I shall have one to spare. I
did not tell you how Pasta charmed me in the *Romeo*
the other night. She sang "Ombra adorata" *divinely*.
They played, also, an act of *Teobaldo e Isolina*, in
which Veiluti sang "Notte tremenda," in a style of
which I had no idea, still, however, he does not please
me. The ballet, *La Naissance de Venus*, was better,
and I believe now I have done with operas. You must
not mind that lying old witch Madame de Genlis' attack
on you in her book. I thought she would not let you
off easily; you were not only a better, and younger
(and *I* may say *prettier*) author than herself, but a
more popular one.

I have seen the Charlemonts, the Charlevilles, and
the old lady of Burlington Street, and most of your
friends, and am charged all over with kindness to you,
and regrets that you are not with me. Parliament will
be up in a few days, and then all will be off. Here
goes my tenth day, and that is half-way through this
tiresome job. I think you may begin to feed the calf,
as I shall be off the moment my business is settled.
Oh this cursed wilderness of a town; you may guess
how bad it is when a man sits down to write to his
wife, *à l'heure qu'il est*, Regent Street like a carnival.
Now I'll trouble you to guess what I am going to tell
you; but I'll be d——d if you do, so to save you the
trouble of making a judy of yourself, I may as well

tell you at once that Capel is going into Parliament to
teach the Premier his "*reading made easy*," and set the
finance at rest. He is to represent Queensborough with
its mayor and freemen. These old boys beat us hollow.
Think of his encountering the heat and fatigue of late
House of Commons work? By-the-bye, I met at breakfast, in the coffee-room, this morning, our old Italian
friend, Dr. Clarke. He is a good specimen of our good
Italians. He told me news of many of our old friends
at Rome and Naples, which I shall keep for you till
we meet. Fashions!! heavens if I have not forgotten
to tell you, from that queen of fashion, Mrs. M'Neil!
bonnets the size of *my* umbrella; your gigot sleeves as
full *as you can make them*. I am reading *Vivian Grey*,
at night, and in bed in the morning. Colburn gets
twelve hundred pounds per annum for the *Sunday Times*,
eighteen hundred pounds on the *New Monthly*, and
shared eleven hundred pounds this year on the *Literary
Gazette*.

Ever yours, whether you believe it or not,

C. M.

PS.— If ever I am caught in this region of smoke
again "all alone, *proudie*," I'll be ——!

In the mention of Lady Morgan by Madame de
Genlis, there was nothing to break any bones nor even
to give a scratch to the most ardent self-love. Madame
de Genlis writes in the character of a Minerva, and expresses herself as though Lady Morgan were one of her
élèves, in the *Tales of the Castle*, who required a gentle
admonition.

"Lady Morgan," says Madame de Genlis, "is not
beautiful; but there is something lively and agreeable

in her whole person. She is very clever, and seems
to have a good heart: it is a pity that, for the sake of
popularity, she should have the mania of meddling in
politics [of course it was natural that Madame de Genlis
who, as she boasts, had educated two princes and one
princess of the blood, should think small things of
Lady Morgan's liberal ideas]. She says gracefully, that
"her vivacity, and rather springing carriage, seemed
very strange in Parisian circles. She soon learned that
good taste of itself condemns this kind of demeanour;
in fact, gesticulation and noisy manners have never
been popular in France. When people go to the pro-
menade it is to take a chair. When she came to me
one day, she told me she had a very interesting lady
in her carriage who was desirous of seeing me — this
was Mrs. Patterson, the first wife of Prince Jerome
Bonaparte. Lady Morgan pressed me very much to
receive her; I consented. I saw a very fine woman —
mild, melancholy, and quiet, who was worthy of a
better fate."

Of course there is an air of affable superiority in
the above which is very amusing, but not calling for
any sympathy, and certainly cannot be called "an
attack."

The following scraps of diary complete the year
1826.

October 27. — Poor Talma!! one of the earliest
and kindest of my French acquaintance. The account
of his death has just reached me. Of all the eminent
men I knew in Paris 1816, there now only remain
Lafayette, Jouy, and Humboldt. Talma died of in-

testinal schirrus. Monsieur Du Puytren was desirous
to perform an operation which he was convinced would
have saved him if he had had strength enough to un-
dergo it, but he was deterred from resorting to it by
the extreme weakness to which he was reduced. The
Archbishop of Paris repeatedly called at his house, but
Talma declined to see him. Talma did not suffer any
acute pain, he only complained of having a cloud before his eyes. Talma refused to see the Archbishop or
any priest, saying that he would not deny the forty
brightest years of his life, nor separate his cause from
that of his comrades, nor acknowledge them to be in-
famous. The present Archbishop has endeavoured to
obtain the repeal from the Court of Rome of the ex-
communication pronounced against actors. Talma was
born in Paris, in January, 1760. His father was a
dentist, who afterwards exercised his profession in
London with great success.

October 30. — A ballad singer was this morning
singing beneath my window, in a voice most *unmusical*
and melancholy; my own name caught my ear, and I
sent Thomas out to buy the song, here is a stanza: —

> "Och, Dublin city there's no doubtin'
> Bates every city upon the say;
> 'Tis there you'll hear O'Connell spoutin',
> An' Lady Morgan making tay;
> For 'tis the capital of the finest nation,†
> Wid charming pisantry on a fruitful sod,
> Fighting like divils for conciliation,
> An' hating each other for the love of God."

Just received the following note from Archibald
Rowan, sending me the history of the "United Irishmen" for my "O'Briens and O'Flaherties."

II. Rowan to Lady Morgan.

Tuesday Evening.

As there is no certainty from what seeds or flowers the bee extracts its sweets, II. Rowan sends Lady Morgan a book, which, it seems, was published after he left Ireland, and, till he met with it the other day, he did not know it existed.

CHAPTER III.

THE O'BRIENS AND O'FLAHERTIES — 1827.

EARLY in 1827 the novel of the *O'Briens* and the *O'Flaherties* was complete. There was a long nego-ciation about the price. Lady Morgan had a perfect conviction of her own value, and she stood out for terms. Colburn wrote pathetically that no other pub-lisher ever would or could feel the interest he did in her works, or make so many sacrifices to insure their success, and as those things did not move Lady Morgan, he wrote on May 7, 1827, and made an offer of one thousand two hundred and fifty pounds, to be paid by instalments. This, Lady Morgan refused, and after some further correspondence, Colburn, sooner than see a rival in possession, agreed to her terms, which were one thousand three hundred pounds down for the copyright, one hundred pounds on the second edition, and another hundred on the third edition, with the stipulation that no edition was to exceed three thou-sand copies.

The work was more popular than any of her former

tales. The pictures of Irish society immediately before
and after the Union, and the characters of the vice-
regal Court under the Duke of Rutland, had a peculiar
interest at the time the book came out, which has now
evaporated; but there is still the perennial interest of
human nature, dashes of Irish humour and Irish pathos,
and traits of manners not now to be found, — for
the Irish peasant of the present day is quite a different
creature.   As a repertory of the manners, customs,
grievances, and society as it existed both in Dublin
and the provinces in the time when Ireland was the
seat of misgovernment and mistake, the *O'Briens and
the O'Flahertics* will always be a standard work of
reference.   As a tale, the plot is too confused, and the
interest too much diffused; the whole story is rambling,
but detached portions of it are inimitable; for in-
stance, the account of the Miss Mc Taafs and their
"JUG DAY," which we have quoted elsewhere, and
which was drawn from the life.   It is a portraiture
perfect in its kind, and like a picture by Hogarth in
words.   The Lord Aronmore is not so interesting a
personage as *O'Donnel*, but any one wishing for a book
full of scenes of racy Irish fun and delicate satire
would find these in the pages of the *O'Briens and the
O'Flahertics*.   The first volume which is occupied with
an account of an Irish feud, might be omitted, as it
damps the reader's interest by too long a prelude.

A certain rebel, General Aylmer, offers the type for
her hero.   The real General, driven from his own
country after the troubles of '98, entered the Austrian
service; distinguished himself; became a general; was
selected to accompany the Emperor of Austria when
he visited England, and, at the special request of the

2*

Prince Regent, he was left behind to teach the sword-
exercise to the British Army. His special pupils were
the 10th Dragoons, and he performed his task so well
that he received a free pardon and a handsome sword
from the Prince Regent himself. He tried to settle
in his native land; but, all patriotic as he was, he
could not be happy in peace and retirement. He
headed a band of Irish sympathizers, and joined the
South American patriots, then in the beginning of their
struggle under Bolivar. He fought hard, of course,
and received a wound in one of their battles, from the
effects of which he soon after died. Some idea of a
real Irish hero may be formed from the incident that
once having got into a squabble with the Duke of
Leinster's gamekeepers, he called on His Grace to complain, attired in his full Austrian uniform, with sabre
and helmet complete!

February. — Death of Lydia White; I received the
account this morning. Poor Lydia had asked a party
to dine with her on Friday, — on Wednesday she was
dead! From economy of eyes and lights, she used to
sit when alone to a late hour without lights. Her
servant having placed candles on the table in the front
drawing-room waited for his mistress to ring to light
them. He thought he heard something fall, but as
the bell did not ring he did not go up, till surprised at
her remaining so long in the dark, he entered, and
found her lying on the floor. Dr. Holland was sent
for, but medical aid was too late. When some of her
party arrived to dine on the Friday she was lying
dead. Poor Lydia! before she was buried she was
forgotten!

The Lydia White so often referred to was a personage of much social celebrity in her day. She was an Irish lady of large fortune and considerable talent, noted for her hospitalities and dinners in all the capitals of Europe, particularly London and Paris. She had remarkable quickness at repartee. At one of her small and agreeable dinners in Park Street (all the company except herself being Whigs), the desperate prospects of the Whig party were discussed. "Yes," said Sidney Smith, who was present, "we are in a most deplorable condition, we must do something to help ourselves; I think," said he, looking at Lydia White, "we had better sacrifice a Tory virgin." "Ah!" replied, she, "I believe there is nothing the Whigs would *not* do to raise the wind."

There are several incidental mentions of her in the diaries of Lord Byron and Moore. Byron seems to have been inclined to shy at what he calls her "*purple parties*," but he does not speak ill-naturedly, though he rather makes fun of her. He tells Moore in one of his letters that Lydia White was in Venice, and had just borrowed his copy of *Lalla Rookh*.

For some time before her death she was in a languishing state of health, but it provoked witticism rather than compassion. Moore says in his diary, May 7, 1826: — "Called upon Rogers; found him in high good humour. In talking of Miss White, he said, 'how wonderfully she does hold out; they may say what they will, but Miss White and *Missolongi* are the most remarkable things going.'"

In consequence of disease she became of a great size during the latter part of her life; and the best her

friends could find to say of her was, that she would
"leave a great gap in society." For a woman who was
so well known in the world, she has passed singularly
out of remembrance.

March 8. — Last night, Laporte, the celebrated
French actor from the Vaudeville, delighted a very
chosen society at our *petite soirée* by his reading of *Les
Precieuses.*

In the dawn of refinement there is always a tendency to the *Précieuse-ism* of the Hôtel Rambouillet.
Louis XIV., that most illiterate of men, was bored alike
with the real and affected superiority of some of his
courtiers; he was protector of Molière, and even the
Jesuits could not hunt down *Tartuffe.*

May 9. — Received in Kildare Street the Duke de
Dalmatia, son of Marshal Soult, and his friend de
Visconti. They were sent to me by the Duc de Monte-
bello.

The diary is resumed in London.

July 27. — Lady Charleville was pre-eminently
agreeable to-day, — we talked over Lady Cork; she is
eighty-one, and gave a dinner to twenty special guests
the other day. Her last intrigue "*aux choux et aux
raves*" was driving a hard bargain with the Tyrolese
to sing at her party. She picked them up in the
Regent's Park, and brought them down to thirty shillings, which she was heard wishing to beat down to
eight, when she stood with them where she thought
there was no one to listen, but they held out for the
thirty shillings.

At the Duke of St. Alban's, where there were all
the opera people, she said, "Duke, now, couldn't you
send me the pack for my evening?" "Certainly," said
he, and they were sent with a grand piano forte.
When they came to her, Lady Cork got frightened,
and said "Je suis une pauvre veuve, je ne saurais
payer de tels talens, mais vous verrez la meilleure
société, la Duchesse de St. Albans, &c., &c." The
Primo Amoroso bowed, and acknowledged the honour,
but intimated that the Duchess always paid them.

Lady Cork went to the Duke and accused him of
taking a word at random, *tout de bon*.

The Duchess overhearing, came forward in a rage,
and scolded the little Duke like a naughty schoolboy.
The angry Duchess took all upon herself. Lady Cork
was very angry at "the show up."

Talking this morning with Lady Charleville on the
report of my having found assistance in Brownlow's
conversations. "Not you, child," she said, "you have
a splendid imagination, but you have no powers of
argument." She was right as to the fact, but wrong
as to inference. Men are always more easily convinced
by images presented to their senses, than by arguments
offered to their reason. Images are facts, arguments
are but words, and impressions are more rapidly conveyed than ideas. I have often failed to excite an interest by argument, — I have always succeeded by a
scene.

There is nothing less amusing than writing for the
amusement of the public.

Lady Cork said to me this morning, when I called
Miss —— a nice person. "Don't say *nice*, child, 'tis
a bad word. Once I said to Dr. Johnson, 'Sir, that

is a very nice person.' 'A *nice* person,' he replied,
'what does that mean? *Elegant* is now the fashionable word, but will go out, and I see this stupid *nice*
is to succeed to it; what does nice mean? look in my
dictionary, you will see it means correct, precise.'"

Lady Cork also told me that on one occasion when
Croker was dining with the King, the Duke of Clarence
was present, who was always indignant at the insolence
of office displayed by Croker in the Admiralty. "When
I am king," said he, "I will be my own secretary of
the Admiralty." The King overheard them and said,
"What nonsense is that you are talking, Croko?"
"His Royal Highness is mentioning what he will do
in case he should become king." The next morning
the King sent for Croker to his bedroom, and reproached him for exposing his brother, and he was
never invited to dinner again.

The following note from Lady Caroline Lamb contains the announcement of the unexpected death of
Canning.

Lady Caroline Lamb to Lady Morgan.

BROCKETT HALL,
Wednesday.

MY DEAR LADY MORGAN,

In consequence of a carrier coming this way, I have
heard to my excessive horror that Mr. Canning is
either dying or dead. I am coming to town in consequence to know the truth, and if I can, to see the
Duke of Devonshire; in the mean time, will you call
upon me to-morrow (Thursday) the moment you are
up, and pray let it be early; you never said good bye,
you never said thank you for my sweet scent. You

never brought me the portrait. I take this note to
town to-night, scarcely hoping to see you. I have
two or three notes from William, evidently not knowing this disastrous news.

Yours most truly,

C. LAMB.

To return to the diary again —

Canning's death makes less sensation than might
have been expected; he had no hold on the convictions of society. His one absorbing idea was to be
the political Atlas of England, to raise her on his
shoulders. His vituperative eloquence, his wit, his
aplomb, his humour were exquisite. When I wrote
my first *France*, and attacked the Bourbons in my
tiny way, Canning was at the feet of the restored
despots, and called Bourdeaux *Le Temple de Madame
D'Angoulême*.

Lady Cork once took me to visit him, but he
was out.

Dublin again. — We have busied ourselves very
much upon the occasion of Talbot's election, and wrote
all sorts of squibs, some of which were sung in the
street the next day.

October 19. — We dined at our new Secretary's
to-day (W. Lamb). We had Curran and Grattan,
names new to the salons of our Irish Secretary.

I was telling Henry Grattan and Mrs. Blachford
that I had introduced their father in my *O'Briens and
O'Flaherties* at the head of his volunteer corps in the
park. Mrs. Blachford said that her father one day
marched his company into the middle of the sea. On

another occasion he was reviewing them with his glass to his eye and Mrs. Blachford was near him; he asked her, "Mary Ann, are their backs or their fronts towards me?" He was very blind and very absent, and his mind full of anything but military evolutions.

Crampton told me that a man repeating to him an observation of a clever person who had said "such a one's mind is still in full force, but he must die, his *physique* is quite worn out," he said Dr. B—— says, 'Mr. —— must die for his physic is out!" * * * The Hon. George Keppel, aid-de-camp to Lord Wellesley, became an *habitué* of our house in Kildare Street. *Il n'y bougeait plus* — at last it came out that he had a manuscript by him of his journey through Persia — in a word, he wished me to *blanchir son linge sale*, or rather to sell his book for him. I always like to encourage the young rising aristocracy to work, for a thousand reasons, so I took his MS., read it, and sold it for three hundred pounds to Colburn, who, but for me, would not have given him three hundred pence. After it was out, his vanity got alarmed lest I should arrogate to myself the "best passages in it!"

November 12, Sunday. — At my once-a-fortnight's Sunday dinners yesterday, I had a strange *olla podrida* sort of gathering. Bunn, the lessee of the theatre; Calcraft, the manager; Sir Charles Malcolm, just appointed to his first place at Bombay; Mr. Cuthbert, and one or two others. In the evening, Sheil, Curran, Crampton (Surgeon-General), Mrs. Corregan, the *prima donna* (who sang charmingly); some of the old Court, an American Corinne, Miss Edgeworth, and the Lakes of Killarney.

Bunn's anecdotes were some of them very amusing.

Talking of Theodore Hook, Bunn said (though Bunn
is by way of being his friend and disciple) "No friendship can bind him, he will show up a friend in his
writings all the same as his foe. He is said to make
three thousand a-year by the *John Bull* and his other
writings. He lies on a sofa and drinks claret all day,
and has a face like a grenadier's cap. He was the
confidential friend of Lord Bathurst."

Here he was interrupted by the frank indignation
of Sir Charles Malcolm. — "He is one of the greatest
rogues that lives unhanged! When Lord Bathurst
engaged him to write the account of Bonaparte's de-
tention at St. Helena, there were among many gross
falsehoods, a calumnious attack upon my uncle, Sir
Pultney Malcolm. He heard this, and said to Lord
Bathurst, 'I hear that there is such a work coming
out; the moment it appears I will publish a counter
statement, in which I will tell the whole truth — *I will
spare none!*' The work, on the day it was to appear,
was suppressed; Lord Bathurst bought it up from
Colburn."

The John Bull, The Age, The Beacon, The Satirist,
and such works may be called into life, and men may
endorse their opinions. They may have partisans,
readers, and patrons. Despotism in politics, corruption in morals, calumny in conversation, degeneracy
in taste, bigotry in religion was "the badge of all
their tribe."

[NOTE, 1847. — In looking over this book I find
all my opinions justified by time. Where now are the
John Bull, The Age, The Satirist? The Quarterly is so
reformed, its name alone remains unchanged.]

The O'Briens and the O'Flaherties. In the dialogue

and tone of manners given to my fair oligarchs in the
second and third volumes, I was dreadfully afraid there
was *de quoi choquer les Prudes*, and I suppressed many
droll things that had been related to me. I was mur-
muring my fears to Lady Cloncurry — severe upon
mœurs and a model of propriety. Lady Cloncurry set
my mind at rest by answering me that I had kept clear
of extremes and dwelt more in the decencies than was
at all characteristic of the time I described. Her
mother, the beautiful Mrs. Douglas, had lived in the
thick of the world in the times I had mentioned; she
had taken the governess of the Duchess of Rutland,
Madame Delval, to educate Lady Cloncurry. They
had many curious anecdotes from her, more curious
than edifying. The Duke had in his route brought
over with him a certain handsome Mr. Bathurst, who,
to the amazement of the Irish ladies, used to enter the
drawing-room in a succession of somersaults, which
he performed with singular agility. Under the lieu-
tenancy of Lord Hardwicke and the commencement
of the Duke of Richmond's, there were in the Castle
circle a *posse* of titled women of bold reputation, who
had the uncontrolled sway in everything. These
ladies introduced a kind of savage dance, or rather
romp, called "Cutchakutchoo;" this was performed
by the parties squatting themselves on the floor, both
their arms underneath their legs, and changing places
with their partners as well as they could in such a
posture. In short, the Dublin court of that period
was like the manners described in *Grammont's Memoirs*.

Morgan has just been in to show me this letter
from O'Connell.

Daniel O'Connell to Sir Charles Morgan.

MY DEAR SIR,

The *Freeman* is a slave, that is plain; he is a mean and paltry dog, also — but that is of course.

I have got your manuscript, but do not leave it because I hope you will allow me to transfer it to committee, which, on the late occasion, has shown some symptoms of reviving honesty.

Faithfully yours,

DANIEL O'CONNELL.

Poor Lady Caroline is worse; here is a note just come.

Mrs. Hawtre to Lady Morgan.

BROCKETT HALL,
November 22.

I am much grieved that I cannot give you a better account of dear Lady Caroline's health. Since the operation, her symptoms have assumed such varied appearances that at this moment we have no confidence of an ultimate recovery; the natural strength of her constitution is very great, and we have all ardent hopes much good may result from that favourable circumstance. The situation is most distressing to the many kind friends that are interested for her recovery, and we must derive consolation from witnessing her perfect calm resignation. Lady Caroline expressed much pleasure at receiving a very feeling letter from you this morning. Mr. Lamb is cruelly situated to be separated so far at this moment. Trusting I have given you a correct account of my kind friend, though a very unhappy one,

Believe me,
Yours truly,
GEORGINA M. M. HAWTRE.

November 23. — Yesterday I went to see Lord and Lady Howth. Howth Castle stands as it did in the time of General Wade, and seems a mansion of Queen Elizabeth's day — not, I should think, older, except one high square tower, within an enclosure — a method common in old Irish castles. This tower appears of great antiquity. The general mansion is a long, low building of many gables, ascended by broad, sheltered, stone steps; the offices spacious, low-roofed — they stand on the ground-floor. The huge metal bells that have stood there from time immemorial, till the date of their being placed there, has escaped all memory. At either extremity of the hall are a few black oak and balustraded stairs — that to the right leads to the state bedroom, a curious and charming old apartment, breaking out into little turret-closets and recesses that are now alcoves and dressing-rooms for the lords and ladies of the day; that to the left is called the haunted chamber, a formal room said once to have been King William's bed-chamber. Opposite the door of entrance in the hall is a little ante-room leading to the grand stairs and to the drawing-room, a long, low-roofed, narrow room, with a fine, carved ceiling, carefully white-washed, a superb mantel-piece of grey marble, rising in a succession of stories to the roof, each storey set off by a profusion of old china. Then there are coffers, cabinets, japan-screens, and other old relics of

old houses and old families that one is ready to fall
down and worship. Above are corridors, with dear
old bedrooms, odd nooks, and niches for nothing at
all; then narrow and winding passages and stairs, popping upon one at every turn; the whole is a perfect
picture of the dreary, unconnected style of domestic
dwellings, — the comfortless, unaccommodating reality
of those times which paint and write so well, but which
one would not wish to have lived in. There is a curious
picture which represents the great front of the old castle
and part of the rock on which it stands. The famous
female pirate, Gran O'Neile, is mounted on horse-back,
holds a faulchion, with her long, silk mantle drawn
decently round her stout limbs, her head well formed,
her shoulders and arms are bare, her yellow drapery
seems to have fallen off; she has a sort of white veil
or bandeau on her head; she is issuing orders to several
men, all employed in carrying off plunder from Howth
Castle; some are rolling up casks, others throwing about
domestic utensils, others are loading asses with difficult
piles of luggage which they are conveying towards the
shore; but the most remarkable person is the young
heir of Howth, an infant child, which one of Gran
O'Neile's female followers is holding up to the fair
pirate, who is about to place it on horseback before
her, at the moment she is issuing her last commands,
and leaving the castle for her ship, which was at anchor
near. Over all, emerging through a cloud, appears the
head and bust, beautifully painted, of some saint.
While I stood gazing on this curious picture, I held
the present heir of Howth, Lord St. Lawrence, in my
arms; beside me stood his young and smiling mother,

not yet of age; on the other side, his French nurse,
herself a descendant of Gran O'Neile.

In Howth Castle, as elsewhere in secluded places,
there were two state bedrooms, rich, cumbrous, and
spacious; all the rest were hovels.

November 27. — Yesterday, we had a dinner-party,
the Honourable William Lamb, Lord Cloncurry, Mr.
Blake, Chief Remembrancer Curran, Mr. Evans, of
Portran, &c., &c. Mr. Lamb was in the lowest spirits
from the bad accounts that had come of poor Lady
Caroline.

Poor Lady Caroline, her life was fast ebbing; but
she had kind friends round her. Here is a letter from
her husband, more than a fortnight later.

W. Lamb to Lady Morgan.

> Dublin Castle,
> *December 12.*

Dear Lady Morgan,
I have been very neglectful lately in not sending
you the accounts which I received. It is with great
pain that I now send you the enclosed. It is some
consolation that she is relieved from pain; but illness
is a terrible thing. Send them me back, that I may
forward them to Lord Duncannon.

> Yours faithfully,
> William Lamb.

The following is the letter alluded to; it is endorsed,
"Dr. Goddard's letter, sent me by Mr. Lamb."

December 13, 1827.

MY DEAR SIR,

I regret very much that I have but a melancholy account to give you to-day of Lady Caroline's health. Saturday she seemed in good spirits; but on that night she began to complain of pain in her side, accompanied with cough and shortness of breath. These symptoms are, I think, partly accidental, and may not continue; but should they, they will certainly give us great cause of alarm. There is another change, also; she is inattentive to what is going on. She speaks with difficulty, and seems unwilling to see many people. You may gather too plainly from all these symptoms the unwelcome news that her ladyship is getting worse; her sufferings she still bears with fortitude, and complains but little.

I remain, dear Sir,
Your obedient and humble Servant,
G. GODDARD.

Lady Charleville to Lady Morgan.

December 30.

You are so kind in the expression of an interest for my recovery, that I must thank you, *au risque*, to take up valuable time with reading a very dull letter. I have suffered from an attack of the chest; a blood-vessel I broke thirty years ago seemed inclined to go over its old train of pain and disease; but it has stopped; and I think if I had air and absence of coal sulphur, I should be well.

Now you know as much as I do myself of my "*physique et morale;*" and I rejoice that you are con-

tent with the success of your novel and of the profits.
People have more time to read away from this town,
I believe, and think more about books of amusement;
but I am quite sure the reviews prevent three parts of
society from going through any book in London. I
fear it will make enemies amongst the survivors of the
cabinet of 1786. You have written powerfully, and
many of great judgment say so when they dare; but
the ladies are vociferous in condemnation of what they
call blasphemy and indecency, and conceive me very
atrocious for not having discovered either the one or
the other defect in the book. The king, I find, was
interested in the lighter parts; but some of the charges
against the Irish government, he said, were too bad,
while God knows they were not half bad enough to
my mind. Now, what I like best in the whole was
Shane; he beats Eddie Ochiltree off the ground. I wish
he had not killed anybody, nor been killed; but all the
poetical fancies will fix upon him, if he had murdered
all the excisemen in Europe. In short, I love him so
that I think he is the hero of the tale, and the Miss
Mac Taafs the heroines. I must, however, tell you
that I am so miserably convinced, by all I have ever
read or SEEN, of the tendency of Roman Catholic tenets
to put down human intellect, to control and guide all
human interests to their own profit, and to create control even in the heart of every private family, that even
independent of Jesuitism, I cannot like any amiable
abbess, or allow of any stratagem, that holds forth one
of those traps for us to put ourselves and our spirits
into the hands of their church.

Our own church has preserved too many Catholic
trappings, which common sense must reject. I regret,

so far as Ireland is concerned, that at the time we had
our volunteers, our patriot hands were not strengthened
to make a division of church lands, which would have
afforded proper provision both for Protestant and Roman Catholic pastors of all ranks; neither of them
could then have stripped the peasant of his mite, —
the first by impoverishing him, and the other by super-
stitious rites.

I think my dear Mr. Grattan was short-sighted in
not getting us over this step when we had *arms in our
hands.*

My Lord (who when he was sixteen was generalis-
simo of volunteers for the King's County) says, "you
have underrated the whole force by two-thirds;" and
also, he says, "there was not one Roman Catholic
received into the original institution." He was also
deputy to the Convention from the King's County.

We had been so enslaved and so impoverished,
that even men like Grattan thought wonders were
accomplished in 1782, by hearing us called free, and
having a ship or two allowed us, and being permitted
to decide finally upon our own cause and in our own
parliament.

They ought to have foreseen that with revived
energies Ireland should naturally become a still greater
object of distrust and jealousy to her *marâtre,* — that
a union would be her best policy. Our private secu-
rities and our people's comfort should have been
looked to when government dared not have refused us
the proper and liberal position which the church lands
would have afforded for the priests, while enough

3*   *i*

would have been left for the ascendancy of the religion of the State.

Whatever objections philosophical inquiry may incline to make, the Church of England is pure in its precepts, and does not, by oral confession, put us into the hands of creatures as fallible as ourselves; whose interest it is to subdue our energies and destroy our judgment, in order to direct into one channel the exercise of intellect and property. But this opportunity is past; we can do nothing now but look on; I hope times will mend, as the old phrase says.

I hear from authority, Sir William Knighton now settles all things here. It is certain the king said he loved Lord Holland as his brother, but it is a new question for a British king to ask what the Emperor of Austria and King of France would say to a Whig ministry! Objecting to Lord Holland is objecting to one of the best friends of Old England. I am, and always was, for liberty, for law, and for full exercise of religious opinion; *but* I would have no man a legislator who was bound to follow the direction of his priest; consequently, no Roman Catholic in either house of parliament.

Many people fancy your enlightened Catholics do not confess or would allow of political control; if they do not, why not conform at once? Their opinion on the metaphysics of religion could not be an objection to their sitting in parliament to legislate for us; but a majority, governed by the Jesuits, would soon put out the sun of England.

Lady Anglesea, I think, will never be able to go. I hope Mr. Lamb will stay. You are right, Lady Caroline was scarcely accountable, and is to be pitied;

but better her poor heart ceased to beat than stand in the way of the good he may do.

I am, ever yours affectionately,   M. C.

My little grandson is JEAN JACQUES!! *Viva!* compliments to your *sposo.*

Hon. W. Ponsonby to Lady Morgan.

ST. JAMES'S SQUARE,
January 26.

MY DEAR MADAM,

The interest which you have felt for my dear sister, makes me anxious that you should not hear from common report the termination of her long and severe sufferings. From the beginning of her illness, she had no expectation of recovery, and only felt anxious to live long enough to see Mr. Lamb once again. In this she was gratified, and was still able to converse with him and enjoy his society; but for the past three days, it was apparent that her strength was rapidly declining, and on Sunday night at about nine o'clock, she expired without a struggle. A kinder or a better heart has never ceased to beat; and it was to her a great consolation, and is now to us, that her mind was fully prepared and reconciled to this awful change. She viewed the near approach of death with the greatest calmness; and during the whole of her severe sufferings, the patience with which she endured them, or her kind and affectionate feelings for those about her, never failed for one moment. Mr. Lamb has felt and acted as I knew he would, upon this sad occasion.

Believe me, dear madam,

Very faithfully yours,

W. PONSONBY.

Diary resumed: —

January 30. — Received this morning a letter from the Honourable William Ponsonby, announcing the death of his sister, my poor dear friend, Lady Caroline Lamb. She expired on the evening of the 26th. She was tall and slight in her figure, her countenance was grave, her eyes dark, large, bright; her complexion fair; her voice soft, low, caressing, that was at once a beauty and a charm, and worked much of that fascination that was peculiarly hers; it softened down her enemies the moment they listened to her. She was eloquent, most eloquent, full of ideas, and of graceful gracious expression; but her subject was always herself. She confounded her dearest friends and direst foes, for her feelings were all impulses, worked on by a powerful imagination; all elements of great eloquence, but not good for guidance; one of her great charms was the rapid transition of manner which changed to its theme. The chief cause of the odd things which she used to say and do, was, that never having lived out of the habits of her own class, yet sometimes mixing with people of inferior rank, notable only by their genius, she constantly applied her own sumptuous habits to them. Here is a specimen: — she called on me one day in London, and struck by my servant, who announced her, being in livery, she said, in her odd manner, as she was going down stairs, "My dear creature, have you really not a groom of the chambers with you? nothing but your footman? You must let me send you something, you must indeed. You will never get on here, you know, with only one servant — you must let me send you one of my pages.

I am going to Brocket, to watch the sweet trees that
are coming out so beautifully, and you shall have a
page while I am away!"

I am sick of the jargon about the idleness of genius.
All the greatest geniuses have worked hard at everything — energetic, persevering, and laborious. Who
has worked so much and so well as Bacon, Kepler,
Milton, Newton? it is the energy that gives what we
call "genius;" that leaves its impression on all it
touches. Nothing but mediocrity is slothful and idle.

Dr. Goddard to Lady Morgan.

February 10, 1825.

It was the wish of Lady Caroline that the portrait
of Lord Byron in the morocco case should be given to
your ladyship after her death. The picture at present
is in my keeping; and if your Ladyship would let me
know where you are, and how to send it you, I would
take care it is properly packed up and forwarded according to your directions.

I beg to be,
Your Ladyship's obedient,
B. GODDARD.

At this time, the Beef Steak Club — a high Tory
political gathering in Dublin — invited Lord Anglesea
to dinner, and there was a rumour that he was inclined
to accept it.

Lady Morgan wrote the following letter to Lord
Aylmer, to induce him to use his influence with the
Marquis to keep him from attending.

DEAR LORD AYLMER,

The esteem and admiration I have heard you express for Lord Anglesea, and the generous sympathy I know you have always felt towards Ireland, induces me to state to you, *sans préambule*, the following facts. A rumour prevails at present in Dublin, that Lord Anglesea means to accept the invitation to be given to him by the *Beef Steak Club*. The circumstance is apparently so insignificant, so utterly unconsequential that it is necessary to be utterly Irish, and to know thoroughly the state of this unhappy country to attach the smallest consequence to it, or for a moment to suppose that the well merited and universal popularity of Lord Anglesea could for a moment be shaken by such an event. The fact, however, is so much the contrary, that should Lord Anglesea take his place in a Society which has so long offended the nation, and so utterly insulted the King in the person of his representative, the Marquis of Wellesley, not all the efforts of the Catholic leaders now disposed to support and uphold the popularity of Lord Anglesea's government, would suffice to keep quiet that nest of hornets the Catholic Association, who, emblematic of the rest of this susceptible but injudicious nation, are more willing to submit to injuries than to insult. I need not tell you, my dear Lord, the effect of the unlucky facility of Lord Wellesley in yielding to the request of the Beef Steak Club, impeded his subsequent efforts at tranquillising Ireland, nor into what annoyances it betrayed him. For the party to whom his unguarded concession was so flagrant a triumph, has acted more like a froward child, that pouts the more it is petted. With respect to the liberty

I have taken, and the mode I have chosen to com-
municate this to your Lordship in preference to any
person in an official position about Lord Anglesea, my
selection has arisen from your holding no place, and
from knowing that you are equally the friend of Ireland
and of its gallant and excellent chief governor.   I
leave it entirely to your Lordship's judgment and
kindly feelings to act as your excellent judgment may
dictate, and

I am,

Your Lordship's very truly,

SYDNEY MORGAN.

The letter effected its purpose, and Lord Anglesea
did not go to the dinner.

The diary returns to the subject of Byron and Lady
C. Lamb: —

I was showing my picture of Byron, this morning,
to Mr. Lovett, of Lismore, of literary notoriety, and
the conversation naturally turned on the extraordinary
liaison of Lady Caroline and Lord Byron *à propos* to
which, Mr. Lovett told me the following anecdote.

"One morning I sauntered into Scroope Davis'
lodgings, and threw myself on a sofa; but finding both
ends full of heaps of books, I said, 'Why the devil
don't you put up shelves, and leave your friends a
place to sit on?' 'Oh,' he said, 'those were books left
me by Byron, when he was going away, and I have
not yet disposed them.' I took up some of the volumes
with interest, and lighting on *Vathek*, I said, 'Oh, you
must lend me this, I have never had it;' and turning

over the leaves, I found a poem in MS. addressed to
Lady Caroline Lamb, with some allusion to her conduct to her husband. I read it aloud, and Scroope
Davis, snatching the book from me, said, 'No, you
must excuse me, I cannot let you have that.' He would
not even permit me to read the poem a second time.
It was atrociously bitter and cruel. A woman was never
so treated in poetry or prose.

Thou false to him, thou fiend to me.

This is the only line I can recollect."

By-the-bye, Lady Caroline assured me, last August,
that Byron's last letter to her was sealed with Lady
Oxford's coronet and crest. That she had a presentiment, on receiving it, of its contents, and that having
read it she fell into a swoon, and took to her bed in a
wretched hotel in Dublin; and that her head and heart
never recovered the shock, and never would.

August 10th. — Olivia and her three girls still at
Jenkinstown, Kilkenny — well for them! whilst I am
perched up in my two-pair-of-stairs dressing-room,
breathing dust, and seeing nothing but neighbour
Sweeney's old house, and the carpets up and the
curtains down, all ready for the workmen and our
departure. What a pickle to receive Prince Pickle
Mustard in, and on dreary Sunday evening, too, that
direful day in Dublin!

We had just returned from a long, dreary drive,
tired, cold, covered with dust, when a thundering knock
came to the door — J. Thomas flew to open it; enter
a creature, fine and foppish — a sort of a tartar turned
dandy — who asked, in a foreign accent, for Lady
Morgan.

Thomas, sulky as a pig, because he hates "my
lady having them furriners," cried, "I don't think
my lady is at home; but I'll thry, sir. Who shall I
say, sir?"

"The Prince Pucklau Muskan"!!!

Away went Thomas, tumbling down the kitchen
stairs —

> Jack fell down and broke his crown,
> And Jill (Morgan, with a bottle in his hand)
> — came tumbling after.

I, like Miss Polly, tumbled up stairs to the drawing-room and stood in all my dust and dowdiness to
receive l'Altezza, whom *le cher* J., announced as "Prince
Pickling Mustard," (just as last summer he persisted in
calling Prince Cimatelli, "Vermacelli;") Well, I put
on the best face (a dirty one) I could on it, and
endeavoured to excuse things. The Prince put me at
once at my ease. He is a most *finished* fop. *Hélas*, I
shall have to unpaper and unpack my room and ask
him to dinner when he returns from Wicklow.

Thomas Campbell, who had recently lost his wife,
wrote to Lady Morgan: —

Thomas Campbell to Lady Morgan.

10, UPPER SEYMOUR STREET WEST,
LONDON,
August 15, 1828.

DEAR LADY MORGAN,

Will you and Sir Charles do me a kindness, though
I am sensible that in spite of the best feelings towards
you, I have no great claims upon your favour? It is
to receive my young friend Mr. Macdonald, with the

usual attention which you are known to show to respectable strangers. Mr. Macdonald is the son of a
gallant and distinguished General, who has more of the
aspect and character of the true Highland chief than
any man I know. Young Macdonald is, of course, a
Tory, from his Jacobite family, deadly enemies of the
Campbells, by the way; but he is liberal and sensible,
and, therefore, I wish him to see the true-blue liberals
of Dublin under your kind auspices.

I long to see you and Sir Charles once more in
London. Of my dreadful domestic calamity, you must
have heard some time ago. The decline of my Matilda's health was very rapid, and the afflicting blow,
as you may suppose, was agonisingly stunning. It is
impossible to divest the dissolution of a beloved being
of pain and horror to those who watch it; yet thank
God, I had no conception that death could be apparently so little painful to a sufferer. At first her illness
threatened to be exactly like that of four of her sisters,
who died before her, after lingering for four or five
years in pangs of body, not unmixed with mental
alienation. But thanks to heaven, my poor Matilda had
a shorter and gentler fate.

My son continues better, and is so companionable
that I feel his society a great blessing to me in my
lonely house. I have fitted up, since I saw you, a
small and beautiful adjoining cottage into a library,
which opens from my parlour. You must come over
from Ireland for the purpose of seeing me in this retreat, reading your works, and enjoying the self-com-
placency of an old and comfortable author.

I have long intended to send you a copy of my
last edition; but I have always a latent distrust that if

I gave the commission to Colburn, he would neglect it, like everything else. Mr. Macdonald has promised to charge himself with delivering it. Deign to accept, and with best regards to Sir Charles,

Believe me,

Dear Lady Morgan,

Your obliged and sincere friend,

T. CAMPBELL.

The diary continues —

August 19. — What a pleasant evening I have spent with my dear friends the Hamilton Rowans. Captain H——, the gallant commander of the Cambria, was there; he is just returned from Greece, and told me many curious facts. What added to the interest was, that there lay on the sofa his dog Caroline, which had been present at the Battle of Navarino. He brought over with him a little boy who had been saved out of the Capitan Pacha's ship when he burnt it.

I heard a great deal of Mavrocordato, my old travelling acquaintance in Italy.

August 21. — We were engaged to go, last evening, to Maritimo, to Lord Cloncurry's, but Morgan had to dine previously at the Mechanics'. I requested permission to bring Prince Pucklau Muskau with us, which was granted. Whilst I was dressing, I dispatched Thomas and the carriage for his master to the Mechanics', with directions to proceed thence to fetch the Prince. Poor Thomas was kept an age waiting for his master, and he wrote him a note in the hall, which Morgan gave me. It is *à mourir de rire.*

"*Sir Charless!* Me lady will be very unhappy and sariously blame me, for ye not forthcoming."

"Ye most obedient and very humble servant,
                    "THOS. GRANT."

When they went for the Prince, after waiting an
hour, word came out that His Highness had disap-
peared — where, nobody knew; and it was near twelve
o'clock before we arrived at *Maritimo*. I made the
Prince my excuse, and as there were a number of
Englishmen by, there was a general laugh; and they
said, "What! is poor Prince Pickle come *here?* Oh,
he will have you down in his '*morgen blatt*' — he will
pounce on you." In short, I saw there was a ridicule
about him, or a something, but it shall not deter me
from being civil to him. He is a stranger and a foreigner, and recommended to me by Mrs. Beauclerk —
sufficient causes. He comes to visit "remote Ireland,"
and if I shut my door, what house will receive him?
He has the eye of a cat — a sort of mild roguish look,
like his master of Austria.

There is nothing so extraordinary as that the nobility of England should have produced so few geniuses.
Who but Lord Byron? I know not one. Lord Peter-
borough, perhaps, comes nearest; but he was too wild
and extravagant. The Dukes of Buckingham and
Rochester were wits, not geniuses; and their talent, developed by the civil wars, gave them the advantage of
middle life, necessary for exertion. The sharpening of
the faculties, by exercise and exertion, are advantages
denied to the great. The Lord Keepers, and Lord
Chancellors, and other law lords, were clever men, but
they were many of them *le lie du peuple*, and none of
them of noble blood. What a sad show up of preten-

sion and mediocrity is Walpole's work of royal and noble authors!

August 22. — What a splendid head of Arthur O'Connor, painted by Hamilton, I have just been look-ing at! This noble and unfinished picture represents him at full length, with very scanty drapery, and as Demosthenes. He looks like a noble Irish savage of the sixteenth century, with his blanket, mantle, and skewer. There were four of those O'Connors, all fine men as to the *physique*. They were Arthur, and Roger, and Roderick, and — I forget the other name. The two elder full of talent, and champions of Irish inde-pendence. They never crouched to power. Lord Longueville, their uncle, put Arthur into the Irish parliament to uphold the Government of the day, and to speak against the Catholics. He took the direct contrary line, and he was disowned and disinherited by Lord Longueville. When the *Press*, an Irish news-paper of 1797, was burnt by the common hangman, and Peter Finerty, the printer, was pilloried for sedi-tious libel, published in that paper, Arthur O'Connor stood beside him upon the scaffold, and held an um-brella over his head.

I have so little confidence in the certainty of this life, that I always live as if I were going to die. I never stir from home for more than a month without settling my little affairs and altering or adding to my *Will*, as circumstances direct.

I never am in debt one shilling. Poor people ought always to pay ready money, by which means they live as if they were rich. By not doing so, the rich often live as if they were poor and die insolvent.

August 23. — I received a letter, signed James Devlin, which has made me laugh; a blessing, any how! He says he is come up from the country to settle in Dublin; "but being unable to get into any but a beggarly employ," he has, "as his only alternative, and with a boldness, under such circumstances, he hopes pardonable," written a poem; and "snatching fortitude from despair," he sends it to me to get published. I read the poem — *Recollections of a Patriot* — not worth recollecting, and I have written at once to tell him so.

August 25. — Here is a letter from my poet showing a degree of sense that is wonderful in a poet who is also an Irishman. Here it is. What a contrast between the humble confidence that he can make good boots and shoes for gentlemen and the "fortitude from despair" with which he wrote his bad poetry! Oh! why will not every one find out his "last" and stick to it. How much more pleasantly the world would jog on!

James Devlin to Lady Morgan.

DUBLIN,
Thursday.

MADAM,
Finding that I may expect no benefit from my poetry, and feeling that I must use some exertion to get myself out of the difficulties my want of employ has involved me in, I again take the liberty of troubling your Ladyship, requesting, should Sir C. Morgan want any articles in the way of my business (a gentleman's boot and shoe-maker) that he would do me the

kindness of favouring me with a trial, confident, should he do so, of my ability to give satisfaction.

I remain, your Ladyship's
Obliged and most obedient servant,
JAMES DEVLIN.

Thursday, November 19. — To-day, is the Public Dinner given by the friends of civil and religious liberty, and got up at our house on Wednesday.

November 20. — I must get an account of the Dinner. It went off splendidly, but there was some *démêlé* about Prince Pucklau Muskau: first, he was not wanted there; and next, he desired Morgan to find out, if he went, whether the health of the king his master would be drunk (at a dinner given to celebrate freedom!); and next, if he would have the precedence of an Altezza granted to himself. There was a burst of "*noes*" when Morgan read the proposition. Morgan had the indiscretion to advise the Prince *not* to go. He seemed to be struck and mortified. I tremble for the consequences. It is just as well not to be married, for marriage is but another name for suffering.

The conjugal anxiety of Lady Morgan on the subject of the Prince's wounded susceptibilities, was a source of great fun to "the darlings in Great George Street," who wickedly amused themselves with writing challenges to their uncle, with caricatures of "the event on the turf," coming off at "Goose Green," the favourite locality in Dublin for "affairs of honour," as Chalk farm used to be for London. But Lady Morgan's anxiety was *tout de bon* — Sir Charles was the most peaceable man in the world; but she was in continual dread lest "Morgan should be called out;" *à propos* to his strong politics. On this occasion, however, the Prince was quite innocent of any intention to challenge any body.

The next entry in the diary is, "*The Prince is gone, thank God!!!*"

November 22.—Sheil this day from England, after his triumphal dinner and noble speech. At night he was at my tea table, full of fire, fun, spirits, and energy — what a *physique!*

Cobbett, he says, overpowered him with praise in the waggon at Penenden Heath. It was not until he saw five columns of his speech in the papers that his honey turned to gall. It was like Majesty against the *Register*. He cannot bear to be out-printed. Sheil's manner of speaking startled his sober auditors at the London Tavern; he is extremely theatrical in his delivery, and as he says himself, it is too like the stage.

This meeting on Penenden Heath had an immense political importance at the time.

A meeting of the landed proprietors, clergy, and freeholders of the county of Kent, was summoned for the 24th of October, 1828, to petition against Catholic Emancipation. The place appointed for the meeting was Penenden Heath, in Kent, and from the rank and influence of its promoters great importance was attached to it. Mr. Sheil conceived the bold idea of attending the meeting, and making a few statements on the opposite side. He qualified to become a freeholder in the county, that no legal objection might be taken against his right to address the assemblage. He kept

his intention a secret, except from a few intimate
friends, and presented himself to address the meeting.
His appearance caused the greatest excitement and
uproar. No one could hear a word of his speech; but
he delivered it steadily to the end, and then sent an
accurate copy of it to one of the evening papers; and
every part of the kingdom thus heard his arguments
and was penetrated by his eloquence. It was an admirable speech, marked by the soundest judgment in
the selection of its topics, and it was as eloquent as
the man's whole heart could make it. It produced a
great impression in all quarters. A public dinner was
given to him, at the City of London Tavern, by four
hundred friends of civil and political liberty. Jeremy
Bentham, who was prevented attending, expressed in
his letter of apology his admiration of the speech as
"a most masterly union of logic and rhetoric."

November 30. — Sir Walter Scott's sermons. What
twaddle! what logic! what common places given in the
commonest pitiful platitudes! Oh, genius! these are
the things that bring you into disrespect.

December 4. — Dinners in old times! The joyous,
brilliant tables of the Powers, the Grattans, the Bryans,
&c., &c., compared with the sumptuous dulness, and
expensive *menu* of the present style of dinner, what a
difference? I am led to this reflection from the accident
of meeting Harry Bushe, this morning, in the street,
just arrived from the south; and having persuaded him
to come and take *la fortune du pot*, at five o'clock, in
Kildare Street, and go with us to the play. We sat
down to a little round table, barely within the rule, of
not more than the Graces. Coffee was served, and the

4*

carriage at the door before seven, so that there was
not time for much more than a *causerie de désert*, but
I was struck by the humour, memory, reading, and
knowledge of past Irish life and Irish manners displayed; yet Harry Bushe was merely a man of fashion
in that brilliant circle in which we moved twenty years
back; well-educated, and well-bred, full of life and
spirit, fun and frolic, as were all the gentlemen of
that day. His brother, Parker Bushe, the last of the
pleasant gentlemen of Ireland, had more *wit*, tact, and
keen relish of humour than any man I ever knew.
The account of his death recently reached me in London. I exclaimed in the selfishness of my own social
loss, and in the words of Madame de Villette, on the
death of Chamfort, "J'ai perdu en lui mon meilleur
causeur." I might have added, *mon meilleur lecteur*,
for he was one of the men of Ireland *at whom* I wrote
my Irish novels; there were *hits*, and touches, and
traits in *O'Donnel* and *Florence Macarthy* which none
but such as he could appreciate and feel. These two
gentlemen are the nephews of the late Mr. Grattan,
and brothers-in-law to that most perfect of Irish gentlemen, Richard Power, of Kilfane, a class of men now
become extinct in Ireland, they are replaced by a dull
and dogged set.

I was in all the *prémices* of my passion for an antique lamp, which Hamilton, the painter, had got in
the tomb of the Cæsars, and I from his daughter, when
Mr. Wyse dropped in. I turned his attention to my
lamp, which I held in my hand. He observed it was
a true antique — a heathen and not a Christian lamp.
The heathen lamps, he said, are all of a finer and
lighter earth than those made after the Christian era,

when all the arts degenerated. They generally bear the impress of a dove, or cross, or olive branch, whilst those of the antique bore the head of a Jupiter or Mercury.

Poor Wyse! with a woman of taste and intelligence and domestic habits, how happy he might live; but I doubt if a woman of feeling would be happy with him; he married one without either, and whose whole existence was *une sotte vanité*.

CHAPTER IV.

LETTERS AND DIARIES — 1829.

ALTHOUGH Lady Morgan lived through such stirring times there is very little said in her journals about politics. She and Sir Charles were much mixed up in the movement for Catholic Emancipation, and Lady Morgan's drawing-room, in Kildare Street, was the *foyer* of liberalism; her influence over the young men who frequented her house was great, and all the leaders of the liberal party recognised her as a staunch and effective ally. Her salon was a rallying-point where people of all sects and shades of opinion met; she received alike dandies, women of fashion, political agitators, and members of the Government.

No two persons could have been more entirely opposed to each other in their nature, taste, and character, than Lady Morgan and Mrs. Hemans. With all her celebrity, Mrs. Hemans shrank from publicity, to which Lady Morgan had been inured, until it had become her second nature. They had no point of per-

sonality in common, except that both of them were
women of genius. It is very pleasant to see them
meeting on the mutual ground of womanly kindness.
The following letter from Mrs. Hemans must, in great
measure tell its own story. It would appear, that an
impression had gone abroad that the circumstances of
Mrs. Hemans were the reverse of comfortable, and it
had produced a desire amongst many of those who admired her genius and respected her character, to help
her in any mode that might be the most acceptable.
Lady Morgan, in her genuine kind-heartedness, came
forward to do as she would have wished to be done
by; her letter is not on record; but the reply of Mrs.
Hemans is at once dignified and grateful.

Mrs. Hemans to Lady Morgan.

WATERTREE, NEAR LIVERPOOL,
January 2, 1829.

MADAM,

I beg to acknowledge, with sincere thanks, the very
kind interest expressed towards me in your letters both
of which, after considerable delay, occasioned, I
imagine, by my late change of residence, I have just
received. It is indeed, pleasant to be the object of
feelings so cordial, to hear of unknown friends so zealous; nor do I the less gratefully own the services thus
frankly offered, because it is not necessary that I should
avail myself of them. I have recently met with a very
liberal publisher in Mr. Blackwood, and he has just
brought out new editions of two volumes, *The Records
of Women*, and *The Forest Sanctuary*, in which most of
the pieces originally sent to the *New Monthly*, and other
periodical works are collected. I will order copies of

them to be sent to Mr. Colburn's, for Lady Morgan, who will, I hope, honour me by her acceptance of them, and believe me, with a sincere feeling of her kindness,

Very truly
Her obliged servant,
FELICIA HEMANS.

In February, 1829, Parliament having been invited, in the Speech from the Throne, "to consider the condition of Ireland," proceeded to introduce a Bill for the summary suppression of political societies under whatever name they might exist. The duration of the Bill was limited to twelve months; it was passed without opposition, in order that the course might be cleared for the great impending struggle for Catholic Emancipation. It was well known amongst the friends of emancipation, that one of the Duke of Wellington's great difficulties, was the powerful body of the Catholic Association, as a word either of triumph or of threat from that body, would have rendered the King entirely intractable. This Association had been revived in 1827. It was a signal example of the faculty of organisation, and of the all but omnipotence of Association as an engine to carry any object it may have in view. The Catholics in Ireland had attained the perfection of national organisation; they had almost reached the discipline of a regular army. Perhaps the Anti-Corn Law League, many years later, is the only other organised popular machinery which can be compared to it.

The Catholic Association had done its work when the English Government had been induced to consider the best mode of granting political justice to the Roman Catholics. The friends of religious liberty felt that any sacrifice must be made to prevent the least pretext for revoking the good intentions formed with so much difficulty. Lord Anglesea, who had been won over to the cause of emancipation, used all his influence to induce the leaders of the movement to suspend their proceedings. But the members of the Association were somewhat reluctant to give up their position. There were meetings of the leaders, and many hot discussions; the prospect of public affairs was ominous and unsettled. It is mentioned in the *Life of Sheil*, by Torrens McCullagh, that at a party at Lady Morgan's, a letter from Mr. Hyde Villiers, (brother of the present Earl of Clarendon, then Commissioner of Customs to Dublin) was shown to one of the leaders of the Association. This letter reiterated all the pleas put forth by Lord Anglesea, for the suspension of the proceedings of the Catholic Association. Coming, as it did, from one who was supposed to know the intentions of the Government, it produced a great effect. Mr. Woulfe, the member to whom the letter had been specially shown, requested leave to show it to Sheil. A private meeting assembled at Sheil's house, where the important step was resolved upon; and when they separated, Sheil undertook to propose the dissolution of the Catholic Association, at the next meeting. Accordingly, on the 12th of February 1829, Mr. Sheil moved, "that on its rising that day, the Association should stand perfectly dissolved." "The object of this body," said he, "was, and is, Catholic Emancipation; that object, in my judgment, is already attained. Nothing, except our own imprudence, can defeat it. The end being obtained, why should we continue to exist? In a few days the Act of Parliament will put us down. Let us determine to dissolve, and declare our motives for so doing."

The motion was carried, after some debate, and the Confederacy, which had existed under various forms for six years, separated to meet no more.

February 12. — I am just returned from the meeting of the Catholic Association, and faithful to its fire; for so great was the heat, and crowd, and excitement, that I nearly died *under harness. The great question* — the dissolution of the Catholic Association, was the subject of debate; and every ardent mind came worked up to the contest. All the best feelings, cool judgment, and tact, was evidently for the prompt and voluntary extinction of this great engine of popular opinion.

February 13. — Yesterday was memorable for our great meeting at the Rotunda of the friends of civil and religious liberty — the first great thing of the kind since the great era of the northern volunteer martyrs, recalling the public spirit of 1782; there were fourteen peers present; but, for the account, see the newspapers of the day.

The *élite* of the *élite* dined with us the same day. Lords Miltown, Cloncurry, George Villiers, Henry Greville, Charles Brownlow, R. Sheil, John Power, Lord Clements; Lord W. Paget, and Lord Bective were invited, but were engaged, so they came in the evening with Wyse, and others of the notables. Since the Union, no such re-union has been in Dublin.

February 15. — I was at a party last night of the *débris* of the ascendancy faction; but the Orange ladies all looked *blue*, and their husbands tried to look green.

Very shortly after this event, Lord Anglesea was recalled from his Viceroyalty, to the great regret of all the liberal and enlightened portion of the Irish public. Lady Morgan wrote to him the following letter.

Lady Morgan to the Marquis of Anglesea.

KILDARE STREET, DUBLIN,
February 24, 1829.

MY LORD,
While your Lordship is still occupied in receiving testimonials of national gratitude and regrets, it is almost presumptuous in an individual to make claims upon time so importantly devoted; still I cannot resist the desire of soliciting your notice to the little *sketch* of vice-regal popularity in Ireland that accompanied this — for I am neither of a sex nor a country to permit discretion to wait on feeling; and I should be sorry to be the last (however least) of the many whose offerings of respect and admiration are about to follow the ex-Lord Lieutenant of Ireland in the privacy of domestic life. It is a proud, and I may say rare privilege, to be so followed. How few of your Lordship's predecessors have won it, and how dearly they have purchased it, forms the subject of pages which had probably never been written had this unfortunate country never benefitted by your government.

I have the honour to be, with deep sentiments of respect,

Your Lordship's

Obliged and obedient servant,

SYDNEY MORGAN.

This letter followed Lord Anglesea to England, whence he replied —

Marquis of Anglesea to Lady Morgan.

UXBRIDGE HOUSE,

February 28, 1829.

MY DEAR MADAM,

I have this moment received your flattering effusion of the 24th.

I never could bear to keep the ladies waiting, even for one moment, and therefore hasten to tell you, that as my hour of trust is so near its close, I issue no more proclamations.

Why, *the Perry* might take me, and with his two pocket justices commit me summarily! *Gare*, then, your coteries. There may be treason in tea drinking. I advise you to look to it.

But, surely, *you* did not suspect *me* of inditing in rhyme? *You must* have found out that *I* am the most prosaic, perhaps the most *prosy* (I leave you two full months to decide this latter point) of *all* representations of royalty.

Be this as may, I will not shine in borrowed plumes any longer. No, my dear Madam, I am as incapable of making a rhyme as of effecting the quadrature of the circle, or of speech making, and this latter misery is daily inflicted upon me.

March 4.

My DEAR MADAM,

My dismay is great at finding this scrawl amongst my papers. I really thought that it had gone, and been long since committed to your flames.

I now send it as I found it, merely to show, that if I had forgotten my letter, I had not felt indifferent to yours.

Do not let all my good friends quite forget me, and I beg you to

Believe me,
Very truly yours,
ANGLESEA.

Lord Anglesea was replaced by the Duke of Northumberland; hence the allusion to "the Percy."

March 11. — Sunday, dressing room, 12 o'clock. What an age since I put anything into this book! Christmas festivities at Lord Miltown's, Lord Cloncurry's.

My article on "Irish Lord Lieutenants" was sent off yesterday at two o'clock for the *New Monthly.* For five days I had been working against time and scarcely drew breath. To-day I am a lady at large (if not a large lady), and now for my own amusement and edification. Feet on fender — fire blazing away — snow falling — nothing but discomfort without and comfort within! soon will come my darling children and their good little father and dear little mother; and oh, the merry day we shall have in spite of wind and weather! And so please God we begin the new year; for this is our first family *réunion* in 1829.

The letters which follow relate mainly to the Irish politics of the year.

Lady Charleville to Lady Morgan.

My Lord has given the Roman Catholic Committee two hundred feet on the side of the Grand Canal, for two schools and a house, for the Sisters of Charity. As the population of Tullamore is about six thousand, our school (on the Lancastrian principle) holds one thousand, and is never half full, which does not suffice. To read, write, and cypher, and work, is good, come as it may; I will not consider it as an attempt to extinguish mine, but rejoice that anything is about to be done for the lower classes.

Farewell, and always believe how much I am

Yours faithfully,

C. M. C.

Richard Sheil to Sir Charles Morgan.

MY DEAR SIR CHARLES,

Pardon me for not having immediately answered your kind invitation. I intended to pay my respects to-day, and to say that I should wait on you. I saw Colonel Gosset, this morning, who says that Lord Anglesea goes on Monday. Lord Melville has refused the Government of Ireland. It is not known who will be appointed. Brougham omitted, from bad health, to attend two meetings of the Opposition. Lord Holland has written to Blake to say that the lukewarm are excited by Lord Anglesea's recall. It is considered a most improper proceeding Lord Holland has written a tract on Lord Bexley's attack on the Catholic religion!

Present my compliments to Lady Morgan, and believe me,

> Most truly yours,
> RICHARD SHEIL.

March. — So the *Quarterly* has let loose its dogs of war again on me, under the new groom of the kennel, Mr. Lockhart, of John Scott celebrity and Walter Scott's auspices. The Scotch reviews accuse my poor innocent *O'Briens and O'Flahertics* of being blasphemous and indecent — the old charge newly tagged up.

Now I have a right, like other British subjects, to be judged by my peers, and I summon a jury of matrons, of the most intact reputation, mothers "who wear pockets, and don't hold opera-boxes signs of inward grace," to say if they detect in my pages one line that tends to make one honest man my foe. Why, then, if they do, I submit to be branded with that horrible stigma with which a modest woman and a moral writer is now impugned withal. But I have been tried already before that truly Grand Jury, the PUBLIC, from which there is no appeal, and acquitted; and I have before me 'a letter from Mr. Constable, offering me the same terms as Sir W. Scott.

I see in the papers, to-day, the death of Mr. Gifford — the direst, darkest enemy I ever had. We never saw each other; he hated me for my success and my principles.

Mort le bête, mort le venim,

at least *esperons!*

Gifford was, it is said, in the receipt of a large income. During the time that he was editor of *The Quarterly Review*, Mr. Murray paid him nine hundred pounds a year. He received annually, as one of the comptrollers of the Lottery Office, six hundred pounds. He had a salary of three hundred pounds as paymaster of the band of Gentlemen Pensioners, two hundred a year as clerk of the Estreats in the Court of Exchequer; and, in addition to all these sums, he enjoyed a pension of, we believe, four hundred pounds per annum from Lord Grosvenor.

April 4. — Just dispatched to Colburn my preface to the *Book of the Boudoir*, which is to appear immediately. We are off to England, ourselves, and thence shortly to France.

April 6. — Adieu to care and home, to some whom I love, and to all whom I hate! I leave my trash bag behind me.

The Book of the Boudoir succeeded *The O'Briens and the O'Flaherties*. Her own account of it is given in the Preface, as follows: —

"Whilst the fourth volume of the *O'Briens and the O'Flaherties* was going through the press, Mr. Colburn was sufficiently pleased with the subscription (as it is termed in the trade) to desire a new work from the author. I was just setting off for Ireland — the horses literally putting-to — when Mr. Colburn arrived with his flattering proposition. Taking up a scrubby MS. volume, which the servant was about to thrust into the pocket of the carriage, he asked, what was that? I said it was one of my volumes of odds

and ends, and read him my last entry, made the evening before. "This is the very thing," said he.

It was as Lady Morgan says published in April,
1829. It contains short articles, essays, and observations, such as she was in the habit of writing in her
diary — a little enlarged and put into shape; but it
is the book that exhibits all her faults of style, and
manner, in an exaggerated form. It was bitterly
reviewed in *Blackwood*, where she was accused of all
the sins the Tory party could find to lay to her charge
— the worst she deserved to have said of the *Book
of the Boudoir* was, that it was careless, flippant, and
egoistical; it ought to have none but friends for readers;
the public is not accustomed to be treated in the free
and easy tone of this work, and as sins of taste are
always more resented than sins of principle, it is no
wonder that her enemies and detractors found an opportunity for being ill-natured, and availed themselves
of it. There are some admirable articles in *The Book
of the Boudoir;* but it is not the work on which Lady
Morgan's admirers would take their stand.

There is no journal of her visit to France, this
year, nor of her stay in London. There is the
following entry in her journal after her return to
Dublin.

September 1. — After a most delightful and triumphant visit to France, and residence of three months
in Paris; after a most prosperous journey through the
Low Countries and Holland, an excellent and agreeable voyage from *Ostend to London*, and business-like
and satisfactory residence in London, and a detestable

passage across the Herring Pond, we arrived at our
own dear but dirty little home, and a most joyous
meeting with our family in Great George's Street.

Lady Morgan, during her visit to London in 1829,
made the purchase of her *first carriage*, and took it
back to Dublin with great complacency.

Neither she nor Sir Charles knew any difference
between a good carriage and a bad one — a carriage
was a carriage to them. It never was known where
this vehicle was bought, except that Lady Morgan
always declared, "it came from the first carriage builder
in London."

In *shape* it was a grasshopper — as well as in
colour. Very high and very springy, with enormous
wheels, it was difficult to get in and dangerous to get
out. Sir Charles, who never in his life before had
mounted a coach-box, was persuaded by his wife "to
drive his own carriage."

He was extremely short sighted, and wore large
green spectacles when out of doors. His costume was
a coat, much trimmed with fur, and braided. James
Grant, their "tall Irish footman," in the brightest of
red plush, sat beside him, his office being to jump
down whenever anybody was knocked down or run
over, for Sir Charles drove as it pleased God. The
horse was mercifully a very quiet animal, and much
too small for the carriage, or the mischief would have
been more. Lady Morgan, in the large bonnet of the
period, and a cloak lined with fur hanging over the
back of the carriage, gave, as she conceived, the crown-
ing grace to a neat and elegant turn out.

The only drawback, to her satisfaction, was the

alarm caused by Sir Charles's driving; and she was
incessantly springing up to adjure him "to take care,"
to which he would reply, with warmth, after the manner of husbands.

September 11. — This day sat alone clearing out
the dust traps, refitting up from kitchen to garret,
working myself like a galley slave, removed between
two and three thousand volumes, cleaned and varnished
thirty pictures, washed all my old china and knick-
knacks, worked with my servants and the char-women
for three days successively. Talked much to the two
char-women — *such misery!!* Told them how to make
a bouilli instead of eating salt bacon, when they *did*
get meat. One of them, a half naked creature, was a
sentimentalist. I heard her say, in her slang brogue,
to her comrade, "Kitty, dear, did iver ye read Caroline
and Lindor? its an illegant story!" This must be
Caroline of Litchfield. One of the painters said "Did
you get a sup of 'By yer leave, Charley?'" (*read*
whiskey!)

September 12. — Went to Portrann (Mr. Evan's) to
get rid of the smell of the paint.

September 14. — Returned to town; house finished
and beautiful. Received a splendid present from the
Baron Gérard, of his picture of Henry the Fourth
entering Paris, the Tomb of Bonaparte, and Cupid
and Psyche, all framed and hung up along with my
other presents from eminent artists.

September 25. — Received my first invitation from
Duchess of Northumberland. Received a deputation
of weavers in their misery; they presented me a petition
to assist them. I wrote them an answer.

September 24. — Dinner party at home; little *soirée*

in the evening.   Brought in some improvements in
the *menu* of my table, which I have gathered in my
travels.   A *plombière*, first made known in Ireland,
great success.   Busy all day for my weavers.

September 30. — Begun my new work on France
— out of materials in journals; don't in the least
know what I shall make of it; interrupted by a *cours
de toilette;* an hour *bien sonnée* in my dressmaker's hands.
She is making up a fine tabinet dress for the Duchess
of Northumberland's party on Thursday.

The Duchess of Northumberland, it should be said
in explanation of the above, was a great patroness of
Irish manufactures; she made all the ladies of her court
live in tabinet dresses.   The Duke endeavoured to
develope Irish resources, and Tory as he might be, he
made himself beloved during his vice-royalty.

CHAPTER V.

THE SECOND WORK ON FRANCE — 1830.

SCRIBBLING all day; called down to the drawing-
room at near five o'clock.   "It's *Counsellor Curran*, my
lady!"   Morgan, invalided, came up enchanted to see
his friend Curran, though they are at the antipodes of
human feeling — my own Morgan being all heart, &c.

Morgan said, "Curran, we are quite alone, do stay
and dine with us."

(Now this is a most unfair thing in husbands —
this asking to dinner *à l'impromptu*, particularly a man
like Curran, who likes a good dinner). Clever Curran,

5*

who knows all the little *plis et replis* in the human
character better than the great, looked hesitatingly at
me. I laughed, and said, "It is not fair to take you
in; we are invalids; our dinner is an invalid dinner;
soup bouilli and a roast fowl, except we order up the
kitchen *pièce de resistance* — but I dare not mention it."

"If it is not a leg of beef smothered in onions,"
said Curran, laughing.

"No; but is almost as bad — a leg of pork and
pease-pudding," said I.

Quoth he, "The thing in the world I like best."
So he ran home to dress, stipulating we should let him
off the moment we had dined (an old trick of his);
but I chose to make the agreeable, so did he, and he
staid with us, *en tiers*, till midnight. He was, as he
can always be, most clever, amusing, and rational. He
gave us anecdotes and imitations of Steele, the Catholic
demagogue, admirably, particularly his *whacking* the
editor of the *Morning Herald* three several times, each
time observing, "*There!* I don't think I had complete
satisfaction!"

We talked of the good, but coarse Irish novel, *The
Collegians*. The story is a fact, and not only a fact,
but the trial of the hero, and the whole melancholy
event, was given by Curran in the *New Monthly Magazine*, just after it happened — in much finer style
than in the *Collegians*. The hero was a Mr. Scanlan,
a dissipated young man in the county of Limerick; his
family are what the peasants call, "small gentry," we
"gentry." His uncle, Mr. Scanlan, was High Sheriff
last year; Curran dined with him the day of the hero's
execution. Curran said the uncle's *sang froid* and in-

difference were frightful; he shrugged his shoulders,
tucked his napkin under his chin, said "it was a sad
business," and called for soup. In this, one may dis-
cern the same temperament as in the nephew, the
murderer.

The fair, frail girl, whom this Munster Lothario
had seduced, robbed her uncle of eighty pounds at
his suggestion — satiety and avarice were his motives
to marry her. She had given him forty pounds, he
wanted the rest, and to get rid of her.

When he had sent her off in the boat with his
servant, who was first to shoot and then fling her into
the Shannon, he lurked about the shore waiting his return. To his dismay, he saw the party row back —
she, all smiles and fondness, extending her arms to
him. The servant, taking him aside, said, "I cannot
kill her! Sure, when I had the pistol raised, she
turned round with her innocent face, and smiled so in
mine; I could not hurt a hair of her head, the cra-
thur."

Scanlan took him to a public-house; primed him
with whiskey, gave him a fresh bribe, and sent him
off once more, with his victim, to sail on the Shannon
— waited his return on the shore, and *saw him come
back without her*.

The other anecdote was this: — The jailor of
Limerick had been an old and confidential servant in
the Scanlan family, and had nursed this young man
on his knee.

When the moment of execution arrived, and he
knelt down to knock off the irons, his tears dropped
on every link, and looking up in the young man's face,
said, "Ah, Masther John! when I nursed you in

these arms, in your father's house, little ever I thought this would be the office I should do for you."

Scanlan died with a lie on his lips, denying the crime. He had been condemned on the strongest circumstantial evidence; but shortly after his death, the servant, who had murdered the girl at his command, was taken up for another murder and hanged. He gave every link that was wanted in the chain of evidence, and related the whole story a little before his execution.

The Prima Sera, as the Italians call it, is very agreeable. It begins immediately after dinner, or siesta; it includes the drive on the Corso, and the visit before the Opera. We have a prima sera that is suited to our climate and is very agreeable. It has the freedom of evening society with the sociability of morning visits. I mean the two hours which intervene between the fall of evening at four o'clock, and the dressing or dinner-hour — the hour when the pleasant visitors drop in — when the fire burns brightest, and the lamps are few, and one is still in one's morning-dress, and men put their splashed boots, without let or hinderance, where an hour or two afterwards it would be *outlawry* to appear in clean ones [*shoes* were, at that period, *de rigueur* in the evening], and the feet are put on the fender, and the shoulders find a resting-place in the luxurious arm-chair. The news comes fresh in from the ride or the club; the anecdote is still new from the ball or the *soirée*, where nothing is presumed and everything is ventured; when the story of the diner-out is not yet made, nor the sally of the professed wit held back for its *à propos;* when one talks nonsense *best*

and laughs at it *most*. It is enough to know there is
an epoch of the day when one may be agreeable without stimulus,. and enjoy without effort.

17th January. — Just heard of the death of Sir
Thomas Lawrence and of Mr. Monkton, Lady Cork's
brother.

January 20. — Yesterday we dined at Lord Dungarvon's, at Fairfield. Our party, Marquis and Marchioness Clanricarde, Earl and Countess of Howth,
Lady E. St. Lawrence, Master Townsend and his
daughter, Mr. Blake (Chief Remembrancer) and his
wife; Colonel Cruise, and *Dan O'Connell;* this being
the second time in my life that I ever met the re-
doubtable Dan. Dan is not brilliant in private society,
— not even agreeable. He is mild, silent, unassuming,
apparently absorbed, and an utter stranger to the give-
and-take charm of good society; I said so to Lord
Clanricarde, who replied, "If you knew how I found
him this morning; his hall, and the very steps of his
door crowded with his *clientèle* — he had a word or a
written order for each and all, and then hurried off
to the law courts, and from that to the Improvement
Society, at the Royal Exchange, and was the first
guest *here* to-day, when I arrived. Two hours before,
he was making that clever but violent speech to Mr.
La Touche, and now no wonder he looks like an
extinct volcano."

Lady Clanricarde is the only and much-loved daughter of Canning, and is quite worthy of being so, *quelle
tête*, inside and outside! beautiful and clever, every
word an epigram or a thought, pleasant and amusing
with it all! The dinner was charming, with sweet Lady
Dungarvon's warm, cordial manner of doing the honors

in her own pretty house. I had lots of Irish *shanaos* (Anglice, gossip), with these first-rate Irishmen. Lord Clanricarde told us of the burning down of his beautiful castle.

Feb. 28th. — Poor Molly! I cannot drive her or her situation out of my head. She is dying, but well cared for at my dear sister's.

Molly, as the reader may recollect, was the old nurse; one of the heroines of Lady Morgan's autobiography. She retained to the last her fine Irish black head of hair, and a few teeth as white as ever. She had become very *exigeante* and rather given to whiskey in her declining years; but she was still a specimen of a faithful retainer as distinguished from modern servants.

April 28th. — Joseph Lefanu, son of Sheridan's excellent sister, my old, kind friend, came to-day. It is the wreck of a dear old friendship. His visit to Kildare Street marks an epoch; he is broken down in health and spirits, — a premature old age. Dublin is a tomb to him, — all his friends dead. He spent the evening with us, and we gave up going to the birthnight to stay with him. The tint of intellect over all he says is very Lefanu-ish; he told me an anecdote of his uncle Sheridan missing a legacy of ten thousand pounds from a point of honour, refusing to go and see a man in his last illness lest he should suppose he was actuated by mercenary motives. I said, I believe that anecdote is in Moore's *Life of Sheridan.* "Oh, no," he replied, bitterly, "*this* is *authentic!*"

The following is an interesting notice of an ex-

cellent actress and good woman, who still lives warm
in the memory of all who knew her, and who will
always be a name of mark in the annals of the English
stage.

Miss Huddart (Mrs. Warner) was associated with
the best efforts of Macready and Mr. Phelps to renew
the drama and render the stage all that in certain conditions of society it is capable of becoming as a powerful engine for good.

Lady Charleville to Lady Morgan.

MY DEAR LADY MORGAN,

I beg to offer you and your nieces my tickets for
Miss Huddart's benefit; she is the meritorious and
amiable daughter of a lady of real merit, who was
well known to me, and moved in the best society, at
one time in Dublin. I am told this young actress is
very promising, and I can only answer for her being
the best of daughters, and having met with the heaviest
affliction lately by the loss of her father.

A show of patronage from persons of talent would
do much for a *debutante*, and I know you will lend
yourself for a few hours to serve this friendless young
creature on my account.

I beg Sir Charles to join you, and write me a few
lines with your opinion of her. If I could have gone
to Dublin to wait on the Duchess of Northumberland,
I should have been happy to have taken a box and
gone to see this young creature, for her mother's sake,
but *four* deaths have shadowed over my thoughts for
some time, and left me no joyous fancies for the present. I hope the saints may not shut up the theatre,

for it is literally true that I dare not speak of going to
a play to the few I am acquainted with in Dublin of
my lord's family.

I know how pleased you must be with the Relief
Bill, and I trust in God it may promote general prosperity in this country.

Yours,
C. M. CHARLEVILLE.

The reader will not have forgotten Mr. Wallace,
the old friend and correspondent of Lady Morgan. His
wife, who had long been an invalid, died some time
previous to Lady Morgan's marriage, and whether Mr.
Wallace had himself been a pretender to her favour,
or whether, without having made any declaration of
his intentions, he still felt aggrieved that another
should be preferred before him, there is no evidence to
tell; but the acquaintance ceased after Lady Morgan's
marriage. He was now a second time married; and
the following note is endorsed by Lady Morgan: —
"Mr. Wallace sent this note on the 27th, 1830, after
an interruption of friendship from the year 1811."
The month is not mentioned, but it was about this
period.

Thomas Wallace to Lady Morgan.

Monday Morning.

MY DEAR LADY MORGAN,
I was greatly mortified yesterday at finding you
and Sir Charles had called at Belfield, and departed
without asking for me. I was at home, and should
have been very much gratified indeed to have seen
you and him, meaning as you did such very kind

things towards us. Of those kind intentions I most
cheerfully shall avail myself, and shall participate
gladly in the hospitable and *spirituel* gratifications
which are always, I know, of olden time, to be found
with you and in the society which you select.

Mrs. W. will wait upon you.

Yours most truly,

THOMAS WALLACE.

May 20th.— Off to-day for Shangana and my dear
General Cockburn. I am breaking down again under
close air and want of exercise. Morgan, I declare,
loves me very well, but not well enough to break
through his usual habits of indolence, so he don't walk,
and hates driving. — so I have no resource.

May 30th. — Returned home the 27th — Shangana
is a divine spot! how I enjoyed its scenes! I used to
reproach the General for leaving it in these very
words —

> "Oh, how canst thou renounce the boundless store
> Of charms which nature to her votary yields,
> The warbling woodland, the meandering shore,
> The pomp of groves, the garniture of woods;
> All that the genial ray of morning gilds,
> And all that colours to the song of even,
> All that the mountain's sheltering bosom yields,
> And all the dread magnificence of heaven;
> Oh, how canst thou renounce and be forgiven?"

Gray says, "this of all others is my favourite stanza;
it is true feeling, it is inspiration!" How can *I* "hope
to be forgiven?" — saying this at the grove every day
as I returned from my walk before breakfast, when I
yielded to a vice-regal mandate, and came back to
town for the fête of the king's birthday at the park!

It was, however, a splendid scene. I had a deal of funny chat with the lord-lieutenant; what made it most droll was that two orange bishops were looking on; here was part of our talk —

Quoth I, "Lord Anglesea! some admire you as lord-lieutenant, some for your heroism, but I admire you for —

LORD A. "What, Lady Morgan? pray shock us!"

LADY M. "For the cut of your coat; who is your tailor? or is all this your own order?"

LORD A. (laughing) "Oh, I never give an order, I have an old model coat, the great great grandfather of this; I always say 'make it like this coat,' that is all *my* order."

LADY M. "The fact is, you dress better than any one, *et je m'y connais bien!*"

LORD A. "Well! I *did* dress well when I was young, *so well*, that my early and kindest friend, the late king, did me the honour to enter the lists with me; I remember his saying, at a ball at Devonshire House, 'There is that d — d Paget, better dressed than ever.' He went further than this. One day I went to Carlton House, by appointment; we were to go together, the prince and I, to some morning fête, I forget where. I had waited some time in the drawing-room, when a groom of the chambers put in his head, looked earnestly at me, and retired. Presently the valet of H. R. H. put in *his* head, stared, and retired. I began to get a little impatient, when a page entered, walked round, and followed the other two. The prince then made his appearance, *dressed exactly like myself!* I heard afterwards that he was dressed when I arrived, and had sent to see how I was dressed, successively

changing every article, till he was told he was my
double! All this *now* appears ridiculous, but *then* it
was *tout de bon*."

LADY M. "I don't think he would have taken your
excellency *now* as a model in anything."

LORD A. "No, he hated me, at least, he could never
forgive me my conduct in Ireland. I grieved at this,
for up to my first Irish vice-royalty, he was the kindest of the kind, and I loved him much."

LADY M. "Well, but to go back to the toilette,
don't you think one gets more *soigné* as one gets
older?"

LORD A. "I really think one does; in fact, one
owes it to society to make amends for the defects of
time; we ought to shock the younger world as little as
possible."

Morgan joined us, and we got into politics.

Lord A— said, "Much has been done in the way
of reform, but the Tories *must swallow more yet*, the
Church establishment must retrench. If those gentlemen would save anything, they must give up much.
If the king had lived a year longer, you would have
had a revolution, nothing could have stopped it."

June 17. — Off to Lyons.

June 27. — Returned from Lyons — Lord Cloncurry's,
a long, large party — the first day good — Sheil, Curran,
and Jack Lattan. I never saw him in such force; he
thanked me with all the gallantry and enthusiasm of
youth for my allusion to him in the *Book of the Boudoir*. "Forty years back," he said, "it would have
driven me mad, and even *now* it makes my head turn."
His brilliancy overwhelmed all the wit present; Sheil
was silent, and Curran dull. All sat staring and

listening. He is part of a bygone generation, — his wit was, perhaps, *trop fort*. His wit put me in mind of poor Grassini singing in Paris last year, — it would be invidious to say why. After all, Lord Cloncurry is the drollest of the droll, he makes me laugh more than any one. We had the Jocelyn, Percys, and others very charming. Lord Cloncurry made me die, by the simple way he told me that when the Duke of Northumberland was coming to stay a few days at Maritimo, he said to Lord Cloncurry, "Do not put yourself to any inconvenience for my people, (his servants), they never drink either port or claret." "Upon my word," said Lord Cloncurry, "I am very glad to hear it, for with me they will only get very small beer."

July 1st. — I had a few people last evening, — my own family, Curran, General Cockburn, and the ex-judge Johnson; Johnson is a fine specimen of the old wit, talent, and literary condition of Ireland. He was the intimate friend of the celebrated Curran, to whose son he is much attached. Though eighty-five years of age his conversation is full of force, humour, and gallantry, scarcely a trace of age. He told me in the morning he should give up a dinner-party and box at the theatre to come to us.

Captain Arthur Wellesley (the Duke of Wellington's nephew) dropped in. In the course of the evening Johnson told him an anecdote of his illustrious uncle that amused him.

"I dined," he said, "about forty years ago with old Colonel Ross, of Gloucester Street, Dublin; Ross's nephew, a college boy, (the late General Ross,) dined with us; in the middle of dinner, a little aide de camp, a playfellow of Ross's, came in. They amused each

other at dinner with running pins into each other, and
made such a noise that the old Colonel, starting up,
cried, "G—d d—n it, boys, if you cannot be quiet, go
out into the yard and play ball, but don't disturb the
dinner." The boys, were the Duke of Wellington
and General Ross.

Judge Johnson was a judge who was prosecuted
for a seditious libel; it was an attack on Lord Hardwicke, when lord-lieutenant of Ireland (published in
Cobbett's Register), at the moment when he had a seat
on the Bench. The jury found him guilty of the libel;
but an opportune change of ministry between the ver-
dict and the sentence, allowed a *nolle prosequi* to be
entered. He retired from the Bench, on a pension, in
1806. He had a most unprofessional taste for military
affairs, and held some peculiar theories; amongst others,
that pikes and arrows were better weapons than mus-
kets or bayonets; and he prided himself on having
invented a pike with a hollow staff, to contain arrows,
and a leg to support the weapon, and side traces to
unite it with others, so as to form a *chevaux-de-frise!!*

July 5th. — Left town on Friday for Morris Town,
the seat of Jack Lattan, County Kildare; he carried
us off *vi et armis* in his old French *calèche*, with his
old French horses, and his French cook driving us.
He comes yearly from his hotel in the *chaussée d'Antin*
to his old seat in the Bog of Allan; what a transit!
As we passed that vast ruin, the palace built by Lord
Stafford, near Naas, (one of the items in his indict-
ment), he pointed to a field under the window of the
ruin. "There," he said, "begins my estate, we held
it under King John, and never lost or added an acre;
we must have been very mediocre people." Lord

Stafford, in one of his letters, describing this palace as
having been built with the hope of having the king's
majesty his guest, observes, "My close neighbour is
one Lattan, an Irish Papist." The Wentworth property is now Lord Fitzwilliam's. The traditions of
this country are all in Lord Stafford's favour, he did
no violent things here. Lattan said his memory fa-
tigued him by its redundance. What myriads of anecdotes! Here is a funny one. The Duc de Laval
said to him, one day, on the subject of England —
"Ecoutez mon cher, je connais l'Angleterre au fonds,
les fils aînés sont tous riches et ivrognes, les cadets
sont pauvres et volent sur le grand chemin!"

Lord Cloncurry in his *Life and Times*, mentions
Mr. Lattan having been in the French service, 1793;
he describes him as one of a race, now extinct; a genuine Irishman, in heart and purpose; his service in
France, as an officer in the Irish brigade, had added
the polish and gallantry of a French gentleman, while
his manly figure was set off in full perfection by the
air and habits of a soldier of the old school. The
brilliancy of his wit was never clouded, nor his enjoyment of present mirth ever damped by thoughts of
to-morrow. When his purse was full, he drew upon
it without scruple, for self or friends, and when it was
empty he would sit down to translate the *Henriade*,
to help an *émigré* friend with the proceeds of its publication.

French Revolution.

September 5th. — Since I last scribbled in these
pages, what events! I have lived in them, for them,
and with them, even at this distance from the scene of

action! My life, made up of sensations, will be found in the postscript of my new *France*, the publication of which was retarded for the purpose of inserting it. I shall not say a word of this great subject here.

September 8. — The arrival of Moore and his family has *fait epoch*. We had to meet him at dinner yesterday, — North, Sheil, Curran, and my own family; all his old cronies in the evening, and his old love, Mrs. Smith, to whom he addressed the song "If in the dream that hovers." He sang as well as ever, but it made us all sad; all he sang had reference to the past. I felt when I went to bed as if I had been at the funeral of old friends.

Moore refers to this dinner in his diary, September 7, 1830. "Desperate wet day; dined at Lady Morgan's — company, Edward Moore, North, Curran, Sheil, the Clarkes."

Great delay about the appearance of my book, it takes six days to receive and return each proof sheet. It ought to come out to-morrow.

The second *France* was published on the 7th of September, 1830. It is in every respect superior to the first, except that the continent having now been open for fourteen years, the present work had not the peculiar zest of novelty. To the present generation of readers, however, the *France* of 1829-30 belongs as completely to a time gone by as the Gaul of the days of Cæsar. *France* of 1829-30 is a very brilliant book, and it is not so flippant as its predecessor. There is much less self glorification about social flatteries and attentions; Lady Morgan had become more accustomed

to such things, and her own position in society was
both higher and better defined. The points where she
produces herself in the present work, are precisely
those on which her own sympathies and associations
appeal to the reader, and give a special interest to the
topic in hand. Each chapter makes a charming
feuilleton, abounding in wit and shrewd observation. If
we had to point out the work in which Lady Morgan
has given herself and her peculiar genius the fairest
play and the fullest development, we should take our
stand upon her second work on *France.*

The political and social shades of society in France
immediately previous to the revolution of 1830, "the
three glorious days" which have now passed into oblivion along with much other "pomp and glory of the
world," are caught like a rainbow at the brightest
moment. The men and women of the time, — the
politics, the pictures, the music, the drama, the shrines
of historical interest and of social associations — may
be seen as in a magic mirror. The chapter on the
drama brings back the faint echoes of names which in
our youths filled the public ear. When Mademoiselle
Leontine Fay was the young, handsome, charming
jeune première of the Théâtre de Madame, "drawing
fastfalling, unconscious tears and half-stifled sobs from
all Paris in the *Mariage d'Inclination;*" and when
Dumas' *Henri III.* was a new piece, with Mademoiselle
Mars for its heroine, Rossini is spoken of as "overwhelmed with his professional labours," putting the
finish to his *William Tell*, which had been for the last
two months the topic of conversation and expectation
in the musical world of fashion. The chapter on
romanticists and classists is very amusing. Lamartine,

Victor Hugo, St. Beuve, were then *faisant leurs épreuves*, and are noticed as new authors. The chapter on modern literature contains some excellent criticism and sound remarks. The chapter called "Mornings at Paris" is a charming *resumé* of people and things. Names appear on each page with a personal sketch or a *mot*, which makes the reader at once of their society. There is a visit to Béranger in the prison of La Force; and there are two memorable dinners; one at the Comte de Ségur's, with a record of the conversation as fresh and as amusing as if it were not on topics half a century old; the other is a dinner at Baron Rothschild's, dressed by the great Carême, who had erected a column of the most ingenious confectionery architecture, on which he had inscribed Lady Morgan's name in spun sugar. What woman would not have been flattered by such a tribute! The chapter on *The Archives of France* contains a lively account of her pilgrimage to shrines, dear from historical associations, but not set down in any guide book, and disappearing under the march of imperial improvement. It would be impossible to give a detailed criticism on these two charming volumes, but we would advise our readers in their own interest to send for them, instead of "something new from Mudie." The chapters by Sir C. Morgan consist of articles on philosophy, public journals, primogeniture, and public opinion. They are good, and the conscientious opinions of a man whose indorsement is worthy of respect.

This work was, however, destined to cause Lady Morgan more trouble and annoyance than she met with in the whole of literary life put together. It made an event in Lady Morgan's life, and was in itself

6*

a curious illustration of the laws and customs of the
republic of letters, as it existed in the year of grace,
1830.

Sir Charles and Lady Morgan had gone to France
entirely *proprio motu*, without any bargain or under-
standing with any bookseller.

On their return, Lady Morgan set to work to write
her scenes and impression. Colburn took it for granted
that she neither could nor would leave him for any
other publisher; he considered that Lady Morgan was
bound to him in literary matrimony for better and
worse, and he behaved to her with a cool security
which was not altogether suited to her character. She
wrote to tell him she was writing a second work on
France. Colburn, who was always in arrears with his
correspondence, did not reply. Lady Morgan wrote
again, and as her letter produced no answer beyond a
lazy request to be told the size, title, and topics of the
new work, with no definite offer. Lady Morgan then
opened a negociation with Messrs. Saunders and Otley,
just, as years before, when Sir R. Phillips refused, in
the matter of the *Wild Irish Girl*, to give the price she
demanded, she wrote to Johnson, a rival publisher, as
the reader may remember. She wrote again to Colburn
to tell him what she had done. Mr. Colburn wrote an
indignant letter to Sir Charles Morgan, July 4, 1830,
the very handwriting of which testifies to his rage at
her ladyship having opened a correspondence with another house: — "I can only *now* say, that if Lady
Morgan does not break off the negociation (which is
simply done on the plea of a misunderstanding) it will
be no less detrimental to her literary than to her pecuniary interest. As to myself, it is a very different feel-

ing, and not my pecuniary interest that makes me urge
this matter, as I can prove, if necessary, I have lost
considerably by the last two or three works; but I am
ready, and always have been, to give Lady Morgan
more than the value of her works when I know *what I
am to bid for* — pray recollect, that Lord Byron used
to send his works to Murray without hesitation."

This *sourde* threat was not likely to intimidate an
intrepid woman like Lady Morgan, who had stood fire
so many years, and who loved a fight like a true Mi-
lesian. The bargain with Messrs. Saunders and Otley
was concluded. The terms were to be a thousand
pounds for the copyright; five hundred pounds to be
paid down on the publication of the work, the other
five hundred by four bills at different dates.

The work was published in two volumes, the type
and paper were unexceptionable, the appearance of the
volumes was handsome, and a spirited portrait of her
ladyship, as a frontispiece. The first payment was
duly made — and then — there came a full stop! The
new work by Lady Morgan instead of being received
with a lively sensation as usual, encountered a dead
silence. Messrs. Saunders and Otley writing to Lady
Morgan, September 23, 1830, say, "In reply to your
inquiry respecting the sale of the work, we are sorry
to say it has been anything but encouraging; the booksellers having taken very sparingly, and we have had
but a small demand, although much had been previously
done in the way of advertising, &c., the effect of which
must, no doubt, have been greatly impeded by the opposing system practised. The notice in the *Chronicle*,
slight and incidental as it is, is the most favourable
that has yet appeared. A system of indiscriminate cen-

sure appears to pervade all others, while the more in-
fluential remain silent."

Colburn had proved what he could be as a friend,
and he was now showing what he could be as a foe.
Not only was he enraged at losing "one of his authors,"
— his favourite one, too, but he was also exasperated
at the audacity of any other publishers in entering into
competition with him, and he proceeded to let them
see how he could punish them, and to teach Lady
Morgan that her success had been less owing to her
own genius than to his own skill as a publisher.

"The opposing system," referred to in the letter from
Messrs. Saunders and Otley was a series of manœuvres
and advertisements by Colburn, on the announcement
of the new work by Lady Morgan on France.   The
newspapers of the day appeared with this advertisement, — LADY MORGAN AT HALF PRICE. The
advertisement stated that in consequence of the great
losses which he had sustained by Lady Morgan's former
works, Mr. Colburn had *declined* this present book on
France, and that all the copies of her books might be
had at half price.   Nothing more insulting to Lady
Morgan or more damaging to the success of the new
work, could have been contrived.   Sir Charles and
Lady Morgan were powerless to combat this state of
things; and Messrs. Saunders and Otley wrote more and
more piteously about their own loss, entreating to have
a modification of their contract. They proposed to give
up their copyright, to receive back their bills for the
second five hundred pounds, and to bring out a second
edition (so called) of the twelve hundred copies on
hand, Lady Morgan sharing the profits.

Lady Morgan offered to give them an extension of

time, but declined to let them off their bargain, saying,
that a contract was a contract. Her second edition, as
it was called, answered no better than the first; and
Messrs. Saunders and Otley were losers upon every
item, — printing, paper, advertisements, &c., in addition to the five hundred pounds in cash they had paid
to Lady Morgan, and the further sum for which they
were liable. Sir Charles and Lady Morgan obtained
Counsel's opinion as to the chance of making Colburn
amenable for his proceedings. Mr. Wallace, Q. C. (Lady
Morgan's old lover,) gave it as his opinion that a case
would lie against him, as it could be proved he had
used threats; but Saunders and Otley did not choose to
send good money after bad, and declined a lawsuit.
After a tedious correspondence, which extended over a
year, they declared their intention, on the 1st of September, 1831, to go to law to get their contract can-
celled. Eventually, the whole affair came into court.
The curious and peculiar feature in the case was, Colburn's own admission that he had been so enraged at
losing Lady Morgan's work, that he had done everything he could to injure her literary reputation, and to
damage the sale of Messrs. Saunders and Otley's publication; that he much regretted what he had done under
the influence of wounded feeling; and he took that opportunity of retracting whatever he had said in her
disparagement. Speaking of his magazines, he said
that he paid his other contributors according to a fixed
tariff; but that to Sir C. and Lady Morgan he gave
whatever price they demanded. Lady Morgan, in re-
lating this history, always said, that Colburn behaved
like an angry lover seeking a reconciliation with his
mistress. The matter was at length arranged; Colburn

made some proposal that satisfied Messrs. Saunders and
Otley. But Lady Morgan was not to be so easily ap-
peased. She was sorry to have been the cause of loss
and annoyance to Messrs. Saunders and Otley, instead
of the goddess of good fortune, which she had hitherto
been to all. To compensate in some degree to them,
and to show that she was perfectly satisfied with their
conduct, she allowed them to publish *Dramatic Scenes
and Sketches from Real Life*. But neither did they make
this work answer as a literary speculation. We shall
speak of it in its proper place.

Thomas Campbell was at this period the editor of
Mr. Colburn's magazine, the *New Monthly*. Being the
friend of Lady Morgan and of her husband, he was
naturally in an embarrassing position, for at this time
the quarrel between Colburn and Lady Morgan was at
its bitterest. The following letter shows that he did
his best to act uprightly towards all parties.

Thomas Campbell to Lady Morgan.

MIDDLE SCOTLAND YARD,
September 8th, 1830.

MY DEAR LADY MORGAN,

I write to you under the depression of a most
miserable bad cold, but so impatient am I to commu-
nicate the sum and substance of what I have to say,
that I was determined not to delay my answer till the
cloudy atmosphere of head should clear up.

The sum and substance is, that dexterous as the
little man is, he will be cleverer than even himself at
mischief, if he contrives to make the *New Monthly* a
vehicle for his further malignity towards you. I will

watch every sheet and sentence that goes to press, and nothing, with my permission, shall go to press that is in the least disrespectful to you.

If I followed the impulse of my own feelings, I should not limit myself to *negative* conduct in this business. You may easily imagine what I think of Colburn's conduct to you. It shocked and disgusted me when I heard of it, and, moreover, it astounded me, for his conduct to myself has, on the whole, been very fair and liberal. I thought him incapable of such an action as the advertisement, and if he ever enters upon the subject with me, I will tell him my mind in the strongest reprehensive terms. But my interests are, unfortunately, for the present, involved with his, and I have disagreeable subjects enough to discuss with him without entering on that point. On this, however, you may rely, that he shall not get the *New Monthly* to be an engine of his hostility.

God knows when I may be able to accomplish my long-thought-of jaunt to the Emerald Isle. I trust, however, ere long, to see you or Sir Charles, or both of you, on this side of the Channel; you will surely visit us this year. Here you will find me in a far more liveable part of London than I lived in before, which was so remote that it almost kept me out of society. I am now within a bow-shot of what Dr. Johnson called the full tide of human existence at Charing Cross. I beg my best regards to Sir Charles, and not forgetting to congratulate you both on the late glorious events,

I remain, my dear Lady Morgan,

With respect and regard,

Yours truly,

T. CAMPBELL.

September 17th. — Moore brought a delightful man to us yesterday, the fashionable wit, Luttrell, of the Lady Cork and Charleville set, and author of the *Advice to Julia.* The moment Moore got in, he tried, as usual, to get out. Morgan said, "I beg pardon for the proposition, but do sit down if you can." "Oh, you have *found him out,*" said Luttrell; "I have rarely seen him stay so long anywhere." He got upon the public journals: Luttrell said the *Court Journal* was the standard of bad taste, and cited its calling Lady Londonderry "our own Emily." Talking of Hazlitt, my old critic, and of his special dirtiness, Moore told the anecdote of Charles Lamb, saying to him when they were playing cards nearly as dirty as his hands, "Hazlitt, if dirt were trumps, what a fine hand you would have!" Our wits belong to the last century.

My husband wished to get up a dinner for Moore, at his club, here is his answer: —

Thomas Moore to Sir Charles Morgan.

September 20th, 1830.

My dear Morgan,

I need not say to you how much I feel both the honour and kindness of the invitation which you propose to me, but the fact is, my mind is now wholly set upon getting away as soon and as safely as these equinoctial breezes will let me. Having the nervous task of transporting women and children, at this time of the year, either by Bristol or Liverpool, I am preparing to take advantage of the very first appearance of more settled weather, and, therefore, could not form any engagement that would be likely to interfere with this purpose, nor, indeed, enjoy it at all as I ought, if I *did* form it. It is my intention, however, to be here again before the end of next spring, and then (if my kind friends of the Dawson Street Club continue still in the same disposition towards me) it will give me the most sincere pleasure to accept their invitation. I write in a hurry, but you will, I know, have the kindness to convey all this to them in a way that will best do justice to my feelings, and believe me,

Ever, my dear Morgan,

Most truly yours,

THOMAS MOORE.

Moore mentions this dinner in his diary, and says, "It is the *third* dinner that has been in contemplation for me, one of them being a mob feast at six shillings a head, which Jack Lawless wants to get up for me."

October 29th. — O'Gorman Mahon is not a charlatan, but a mountebank — a mountebank on wire. When asked to dine at the chief secretary's, the other day, he arrived when dinner was nearly over, in a chaise and four horses, two postilions, &c., &c., and entering the room, where he was an utter stranger, exclaimed, on seeing Sheil at the further end of the dinner table, "Ah! ah! my little friend, so you are here!" my blood ran cold, thinking what would come next. I blush for my countrymen.

November 23rd. — A *delightful* letter and pretty present of tablets from dear Lady Emily Hardinge. —

A letter from the editor of the *Athenæum*, offering me liberal terms — altogether a pleasant post.

This is Lord Anglesea's day of entry! What an apotheosis! O'Connell has organised all that is false, bad, and ungrateful in the country against him. All through the town are placards ordering "All who love Ireland to stay at home." Some of O'Connell's "two thousand gentlemen" took their stations in different places, and endeavoured to harangue the people against this once idol of the nation; but in spite of this, Lord Anglesea had with him all the intelligence, wealth, rank, and respectability of the country. The cries of "O'Connell for ever!" "Down with dirty Dogherty!" were abundant. Morgan got out of a sick bed to go and meet him (much to my anxiety and apprehension). Lord Cloncurry came home with Morgan after the swearing in of the lord-lieutenant, and afterwards dined at the state dinner at the castle. Amongst some of the odd and pleasant things Lord Cloncurry told us, was, that Billy Murphy wrote to him to say that O'Connell would call on him at Maritimo on Tuesday last, to offer him all the trades to walk in procession, to meet Lord Anglesea on his entry. Lord Cloncurry waited at home all day, but the "Liberator" never came — *en attendant*, he had changed his mind, and absolved the people from all gratitude to their true friend. Ireland seems now organised for revolution. The government has not one periodical organ, — O'Connell's party has all, save the Orange papers, who are equally factious. It is very disheartening. Meantime, parliament at this most critical moment is prorogued.

The "letters" alluded to in the ensuing note from

Lord Anglesea, were in all probability contributions from Sir Charles or Lady Morgan herself, to some liberal journal. Contributions of common sense, and a little tranquil stupidity, administered with discretion, were, doubtless, the best possible remedies for the restless cleverness of the Irish character. There is a great virtue in stupidity, it gives cohesion, and is a necessary quality before cleverness can attain the breadth and solidity of wisdom.

Marquis of Anglesea to Lady Morgan.

UXBRIDGE HOUSE,
December 3rd, 1830.

DEAR LADY MORGAN,

I have been favoured by the receipt of your obliging letter of the 28th of November, and have also received the letters you were so kind as to send. These had already attracted my notice, and very able productions they are. The subject is admirably handled, and cannot fail to do infinite good.

Oh, that Ireland would try the effect of a little quiet! From mere curiosity she should try it. Granted, that bustle and agitation are very charming, but *toujours, toujours perdrix!* is too much. Do let us be very still and stupid, I am fit for that state of things, and for that only, for I am a sad sufferer, and nothing but the restless desire I have to contribute my mite to help you all, could have induced me to quit my arm-chair. You must all compassionate me, and be very good.

Believe me,
Dear Lady Morgan,
Very truly yours,
ANGLESEA.

The following letter from Thomas Moore to Lady Morgan, is about literary matters. Incidental mention of an offer he had once had "to conduct the *Times*."

Thomas Moore to Lady Morgan.

SLOPERTON COTTAGE,
December 22nd, 1830.

MY DEAR LADY MORGAN,

As you seemed to think it better that I should commune *direct* with the publisher, and I had a prospect of being shortly in town, when I could deliver my answer in person, I deferred writing to either you or them till that opportunity should occur. I have now seen your messengers, at least, one of them; a very grave, respectable bibliopolist as I should wish to meet with, and have given him my answer (as I feared all along I should) in the *negative*. I was glad, however, to see that he had not much set his heart upon the plan, and I shall hope that neither have *you* been very desirous of it, as I hate to refuse anything that *any* body (how much, therefore, such a luminous lady as yourself) wishes me to do. The fact is, it would not be worth a publisher's while to give me such a sum as *alone* would make it worth *my* while to put myself so much out of my way. I was once offered at the rate of one hundred pounds a month to conduct the *Times* for a certain period, and at another time had a proposal from Croker to edit the *Quarterly Review*, at a thousand pounds a year, but neither tempted me. Talking of the *Times*, I have no conception of who was the author of that malignant attack upon you, but meant

to have asked the editor, had I seen him when I was
in town. That great machine and I have long parted
company; their politics under the Duke of Wellington
(as I took care to tell them), being everything that I
most detested. I shall be always glad, however, when
they are in the ways of orthodoxy (as they seem to be
just now), to put a helping hand to the lever, for such
it is of the most massive kind.

Mrs. Moore begs to be most kindly remembered to
you and Sir Charles, who is, I trust, by this time, quite
himself again.   Ever yours, most truly,

Thomas Moore.

PS. — People express a little alarm about my *Life
and Death of Lord Edward*, and I get hints from all
sides that it would be prudent to defer its publishing;
but I shall not mind them.

Christmas-day. — My birth-day — *à quoi bon?* —
still I have great cause to be thankful whilst all I
love live. What a cordial greeting from the Clarkes;
how soothing! how cheering! what a beautiful aspect
of life! Love and the arts — I found them all round
the round table, the blackest frost without; all warm
and sunshine within. Flaxman's illustrations of Dante
on the table, Morgan strumming Rossini at the piano,
Josephine with her pencil, sketching the group, &c.,
&c. Alas! how long will this last? We returned
home better in health, feelings, and spirits, forgot
O'Connel and the Irish Rebellion, the calumnies of
authors, the envy of critics, and soon the whole world,
in the calm, deep sleep of temperance and kindly
feelings.

CHAPTER VI.

LAST YEARS IN DUBLIN — 1831.

This note from Lady Morgan to Moore, at the period when there was an Irish Coercion Bill in prospect gives a picture of a state of things which we hope is never likely to return.

Lady Morgan to T. Moore.

KILDARE STREET, DUBLIN,
January 2nd, 1831.

DEAR MR. MOORE,

I am tempted to put your *good nature* at *rest*, with respect to the *refusal* of the *editorship.* Your friend Crampton (whom I met at dinner yesterday) has offered to forward a note to you by *his* packet. So I am tempted to write. *My* opinion is, that it would be for the advantage of literature if *periodical* publications were put down for ever. Mr. Crampton and I agreed last night that we should be inclined to "put on the *list of friends those whom you say have advised you not to publish* your *Life of Lord Edward*, at this most *mal à propos and inauspicious moment. Ireland* is no more the *country you left* three months ago than it is *Cochin China!* To judge by the outline and aspect of things, a *connoisseur* in *revolution* (and I am *pos mal* in that species of *virtù*) all would say we were on the eve of the worst and most perilous political commotions *one* coming from *below*, and such elements! Imagine countless thousands of the lower classes pouring through the streets, silent, concentrated, *worked* by a nod, a sign; and this, the day after a proclamation from the government, forbidding *all* meetings. (!) All other classes are *paralysed*; government is without *one* organ to address to public *opinion; not one newspaper* in its service — *terrorism* the order of the day and a parliament *dispersed* for six weeks at least, and the nation left to the prayers of the Archbishop of *Canterbury* and the black *Pasto* of Mr. Percival. It is clear that they know nothing about us in England; by this time, however, Lord Anglesea has probably *given* them a *hint; his reception* is a stain upon the country, which can never be effaced; peace or war (*civil war and extending woes*) now lies in the influence of O'Connell over the passions of the people; "*to this complexion are we come at last.*"

In haste,
Dear Mr. Moore,
Yours truly,
S. MORGAN.

January 26th. — I made a very agreeable sort of Donnybrook fair party on Friday last, — 20th. My women were all pretty, and my men all pleasant, and *pour comble* we got up a proverb *en action*, in very good style, all *à l'improvisé*, and though almost strangers to each other in this line, they were acted *à merveille.*

The proverb — "Poverty comes in at the door, love flies out at the window."

What shouts of laughter and fun! — our audience — Lord Douro, Lord Headford, Sir Guy and Lady

Campbell, Sir E. and Lady Blakeney, Augustus Liddle,
Colonel Bowater, Lord F. Paulet, Mrs. Caulfield, Miss
Armitt, and Miss Crampton.

Had a letter to-day from David, the sculptor,
sending me my own bust in marble, and that of
Lafayette!

February 15th. — Sitting all alone to-day; just
before dinner enter T. Moore! *pardi!* I could not believe my eyes. "Why, what on earth brings you
here? is it to dine with me to-day?" "No, I'll dine
with you to-morrow." "My mother was dying, I was
sent for, she has seen me, and has revived." Morgan
came in. Moore sat all the time; I never before saw
him sit for ten minutes together; he was cordial, and
pleasant, and confidential. He told us many strange
things. Poor fellow, he has never been able to get out
of debt. He told us Rogers had expended three thousand pounds on the publication of his dandy book. Oh,
these amateur authors who write for fashion, while *we*
write for fame or famine! Moore says he thinks Murray
would like to publish for me.

February 17th. — I had a little dinner got up in a
hurry for Moore, yesterday; it was got up thus. I
threw up my windows and asked the inmates of the
cabs and carriages of my friends as they passed the
windows, and sent out some penny porters, and lighted
up my rooms. Moore was absolutely astounded when
he saw my party! He sang some of his most beautiful
songs in his most delightful manner, without stopping;
some of them twice over, and all of them as if every
word was applicable to the people around him. Many
of his old friends were around him; I said, "if you

stay a day or two longer, I'll do better than this."
"No, no," he said, "never again can such a thing bo
done. This is one of the few happy accidents which
occur rarely; besides, I don't want to efface the impression even by something better."

I never saw him more natural or agreeable. He
praised Murray to the skies, and said ho was princely
in his conduct to authors. Moore disliked me in my
youth; he told me at Florence that he thought Byron
did not wish to know *me*, and *did* wish to know
Morgan.

April 1st. — Poor Molly! I went to see her, and
the whole was too much for me — my dear Morgan
just returned from her — we are with her every day!
What a scene! her whole anxiety is about her funeral,
her coffin, &c. I have promised her to do all, and
now she is at peace, although her drunken sister (who
is looking forward to a glorious wake) has brought
her priest, who told her she could not be saved. My
sister is all goodness to her, and nurses her like a
mother!

Morgan and I have just had a *battle royal!* The
subject was, as usual, one of my improvements in the
house. All, however, of my improvements have been
made at *long* intervals; the *last* I was five years working at. The present point at issue is, *I* want a little
greenhouse to put my plants in on the *open space* at the
back of the stairs; I want this done, and have offered
to pay for it. Morgan vows I never shall have it, and
is gone out in a passion; but I don't despair. Upon
this occasion I am a bore, and he is — a bear.

Mrs. Hemans had at this period settled in Dublin.

7*

Friendly acquaintance and interchange of well disposed
civilities went on between herself and Lady Morgan,
in spite of the differences of their habits, for Mrs.
Hemans was then an invalid, and inclined to withdraw
from general society, in which Lady Morgan found her
element.   These distinguished women regarded each
other with high consideration.

From Mrs. Hemans to Lady Morgan.

UPPER BAGOT STREET,
May 7th.

Mrs. Hemans presents her compliments to Lady
Morgan, and returns the "Metropolitan," with many
thanks for all the pleasure it has afforded her.   She
trusts that her little messengers may be able to bring
her an improved account of Lady Morgan's health,
and that the particulars of the *Macaw's début* in
fashionable life will not be long withheld.

This Macaw was the pet of Lady Cork and Orrery,
and Lady Morgan was writing a *jeu d'esprit*, called
Memoir of a Macaw of a Lady of Quality.

A letter marked private has always an attraction;
the present note from Sheil is about public affairs, and
though time has deprived them of all the uncertainty
that gave them their emphasis, at the moment it is
interesting to see events as they pass in incidents day
by day.   Lady Morgan was always deeply in earnest
about politics.   Parties were running fearfully high
upon the Reform Bill.

R. Sheil to Lady Morgan.

Tuesday, July, 1831.

MY DEAR LADY MORGAN,

Your letter to me is most gratifying; it is another
and a greener leaf in my parliamentary chapter, a
thousand thanks to your good heart. Believe me you
mistake me much if you try me by my observance of
the rules of etiquette; I know how to value your faculties and your character. There is no one whose friendship and praise I prize more than yours and Sir
Charles's. I have received a series of kindnesses from
both, which I cannot readily forget.

There is no news here in the political circles to
which I can give implicit confidence. It is *said* that
there are dissensions in the cabinet, and that the king
has had a fit of apoplexy. Party runs so high that I
can attach no credit to what I hear, even from the
highest quarters on *both* sides. I *believe* that there has
been a great defection among the Lords, but that it is
quite possible that some of the ministers may ultimately
become terrified at their own reform. Lord Melbourne
was great. Charles Grant did not speak with the cordiality of strong conviction.

Lady Cork was last night making special inquiries
about you; she asked me whether it was true that you
were writing the adventures and observations of her
Macaw. It lately bit off the toe of a countess, but on
the calf of a minister it could make no impression.

I met Jeffery and Macaulay here at dinner; Jeffery
has the most astounding volubility I ever witnessed;
he will not do in the house, I fear. I witnessed at
Sir J. Mackintosh's his introduction to Wordsworth, for

the *first* time. The latter grinned horribly, a ghastly smile.

Remember me to Sir Charles, and believe me,

Yours most truly,

R. SHEIL.

August 13th. — We are invited to the regatta; but we shall go to Lucan instead [Lucan was a watering place near Dublin, fashionable, and much frequented at that time] to repose from country house dissipations, and then I shall set to work at my Irish histories. My dirty house is to be given up to workmen, and I am to have a French window at the head of the stairs, opening on the balcony; the greenhouse question is still laid on the table, but I will have that too before I die, but not long before, I fear.

The review mentioned by Lord Anglesea in the ensuing letter was an Irish one, written to serve some question of the moment; the times, both in England and Ireland, were threatening, and every small contribution of common sense was thankfully received by those who had the guidance of public affairs.

Lord Anglesea to Lady Morgan.

BLACK ROCK,
September, 12, 1831.

MY DEAR LADY MORGAN,

I ought to have thanked you sooner for the Review you sent me, and for calling my attention to the well-written article in it by Sir Charles Morgan. I had already seen *extracts* from it, with which, to be honest,

I was better pleased than with the *whole*, for it happens that I go the full length with him in what I had before met with, whereas, in part of that which was new to me, I differ. I am sorry — you, probably, glad — that I have not time to explain myself.

Lady Anglesea showed me your note regarding an Italian opera, in Dublin, during October and November. If the thing is likely to take, I shall be delighted to promote it, and all my family will join. I think every encouragement should be given to those who will render Dublin gay. We want a little *déjourdissement*, because too much entangled in sombre politics. We may be vastly good patriots, and yet be always lively and good humoured; but before Messrs. Calcraft and de Bégnis embark in this undertaking, they should well calculate their means.

Believe, me,

Dear Lady Morgan,

Very faithfully yours,

ANGLESEA.

October 1st. — I thought the child's ball, at the Stanley's, a *triste* affair, or the contrast with Lady Emily's child's ball made it appear more so.

They were very civil; and Mr. Stanley seemed as if he wished to be as unlike a *minister of state* at a child's ball as possible; he ran about and was even *frisky*, and at the ponderous supper (where there was a smoking sirloin of beef at the head, and a cold round at the foot, two turkeys and ducks at the side); he kept crying, "Why don't you eat; pray eat," as if he was feeding the poor Irish at a soup kitchen.

October 16th. — On my return from Lucan, I find

mon bon ami the black volume, my journal white or
blue, and unwritten still, on the writing desk in my
dressing-room; there it has lain for a month, and it
actually requires an effort of will to open and scribble
in it. My life at Lucan was an odd one, I was placed
in a set I never was in before, such a place is the
mutual rendezvous of quizzeries of all sorts, and I
should have died of it, but for my Dominican monk,
Father Fitzgerald, of Carlow (of whom and our romance
more hereafter), and his friend the head of the Domini-
cans, Father Harold, and our own odd, clever, para-
doxical friend, Professor Macartney. We made a delightful little coterie, and all the mediocrities were
frightened out of their stupid wits. Holy St. Francis!
what a conclave in the midst of their sanctity! for they
were all saints, and vulgar saints. My arrival caused
universal dismay. Miss M—, the archbishop's daughter, ran away, others were about to follow her, but I
tamed them all. No Lady Huntingdon, had she dropped
among them, could have been more in the odour of
sanctified popularity than I was, after a while, and my
life there was, in some respects, most delectable, —
air, health, temperance, and occupation. I wrote there
my two most arduous Irish articles for the Metropolitan.
Since our return, we have been in perpetual agitation
about the Reform bill, but I picked one gay, light-
hearted, agreeable evening out of the bustle, — a
dinner and soirée for Paganini. I asked him, not as
a miraculous fiddle-player, but as a study. He came
into the drawing-room in a great coat, a clumsy walking stick, and his hat in his hand (quite a Penruddock
figure), and, walking up to me, made a regular set
speech in his Genoese Italian, which I am convinced

was taught him by his secretario; it abounded in *Donnas celebritissimas*, and all the superlatives of Italian gallantry. At dinner, he seemed wonderfully occupied with the dishes in succession, and frequently said, "*ho troppo mangiato!*" at each dish, exclaiming, "*bravissimo! excellentissimo!*" The fact is, I had copied a Florentine dinner as closely as I could, having had a Florentine cook all the time we were in Italy; so, we had a *minestra al vermicelli; maccaroni*, in all forms, &c., &c. I asked him if he were not the happiest man in the world, every day acquiring so much fame and so much money. He sighed and said, he should be but for one thing "*i Ragazzi*," the little blackguards that ran after him in the streets. In the evening, I took him into the boudoir; we had a *tête-à-tête* of an hour, in which he told me his whole story; but in such an odd, simple, Italian, gossiping manner, half by signs, looks, and inflections of the voice, that though I can take him off to the life verbally, I can give no idea of him on paper; — still here is the outline. His father and mother in humble life in Genoa, fond of music — no more. At four years old, he played the guitar, and, untaught, attended all the churches to sing, and at seven years of age, composed something like a *cantata*; then he took up the violin and made such progress, that his father travelled about with him from one Italian town to another, till he attracted the attention and attained the patronage of Elise Bonaparte, then Grand Duchess of Tuscany. He was taken into her family, and played constantly at her brilliant little court; there he fell in love with one of her *dames d'honneur*, who turned his head, he said, and he became *pazzo per amore*, and found his violin expressed his passion better than he could. Mademoiselle B— became his guide and inspiration; but they had a terrible *fracas*, they fought, fell out and separated. One day, in his despair, he was confiding his misery to his beloved violin, and made it repeat the quarrel just as it happened; he almost made it articulate the very words, and in the midst of this singular colloquy, Mademoiselle de B— rushed into the room and threw her arms round his neck and said, "Paganini, your genius has conquered;" their reconciliation followed, and she begged he would note down those inspirations of love; he did so, and called it, *Il Concerto d'Amore.* Having left it by accident on the piano of the grand duchess, she saw, and commanded him to play it; he did so, and the dialogue of the two strings had a wonderful success. He married afterwards a chorus singer at Trieste, and she was the mother of his little Paganini, whom he doated on. The mother, he said, abandoned them both, and that he was now no longer susceptible of the charms of the "*Belle Donne.*" His violin was his mistress. While telling me all this, he rolled his eyes in a most extraordinary way, and assumed a look that it is impossible to define — really and truly something demoniacal. Still, he seems to me, to be a stupified and almost idiotic creature.

Here is a letter from the Countess of Cork and Orrery, still harping on her macaw.

Lady Cork to Lady Morgan.

TUNBRIDGE WELLS,
October 25.

It is actually nine months since I received a letter

from dear Lady Morgan. I immediately conceived a
letter of thanks, but never had it in my power to bring
it to light. Lucina is not at hand, nor any other
friendly assistant.

The bantling with bright thoughts is quite decayed,
and I remain your stupid old eighty-six, without a
second idea.

I should not venture to intrude upon you to-day;
but that I really am anxious to be regaled with one
of your pretty greetings. Tommy Moore told me my
macaw had spoke both witty and clever. Bulwer, &c.,
&c., said the same, and that they would send it to me.
I have never seen it. When can I hear of it —
answer this, and tell me, when you come to England.
I don't wish it till April, when I promise you constant,
pleasant *réunions*. I am more *chez moi*, and go out
less than ever. I collect pleasant people, and like this
last act of the play as well as any part of my life. I
am in good health, and have many kind friends, among
whom I trust you'll allow me to set you down in the
first class.

For I am, very truly,
Your faithful and obliged servant,

M. C. O.

A true Whig.

PS. You must write some beautiful panegyric on
my sweet friends, Miss Foleys.

This macaw, which has been several times alluded
to, who spoke both witty and clever, was a bird of
wisdom belonging to Lady Cork, and Lady Morgan
wrote a charming paper entitled *Memoirs of a Macaw*

of a Lady of Quality, which first appeared in the *New
Monthly*, and afterwards was republished in *The Book
without a Name*. It is a model for the kind of writing;
it is full of good feeling, and has caustic, lively touches
of society which give a pleasant sharpness; and there
is a sketch of a poor "Younger Brother," that is
quite touching; altogether, it is one of Lady Morgan's
happiest efforts.

October 30. — In that coarse, dashing, but not
altogether ill-written novel the *Staff Officer*, there is a
picture from the life of my dear old friend Joe Atkinson.
The author wrote me a fine letter under the signature
Oliver Moore, presenting me his book and saying lots
of civil things.

This moment the news came in that our excellent
friend, Wallace, is returned at last for Drogheda. I
worked hard at this, and wrote to all whom I thought
could or could not, assist him. Poor Wallace is very
ill, and got his fever at his odious election.

November 2. — My poor dear old friend, Hamilton
Rowan, is fast going; Morgan saw him the day before
yesterday, lying in his chaise-lounge, feeble, but still
full of spirit and interest in the passing events.

November 7. — The cholera is approaching. I proposed to Morgan that we should retire from Dublin;
he stopped me short by saying, that where there was
most danger that was his post. His view of the case
changed my whole feeling on the subject; *he must* stay,
and therefore, *I* will stay, so last night we set about
thinking what was wisest and best to be done for the
preservation of the poor prisoners of the Marshalsea.
We think we have succeeded. He has gone to examine

the state of the prison, and then to make his proposals
to the Lord Lieutenant.

A letter from one of the horse-riders of the Royal
Arena, to beg I will command his benefit and give him
my name; of course I refused. How people mistake
my energy for influence!

November 14. — Yesterday was a day of offerings.
Robertson presented me with a good miniature of myself. It is a nice picture; but much thinner, graver,
and more sharp and *collet monté* than I ever was, or
ever shall be *secula seculorum*. Offering the second —
A fine bronze medal of Walter Scott, brought me from
Edinburgh. Third — a brace of superb pheasants from
Capt. Jekyll, of the Grenadier Guards. Lady Elizabeth
Clements and Mrs. Caulfield have just walked in with
a present of twelve yards of white satin, embroidered
in flowers by the late Countess of Charlemont for a
court-dress. They made me swear that I would act a
proverbe for them in it some evening. This is the fun
of the thing — the philosophy of it is the embroidery;
it must have taken a life to do, and is a fine illustration
of the life to which ladies of quality were put to formerly
to get rid of their time. I have been thinking to what
use I can put it — as curtains for the boudoir it would
have no effect, except that of soiled, flowered linen.
Draperies of white satin, embroidered in flowers, sounds
"sweetly" in a novel; but for effect, masses both in
colour and material, an adaptation of light and shades
are the things; thus, some fifty yards of scarlet or rose-
coloured moreen, at two or three shillings a yard, would
have more effect than all the embroidered satins in the
world. Furniture should be rich, simple, voluminous,
and capable of falling, or rather melting, into deep folds;

the effect of the rich masses and lights and shades produced by a drapery of this texture is surprising. I think I shall make a *douliette* for my French bed, dye it green and stuff it with eider down.

November 27. — All the early part of the day house-keeping, looking over table cloths, cutting out dusters, and what not of the huckaback order.

Prince Pucklau Muskau's book just come! I am properly trotted out in it. It is too horrible to think there is no doing good without paying the penalty. The prince's book, the Prince of Darkness, I should say, if it did not bear the name and impress of the Prince Pucklau Muskau. At the very time we were showing him hospitality, he was concocting this book, in which I was to be misrepresented and belied. The conversation he describes, was utterly false. I never again ought to receive a foreigner into my house; this is the fourth time I have been the subject of attacks written by such guests. It is rather curious that at this particular moment another foreigner should be presented to me, Count Charles O'Haggerty, *écuyer* to the duchess of Angoulême, at Holyrood; but I am sick and weary of it all.

December 20. — I cannot endure the sight of this book (my diary), I have nothing but botherations to enter. But what a glorious triumph! The Reform Bill passing through the House, two to one against the Tories.

December 25. — Christmas-day, my birthday. Hélas!!

December 26. — Yesterday I dined with my own dear family; what a cluster of clever, handsome and beloved heads!

To-day, off to Malahide Castle where we spend our Christmas.

CHAPTER VII.

A FLYING VISIT TO ENGLAND — 1832.

January 2. — Kildare Street. We had a cordial household, hospitable time at Malahide — all old friends — the Talbots — the Evans of Portran, my old lover and friend, Edward Moore. The fine old Castle is always my delight. I finished my article on it, for the *Metropolitan*, in the old library, with a Grant of Edward IV. lying beside me, bearing his own signature. Drove to Howth Castle — more antiquities — promised Lady Howth we would dine and stay there next Thursday, then to General Cockburn's for the rest of the holidays.

So enchanted to get back to our snuggery in Kildare Street, with all its warmth, comfort, and enjoyment. Those great castles are so cold and dreary, one has so many miles to walk between drawing and dressing-room that the contrast to my little china closet is very great, and then my agreeable droppers in, from three to five.

January 4. — A pleasant levee to-day, clever Mrs. Caulfield, and wild, but pleasant Edward Bligh; a tremendous set-to in politics.

January 5. — Working hard at old chronicles for my intended new novel, *Grace O'Mally.*

January 16. — Went to see the lions and boa constrictor figuring away at the theatre, most wonderful!

Martin played with the lion, or rather the lion with him like a great Newfoundland dog romping with a child. Martin has been predestined by his temperament to tame savage beasts, and to be eaten by them some fine day.

January 24. — All going on cheerily, good company and good spirits, when arrived the last number of the *Quarterly.* The acrimonious spirit of old Gifford still survives, and all the bitterness and weakness it exhibited against me twenty years back, more violent than ever. Prince Pucklau Muskau's vile book furnishes forth this new attack on me; the worst thing they can find to say against me is that my father was an actor, the miserable creatures!

January 27. — By-the-bye, this has been a merry week — a gay ball at Lady Kingsmill's; yet a more brilliant assembly at the Marquis of Headford's. I flirted with Sir Harcourt Lees, and Lambert of Beaupark, the high priests of Orangeism. One of them told me that the *cicerone* of the cathedral of Cashel, showing it to him the other day, said, "And here, sir is the ould part, built by the pagans, and these statues were the *pa-*gods!"

Our new Archbishop Whateley has astonished, outraged, maddened the clergy by advising in his last sermon that some passages, and *some* only, be selected from the Bible and given to the people. They left the church in convulsions, exclaiming, the Bible, the *whole* Bible, and *nothing but* the Bible!"

January 28. — Last night, sitting with the Earl of Rosse, he told me many strange stories, picked up when he was a child from his father, who lived to be a hundred. He described a ball at the great O'Moore's, where the company, exceeding the number of beds, the ladies lay down round the capacious hearth, their feet pointing towards the fire. An old woman came in with an immense quantity of woollen cloth, which she flung over them, and so they slept!

The "madder," so often mentioned in Irish song, was a wooden tankard, made square; there were then no tools for turning. Wooden noggins and wooden dishes were universal; they are still much used in country parts.

When Lord Rosse was Sir Lawrence Parsons, he wrote some learned works on Irish antiquities; his son, Lord II. Oxmantown, is a great mechanician, he is now occupied on a telescope of great power.

February 1. — I began another new work to-day on *The Ignorance of Women*, — shall I ever finish *any?* I doubt it, the motive no longer exists, and perhaps, too, the working material is worn out — this frittering away of mind is very like it.

February 20. — The Whigs and the ministry going the way of all flesh; these mongrel Liberals will never do, — never did do.

Lord Grey's speech on the enforcement of the tithe is conclusive. Lord Plunkett is at the bottom of this, one of the old set of Irish politicians, *rompus et corrompus.* Family aggrandisement is his great motive in all. Somebody said to old Norbury some time before he died, "It is odd that Plunkett cannot see his way clearly about the tithe." "Sir," said Lord Norbury, "he has the *son* in his eyes."

Lord Plunkett is an acute, eloquent, and clear-sighted man, to the extent of his views; but they are not extensive. His politics are simply, rigorously *British*, not European.

Lord Grey is the screw loose.

February 27. — Parties and balls galore this last week — no need to specify.

March 23. — Ever since my last entry, "with darkness compassed," shut up, a dark room, a horrid state, a tax upon those whose charity leads them to come to me. The kind Talbots carry me off to Malahide on Saturday.

April 8. — The other day I took a party to see Malahide Castle. As Lady Chapman's carriage had been broken at a *soirée* the night before, I drove her in my phaeton. Compare this with my *début* in Dominic Street, when I went to be hired as a governess! I did the honours of the castle in my old quality of *Custoda*.

We had an excellent luncheon, and we came home loaded with flowers and vegetables, *à l'ordinaire*. In short, nobody can grow old more agreeably than I do; I sit with the picture of the immortal Ninon de L'Enclos hanging over my head, a sort of votive shrine raised to the art of remaining young through mind when youth has passed away!

I am getting on with the learned opening of my new book on Woman.

April 19. — The cholera is making fearful strides among the filthy dens of the wretched lower orders! many of the higher are panic-stricken.

May 17. — Tory ministry out! just as Lord Anglesey was packing off.

What emotions this event has raised in my mind!

and what an interval! Yesterday — Europe — mankind seemed thrown back on the horrors of past and dark ages; and now they are not only restored, but advanced by centuries. I could not resist writing to Lord Anglesey. Here is a rough draft of my letter.

Lady Morgan to Lord Anglesey.

May 17, 1832.

My Dear Lord,

In moments of great commotion and great emotion, all forms of etiquette must yield to the expressions of strong feeling which acknowledge no masters of ceremonies. My husband and I were at the Park a day or two back, to pay you our deep regret at your leaving. To-day, under a far different excitement, I venture to obtrude the expression of our congratulations ou the greatest triumphs that freedom and knowledge ever obtained over despotism and bigotry. England is saved, and great and good men again take those high positions in which they may best serve the interests of mankind. Of course, your excellence is left with us to revive hopes for Ireland, who, like a capricious mistress, although she may sometimes *bouder*, the object of her passion has no desire to change.

I am, my dear Lord,

With sincere respect and congratulations,

Your Excellency's devoted subject,

SYDNEY MORGAN.

I have just had a letter from Moore, proving that it is equally true of one who becomes rich, as of a poet, that he must be *nasciter non fit*.

8*

Thomas Moore to Lady Morgan.

May 24th, 1832.

MY DEAR LADY MORGAN,

At the time I received your letter, I was not very well able to answer it, and, indeed, till within these two days, have felt by no means well, or like myself. I am, however, now much better. I have been in correspondence, during part of the time, with your friend of the *Metropolitan*, Captain Marryatt, and if the most cautious and flattering liberality, on his part, added to your kind persuasions, could have made a contributor or editor of me, I should have been one at this moment. But I hate to be *tied*; it is this, far more than what you call my aristocratic (God help me) prejudices, which makes me reject so often the golden bait flung at me. If I were to judge, indeed, of the state of literature from my own experience, I should say it never was more prosperous, as I have actually turned away from my *door* (as the shop-keepers say) fifteen hundred guineas and a thousand pounds a year within the last three months; all the time, too, wanting money most pinchingly. From what you said in your letter I took for granted that Campbell had intimated some intention of abdicating the editorship; but this I find not to be the case, and if I were ever so disposed to accept of the chair, I should shrink from the slightest step, on my part, that could be construed into a wish to supplant him. I lament to hear of his present state, but he *has* been a noble fellow. You will think it looks very like contributorship when you come to see some verses of mine announced for the next number of the *Metropolitan*; but, besides my wish to show, by

some trifling mark, how much I felt the kindness both
of Captain Marryatt and Dr. Saunders, these verses
were of a kind that would not *keep*, being a good deal
circulated, or, at least, shown about by those who are
interested in them, and, therefore, likely to get into
print. All I have told you about *shop* business here is
for your private self alone; for, though vain enough,
God knows, at being praised so much higher than I
am worth, I think it, in general, not right to pro-
claim the particulars of my negociations with the biblio-
polists.

Give my best regards to Morgan,

And believe me, very truly yours,

THOMAS MOORE.

May 27. — A bright summer morning. Morgan
took up his guitar at breakfast, and began to *frédoner
La Biondina, in Gondoletta*, and an hour afterwards,
under the combined influence of sunshine and green
tea, Morgan, who is in as high health and spirits as I
am *out* of both, ran up to my dressing-room, where I
was prosing over my *Women of the Church*, with a
handful of MS. music. "See what I have composed,"
said he, and laying it down on my tiresome writing-
desk, he played and sang a pretty *cavatina*.

May 28. — I am suffering beyond all conception
from want of air and exercise. My house is small and
confined; there is no thorough air, and I am never allowed to open a window to obtain it. When summer
comes, Dublin is a dreary desert inhabited only by
loathsome beggars, and I feel suffocated; I complain,
and think and say, "this is a hard fate." My com-
plaints are met with ridicule and vehement argument

— sometimes with harshness; they are not borne with, because their cause is not felt, and all that makes *my* misery makes the happiness of one who, by law and custom, is the master of my actions, while books and easy chairs make up his whole wise scheme of happiness! All he says *may* be true, and I *may* be wrong; it *may* be weakness, caprice, an appetite for excitement; but still it is misery, and there is no reasoning with sensation. Men feel this, and plead it for the indulgence of their own whims — poor woman is commanded to suffer, and be silent, if she is so weak or wicked as to have no control over her sensations. This has been and will be my little personal narrative *in secula seculorum.*

[There is the following note at the bottom of this page of the diary, which is an amusing commentary on the above. *October* 29, 1832. — Looking back on this page, I can scarcely believe I am the person who wrote it; for *now* I am in high health and spirits, and in great vigour of body and mind. My trip to England, and air and exercise, have restored the balance of affection between us!]

London, July 1. — I thought I was past all enjoyment; but well may I enjoy so cordial and gracious a reception from all my old and new London friends. These pleasant and fresh apartments in St. James' Place, close to the parks, and within reach of everything that is best is very enlivening. My visitors begun at ten o'clock this morning — authors, publishers, booksellers, and artists; afterwards, some new and old cronies — Campbell, Captain Marryatt, Bulwer, Dilke, and Wentworth Dilke; Lardner, Miss Sheridan, Sir␣M. Shee, Valpy, and Bentley; then in the afternoon, Ladies Charleville and Charlemont, Lady Stepney and others. This is pretty well for one day. Perhaps what is most delightful of all, is to find the old friends I had early made in my youth still at their post. Lord Nugent was one of my visitors, and more agreeable than ever.

I was carried off to the parks and zoological gardens, by Mrs. Webster, and have now a late eight o'clock dinner to dress for. In short, this is a second spring, an after crop!

July 2. — Yesterday, a charming dinner made for me at Mr. Dilke's. Amongst many celebrities, Hood (of the *Comic Annual*) a very grave person, looking the picture of ill-health, was presented to me. Morgan quite happy — good music in the evening. The cordial hostess, full of kindness — pretty house — full of good pictures and old curiosities.

Lady Cork still in town, still well disposed, but is so *bent* on *getting up a dinner*, that all her lingering forces are summed up in that.

Mrs. Charles Gore, the authoress of the thousand and one fashionable novels (her last, *I'm Money*), and a very successful writer; is herself, a pleasant little rondelette of a woman. I found her something of my own style. When I went to pay her a visit, I found her preparing for a dinner party in a pretty little bit of a boudoir house; we talked and laughed together as good-humoured women always do, and agreed upon *many points*. She made some *clever hits*. Trelawney, D'Orsay, and some other brilliant villains were to have been presented to me to-day, but I was out when they called.

I have little time to write my journal, and so merely

jot down people and things *as a reminder.* As thus: Lady Aldborough has just been — wonderful still — her own hair, graceful figure, and *such a toilet!!* her wit (*un peu trop fort*) most racy, she might *almost* be my mother!!

The following note from Countess Guiccioli is very interesting in its broken English; she had not yet become a great lady at the French court, nor taken up the dropped stitches of her "respectability."

The Countess of Guiccioli to Lady Morgan.

July 9th, 1832.

[With Lord Byron's hair and autograph.]

The Countess Guiccioli presents her compliments to Lady Morgan, and sends to her some lines of Lord Byron's hand-writing, together with some hairs of him. She adds to that a ringlet of her own hair, only because Lady Morgan asked it. But she cannot do that, without a sort of *remords*, as it was a profanation to put together in the same shrine so holy relics with so trifling a thing as it is; for the rest, the few lines of Lord Byron's writing hand are directed to the Count Gamba, Countess Guiccioli's father, and are written in a playful style, as he did frequently, and always when he talked about the laziness and not extraordinary cleverness of his minister, Mr. Sega.

The Countess Guiccioli wishes and hopes that a better opportunity will be presented to her, in order to show how high is her esteem and admiration for the illustrious and amiable Lady Morgan.

August 16. — At last arrived at the original part

of our pilgrimage, *Leamington!* found it a twaddle —
people taking physic to slow music, and returning to
quick; but oh, for Warwick Castle! and Guy's Cliff!
enchanting! My old flirt in my priory days, "the lord
of the castle," was not at home; the Bertie Percys
were, and they were all kindness and hospitality.

August 30. — We are now back to dull, dusty
Dublin; we have been to pay our respects to the vice-
royalties, and saw Lord Anglesey and Lady Mary
Paget, and had a long and pleasant confab. Lord
Anglesey said, "will you dine with me to-day, to-morrow, or Monday." We said, "Monday, if it suits your
Excellency." Lord Anglesey. — "Who will you have
to meet you?" I was *going* to say, "Pat Costello and
Dan O'Connell;" but thought that would be *too* agreeable, so, said, "your Excellency's family." Lord Anglesey. — "Oh, poh, you must have somebody!" At
this moment, in came Mr. Secretary Stanley. Lord
Anglesey said, "You shall have him." Stanley bowed
and smiled, and so it is settled we dine at the Phœnix
on Monday.

Tuesday. — Our dinner was rather *triste*, *dull*, and
fine. Lord Anglesey not in spirits, one of his bad days.

Lady Morgan piqued herself on her influence over
the young men of her circle. She always endeavoured
to rouse them from their desultory habits of amusement,
to a sense of their duties as land owners and Irishmen.

October 25. — I have just got a fine new cloak,
and am so smart! Went to Riversdale, to see Lady
Guy Campbell in it. [Lady Guy Campbell was the
daughter of Lord and Lady Edward Fitzgerald.] She
had just got a picture of her old granny, Madame de

Genlis, and of her mother, Pamela, which had belonged
to the ladies of Llangollen, and which I put her in the
way of getting.

Lady Guy Campbell told me some curious anecdotes of her mother's birth. She has no doubt that
Pamela was the daughter of Egalité and Madame de
Genlis, and she told me that she has a paper signed
by them both, being a contract of adoption of the child
Pamela by both. She recollects an angry dispute between her mother (Lady E. Fitzgerald), and Madame
de Genlis, when the latter said, "*ne vous vantez pas
d'être ma fille vous ne l'êtes pas.*" "*Pardi,*" replied Pamela. "*Il n'y a pas de quoi s'en vanter!*" Pamela
was born whilst Madame de Genlis was in the West
Indies. She sent for the child to London to speak
English with Mademoiselle D'Orleans, and Lady Edward said that when she arrived in her little English
Red Riding Hood cloak, Madame de Genlis was sitting
with the D'Orleans family, and surrounded by the
court. The child looking about it, and astounded by
so fine a party, flew to Madame de Genlis's arms, whom
she had never seen since she was a baby. "Such was
her sagacity," said Madame, "that she knew me from
my reputation!"

I see a great likeness in the upper part of Lady
Campbell's face to Madame de Genlis; but *en beau*,
very pretty from expression and movement of countenance. The King of France was present at her mother's
marriage with Lord Edward Fitzgerald, at Tournai;
he was *then* the Duke de Chartres, and Fitzgerald was
in Dumouriez's army.

November 2nd. — Just returned from Bray Head,
its delicious scenery, and its beneficent mistress. But

what a neighbourhood to live in with its *cagoteries!*
What society! all effete races worn out. The very air
breathes Methodism, and every tree looked like a
preacher. I walked in the sweet Dargle, but not before
the evangelical gate-keeper received half-a-crown from
Mrs. P—— for letting us into Powerscourt. I went to
Holly Brook to see my old friend and Livy's old
schoolfellow (Lady Hudson still deep in mourning for
her favourite child, Sir Robert); I was delighted with
Holly Brook. The old tottering mansion full of the
tippling memory of *Robin Adair.* His glass, half a
yard high and half a yard round, was shown to me,
and his drinking bout with a Scotchman related. The
low, dark room is covered with divine pictures. Lady
Hudson was Miss Novil. We have often spent our
holidays together.

William Plunket (the hon. and reverend), who sat
beside me at dinner to-day, at Bray Head, told me he
had been with his father, Lord Plunket, at Holland
House, which was almost their home when in London.
"One day," he said, "we were the only guests at
Holland House, when Prince Talleyrand came in."
"Where do you think I come from?" he demanded of
Lord Holland. A hundred vain guesses were made.
"Well, then, from dining and passing the day *tête à
tête* with Jeremy Bentham."

I have often thought of this *tête-à-tête.* How could
they understand each other? The extremes of sensibility
and insensibility, of honesty and roguery — philosophy
and philanthropy against diplomacy and villany!!!

November 28th. — Just returned from Lord Cloncurry's, a vastly gay party for Lyons. "Dear Lady

Morgan" and her "agreeability," all the rage once more. Why? *Dio lo so!* Why did she *lose* her popularity? I know not. Take the world as it runs, it is never worth a thought; whims, passions, interests, *any* thing but feeling, truth, reason. Lord Brabazon was deputed my cavalier — a cold, sensible, travelled, electioneering young gentleman, far better than his race. I was thought quite charming! "Adieu, dear Lady Morgan, and may you long continue the agreeable creature you are now!" The other day only, "the agreeable creature" was *toute au contraire!*

November 30th. — Met a poor starved beggar child, and gave him a penny. "Och, the Lord pour a blessing on your honour!" "And how does your poor mother live?" I said, among other things. "Och thin, by ating cowld victuals, marram!"

By-the-bye, this reminds me of a blessing I once received from an old beggar woman, to whom I had given a sixpence. "Och thin! the Lord bless yer sweet honour, and may every hair of yer head be a mould four, to light yer sowl to glory!" What an imaginative race they are, (!) would sixpence ever have stimulated an English beggar to such an invocation!

A note from Mrs. Hemans, endorsed by Lady Morgan, "she would and she would not."

The friendly relations of Mrs. Hemans with Lady Morgan were maintained to the last. Lady Morgan's high spirit delighted and attracted the more delicate and reserved lady.

Mrs. Hemans to Lady Morgan.

December 3rd, 1832.

DEAR LADY MORGAN,

I would have come to you *for pleasure* on Saturday evening, but nothing that is not brilliant ought to enter your boudoir, and my eyes and intellect grow so dim together as evening approaches, that I could only take the refuge of an *owl*, in the shade. To-morrow evening, not for business, but for pleasure, I will come if I can; but I must tell you how I am situated. A gentleman was engaged to pass the evening here, and I must either beg your leave to make him my escort, or give him his *congé* till another time. If neither of these expedients will do, you must again kindly excuse me. You are very good for including my little artist in your invitation; the last time I called upon you, I brought with me some of his drawings from the antique to show you; I will beg your acceptance of one, should you think it worth receiving, the next time I have the pleasure of seeing you.

Believe me,

Dear Lady Morgan,

Very truly yours,

FELICIA HEMANS.

December 6th. — So ends my hospitalities for the year 1832. The thousand details necessary for getting up a recherché dinner with few servants is Herculean labour, and, besides, I have to empty my room for space, and yesterday I had upholstery to put up myself, and pictures to move and change, and poor old Mrs. Casey *broke down* from nervousness (or *whiskey*) in the kitchen, and I had to dress *half* the dinner myself, which every body allowed was supreme, particularly my *matelotte d'anguille*, and my *dinde farci à la daube!* It matters little how *great* dinners are dressed, but *small* ones should be *exquisite*, or not given at all.

To-morrow we dine with the gay young Vaughans in Merrion Square (he is brother to Lord Lisburne). We are to be few and merry. Last Monday we dined at the P——'s, and were many and dull. Society here is all bad: dearth of mind, and want of Europeanism everywhere, to say nothing of party faction and religious acrimony. Miserable country!

December 10. — Yesterday we were at an *amateur concert*, at the castle. Lord Anglesey and I fell to discourse as usual — politics and *badinage*. The Duke of Leinster played his "big fiddle," and looked happy and amiable, and after each act, pottered about, gathering together the music, settling lights, and, in short, enacting the part of "property man" in a theatrical orchestra *to the life.*

I had the pleasure of taking my two girls with me after a *long dispute* and *struggle* (and a *little intrigue*) with their mother *as usual.*

December 14*th.* — Dined last evening at Mr. Stanley's, the Secretary of State, Phœnix Park. A large official party. It would have been a heavy one, but I put my shoulder to the wheel, and away it went! It turned out a most joyous good humoured party. Stanley was sharp and mordant, though agreeable.

He said in the midst of a silence, with a half sneer on his face, "Oh, Lady Morgan, you are a great Irish historian, can you give me a census of the population of Ireland in the reign of Henry II."

I affected confusion, and said, "Well, no, Mr. Stanley, not accurately; but may I presume to ask *you* what is the census of the English people in the reign of William IV.?"

CHAPTER VIII.

DRAMATIC SCENES AND SKETCHES — 1833.

THE work on *France*, in 1829-30, was followed by *Dramatic Scenes and Sketches*, which were also published by Messrs. Saunders and Otley. Lady Morgan gave the work to them in the hope that it would prove some compensation for their disappointment about *France*, but they had not Colburn's genius for making books sell, and though the *Dramatic Scenes* are amongst Lady Morgan's best works, they had not the brilliant success which they deserved. The sum she received and the terms on which the work was published are not on record, but she retained the copyright for herself.

These *Dramatic Scenes and Sketches* are written in a very forcible and effective manner. They show the condition of Ireland as a country, and the state of the Irish peasantry, their sorrows and ignorance, the evil influence of agents and middlemen in the absenteeism of the landlords; the clashing pretensions of the High Protestant Church party with the priests, are excellently shown. The chief aim is to show the ignorance and misconception which prevailed in England of the real condition and necessities of the country; the difficulties, almost impossibilities, thrown in the way of Irish landlords wishing to do their duty and

to see with their own eyes what measures of reform
and relief were urgently needed. The first *Dramatic
Sketch* is called Manor Sackville, and the dramatic
form of scene and dialogue allows every shade of
character and situation to pass as over a magic lan-
tern. For vigorous delineation and dialogue, it excels her novels, — the form gave her free scope. The
dramatic sketch of Manor Sackville is the longest and
the most important. It gives a lively picture of Irish
country life, an old Irish mansion unexpectedly visited
by its proprietor, an enlightened and benevolent man,
accompanied by his wife, an amiable, fine lady, and a
party of fashionable friends from London. The politics, cliques, and condition of the country, from the
Honourable and Reverend Dr. Polypus, rector of New-
town, down to Cornelius Brian, a leader of White Feet,
with agents, tithe proctors, Catholic priests, &c., are
all vividly described and put into action. The result
is, a picture of Ireland as it then existed.

The Irish politics and grievances make rather heavy
metal for a book of amusement, but it is enlivened
with some of the best touches of Lady Morgan's Irish
fun and humour. The other dramatic scenes are
shorter, and are illustrations of different phases of
English fashionable life.

Lady Morgan was peculiarly skilful in her delinea-
tions of English fashionable life. Her "great ladies"
have all a *cachet* of belonging to the class for which
they are intended; and there is, in all Lady Morgan's
"fine ladies," an air of good breeding which dis-
tinguishes her fashionable scenes from the ordinary
type of fashionable novels, and gives them all the air
of scenes of real life. Although *Dramatic Scenes and*

Sketches had not the high tide of success which attended the *O'Briens and O'Flahertics*, it is a work which deserved it.

Here is a letter from M. Prosper Merrimé.

The graceful turn of the original is lost in the less flexible power of an English translation; but the style of M. Merrimé has a charm of its own, which cannot be altogether disguised by any disadvantages.

M. Prosper Merrimé to Lady Morgan.

January 2nd, 1833.

I feel very guilty, Madame, for not having sooner replied to your charming letter, brought to me by Mr. Chapman.   Believe, however, that although I may have been slow to thank you for it, I have not felt the less sensible of your kind remembrance.   I could have wished to be able to go in person and lay my works at your feet, to beg that you would grant me at once your pardon for my idleness, and your protection to travel in the route of Erin, of which land you are the fairy.   Unhappily, bonds which are neither of silk nor of gold retain me in Paris.   I can scarcely leave it, even for a day, to breathe the fresh air of St. Germains or St. Cloud.   For the last three months I have been a creature half a man, half an arm-chair, feeding upon *bulletins des lois*, gravely renewing solicitations, and laughing sometimes when alone at the strange administrative face which is the result!

Public affairs will, however, Madame, leave leisure to read your works upon the present state of Ireland. The form you have given to it confirms me in an

opinion I already held, that true talent can apply itself to every species of literature, and that you are
as sure to charm your readers by your dramas as by
your romances or your travels. Accept, I beg, Madame, all my own congratulations, and permit me to
be the interpreter of those of my countrymen who have
not, like myself, the honour of knowing you, but which
they would address to you if they had.

I beg you to recall me to the remembrance of Miss
Clarke, and of Sir Charles Morgan, and pray accept
the expression of my respectful homage.

PR. MERRIME.

The following notes of good-humoured *badinage* explain themselves. It must have been a great relief to
the thorny State kept by a lord-lieutenant to be treated
occasionally like a natural human being. The joke
about Cæsar alludes to a "command night" at the
theatre, where the play had been very hazardous, from
its allusions.

The Marquis of Anglesey to Lady Morgan.

[No date.]

DEAR LADY MORGAN,

I beg you to thank Mr. Bate *doubly* for me, as well
for his having presented me with a portrait of my
favourite boat, as for having sent it through your
hands.

As you say he is an artist, may I not be permitted
to remunerate him for his skill, and can you not help
me to guess what will be acceptable?

But why quarrel with *Cæsar?* Cæsar *was* borne out

by the results of last night. Cæsar took the bull by
the horns, and he vanquished him. Depend upon it,
it is the only *safe* way. See how the bull was tamed.
He made no fight at all. But I must again defend
Cæsar from the imputation of *imprudence.* He really,
strange to say, knew nothing of the gist of the piece.
Knowing it, however, he could not have chosen better;
he gave his enemy fair play — fought him, as it were,
upon his own ground, and beat him.

Seriously, I never was more surprised than last
night. I own I fully expected a most tumultuous
uproar, and lo! all was good humour, loyalty, and
almost *couleur de rose,* as I shall be when I get my
soirée.   I remain,

Dear Lady Morgan,
Very faithfully yours,
ANGLESEY.

Lady Morgan to Lord Anglesey.

KILDARE STREET,
Wednesday.

Cæsar is a very dangerous person to engage with,
whatever ground he takes! His *desperate pas de charge*
is sure to be borne out by the consciousness of his *old*
"*veni, vidi, vici;*" and "*aut Cæsar, aut nihil!*" turns
out in the *end,* to be a very discreet determination;
Cæsar must therefore (to borrow his *own favourite*
image), "like the *bull* in the china shop, *have it all his
own way.*" So much for Cæsar! Now for the *Lord-
Lieutenant.*

Lady Morgan assures His Excellency that Mr. Bate
will feel himself *overpaid* by an acceptance of his sketch
of the Pearl, and by an approbation so flattering; to

9*

offer any other remuneration would wound rather than gratify the feelings of the venerable artist. Mr. Bate is an eminent *enameller*, and should His Excellency *ever* desire to bequeath to posterity one of the "*thousand and one*" beauties of his *own private collection*, after the manner of Charles II., or Louis XIV., some little order to *eternize* eyes that once *conquered* the *conqueror*, will *faire les délices* of one of the best artists in his line, that England has produced. With respect to the *couleur de rose* passage, in Lord Anglesey's note! Should it *really* be the intention of His Excellency to honour the *thatched roof of an Irish cabin* with his presence, the mistress is ready to *receive* him with that *hearty*

Cead mille falthae,

which he so well deserves from every Irish heart. It is, however, for *him* to *command* the evening. His Excellency's secretary mentioned last night, that every night in the ensuing week was taken, except that of *Monday next*, the 11th. On *that* or any other *evening*, Lady Morgan is sure to be "*at home*" to so illustrious a guest.

For this year, the only diary of any general interest was kept during her visit to London, and her sojourn at Brussels. It begins abruptly:

June 18. — Arrived in London on Monday 10th, by Liverpool, a prosperous passage of eleven hours. From Liverpool to Leamington, where we rested two days, the country one continued garden; no beggary, no poverty. It struck us that the face of the country was much improved since we last travelled this way. We found invitations waylaying us on our arrival.

June 24. — To-day had a visit from Madame Pasta, more naïve than ever; she told us she was near getting into prison at Naples, for singing out of *Tancredi*, *Cara Patria*; and she said orders were given to omit the word "liberta" in all her songs. Her happy temperament shows itself most in her tender affection for her mother and her daughter; she says that nothing, neither fame nor money, consoles her for their absence.

Bellini came in, and Pasta, Bellini, and José went through one act of his *Norma*. Bellini was charmed with José's voice.

I had a curious scene yesterday; Bentley and Rees (of the long firm, Longman & Co.), at the same time, one in the back, the other in the front drawing-room. Each came to negotiate about my next book; Bentley is to have it.

Pasta and I were disputing to-day about reputations. I spoke of her *Gloire*, she said, "*Gloire passagère*, it is here to-day and gone to-morrow, yours endures." I said, "*Je voudrais bien troquer mes chances avec la posterité, pour la certitude de votre influence avec les contemporains.*"

June 28. — To-day, took my girls to Lord Grosvenor's gallery. At night we went to a literary party at Lady Charleville's. Campbell, the poet, said to me, "I am copying out my *Life of Mrs. Siddons*, for which I am to get a price, which, if any bookseller had offered me a few years back, I would have flung in his face, and the MS. into the fire."

The party at Lady Cork's had some curious contrasts. There was Lady Charleville herself, the centre of a circle in her great chair. Lady Dacre, author of

— everything; plays, poems, novels, &c., &c. Lady
Charlotte Campbell, author of *Conduct is Fate*. Miss
Jane Porter (*Thaddeus of Warsaw*), cold as ever,
though the muse of tragedy in appearance. Mrs.
Bulwer Lytton, the muse of comedy. Lady Stepney,
author of the *New Road to Ruin;* lots of lay men and
women, a crowd of saints and sinners. The men
were still more odd. Sir Charles Wetherell, Prince
Cimitelli, D'Israeli, who ran off as I skipped in, some
other remarkables, and one young man, Lord Oxmantown, an impersonation of a "Committee of the House."

July 1. — Pasta and Bellini jumped out of a
hackney-coach at our door to-day, with a roll of music
in their hands, — it was the score of the *Norma*, they
came, Pasta said, from the second rehearsal. Bellini
scolded his great pupil like a *petite pensionnaire.*

July 6. — Days later. Till this morning I have
not had a moment to spare to fill up my journal.
What a loss! Pleasure, business, folly, literature,
fashion. Pasta often calls on us; this is her own
account of herself. "I was a *petite demoiselle*, playing
and singing in the amateur theatre at Milan. Pasta
and I played the Prince and Princess di Jovati, fell
in love, and married. Paer, who heard us, or one of
us, wrote to us to come to Paris, and play in the
theatre of Madame Caladoni. I so wished to travel,*
*que j'aurais allé même à l'Enfer! mes parens étaient dé-
solés!* I went on the stage, and was engaged for
London; came out in *Télémaque.* I was so ashamed

* Mr. Sterling, of the *Times*, told me, that when Pasta was playing
Cherubino, fifteen years ago, in London, she could not procure an order
for a friend to the pit!

at showing my legs! Instead of minding my singing,
I was always trying to hide my legs. I failed!"

"Do you," I asked, "transport yourself into your
part?" "*Oui après les premières lignes. Je commence
toujours en Giulitta (mon nom) mais je finis toujours en
Médéa ou Norma!*"

July 14. — I had a peep at club life, — the Travellers. It is the perfection of domestic life! Every
comfort at once suggested and supplied; good reasons
for not marrying! Women must get up to this point,
or they will only be considered as burthens. Some of
the young husbands of the handsomest wives live at
their clubs.

Went to see the hydro-oxygen microscope, which
has extinguished the solar light. It shows the objects
in a drop of water magnified 800,000 times. The
wonders of the microscopic world illustrate all the base
passions of the whole great system. The animalcules
tear each other to pieces, and are agitated by all the
worst passions; they are of monstrous and disgusting
forms, the water devil, the water lion, with their great
heads, and the strange motions of others, are all images
of crime and weakness; to illustrate the same state by
this exhibition, would be a sermon and a bore; to
illustrate the world by the microscope would be an
epigram.

July 16. — Amongst the notabilities who have
sought us out, are Gabussi and Vaccai, the composers,
and Taglioni, *la déesse de la danse*, she was brought to
us by her husband, who is the son of a peer of France,
and ex-page to Bonaparte. She was quiet, lady-like,
and simple, her dress elegant, but simple. She told
me her father was *maître de ballet*, and had early in-

structed her; but she had so little vocation, that when she came to Paris, she had no hope of success. Of her habits of life, she said, she lived temperately, dining on plain roasts, at three o'clock, never sleeping after dinner, nor taking anything till after her exertions at the theatre were over, then, she supped on tea. She practices two or three hours a-day. She said that the moment force was introduced in dancing, grace vanished; her rule was never to make an effort, but to give herself up to nature, and the great delight she had in dancing. She said she never was so happy as when dancing. The moment she came off the stage her ancles are wrapped in woollen socks, and when she goes home her feet are bathed in arrow-root water.

Last Monday we went to the British Institution, a very mixed society, everybody coming to be seen, and nobody to see the pictures.

After the gallery, we went to a select *soirée* at Lady Cork's. All dukes, duchesses, lords, ladies, and bores; the dresses were bad. D'Israeli shuffled along with his ivory cane, like the ghost in *Hamlet*, and the only amusing thing was a little boy from Ireland, who attacked us all at the door.

July 29. — Yesterday we went to the House of Lords to hear the last debate on the Church Temporalities Bill. We sat in the Peeress's box. The first thing that struck me, was the theatrical set out of the place. The stage below, the gallery above, the dropping in of the actors. To the right from the gallery, in the centre of the lower bench, sat the Dukes of Wellington, Cumberland, Newcastle, and Lord Winchelsea; behind them, Lord Ellenborough, Lord Wicklow, Lord Aberdeen; opposite were Lord Grey, the Duke

of Rutland; opposite to us, on the woolsack, sat Lord
Brougham, bound up like an Egyptian mummy, his
countenance as impassible as Talleyrand's.   When a
note was presented to him he drew his hands out of
his sleeves, in which they were folded, and used glasses.
The debate opened with the Duke of Newcastle, who
stuttered, stammered, and looked frightened.   Lord
Winchester followed, who roared and bellowed; he addressed the Bishop of London, whose manner, in reply,
was cold, collected, but quite as mad; no eloquence,
wit, energy, or originality.   Lord Eldon, an old state-
property actor, with a conventional manner; his speech
was gag — all referred to himself; he was of the
people once — he was still of the people, though
now he was a peer of the realm!   He had filled
the woolsack for twenty years; he respected and
admired the Duke, but he was angry with him for
emancipating the Catholics; he would soon appear before the throne of Heaven (and he took out his blue
pocket-handkerchief and wept through the rest of his
speech); *he* must soon die; but dying, he foresaw the
fall of that glorious assembly; if the bill passed, it
must be swept away, it could not last, except on the
stability of compacts (for compacts are made for man,
not man for compacts) &c. &c.   The whole speech,
that of an old rogue, but a very good actor.   "Pity
the sorrows of a poor old man."

In the box with us was the Duchess of Richmond,
who never misses a debate.   She had been here since
five o'clock, and desired her daughter to keep her
place when she went home for an hour to meet the
Duke of Gloucester; the box holds twenty-five.

The Duke of Wellington's manner and matter were

equally bad. He spoke so low and indistinct, I scarcely
heard him. The effect produced by these scenes was,
the error of erecting a barrier against progress by giving sanction to an assembly, composed principally of
old and infirm men. The number of young men is so
small as to make every man under fifty conspicuous.
Nearly all, as I looked down, seemed bald; many
were infirm, and walked with an arm — Lord Holland
was wheeled in; they were all men without fathers —
consequently, of a certain age. Lord Ellenborough,
and two or three others of his standing, represented
the middle-aged.

Monday. — Last night, at Mr. Perry's, son of the
editor of the *Morning Chronicle.* House after Louis
XIV. style; company, Fonblanque, of the *Examiner;*
Kenny, the dramatist, &c., &c. The manner of all the
men cold and languid; reserve, shyness, and *morgue*
make up the character and manners of English society.

Mrs. Bulwer Lytton, handsome, insolent, and un-
amiable, to judge by her style and manners; she, and
all the *demi-esprits*, looked daggers at *me;* not one of
them have called on me, and in society they get out of
my way. How differently I should behave to them if
they came to Ireland!

July 31. — Last night an agreeable party at the
Countess of Montalembert's. Renewed my acquaintance with the once famous Lady Clare; Lady Dudley
Stewart (Lucien Bonaparte's daughter), in the most
extravagant of dresses; but *très aimable.* That egregious
coxcomb, Disraeli, was there, too — outraging the
privilege a young man has of being absurd.

August 4. — We have had a cordial visit from Captain Marryatt — there had been a coldness since we

withdrew from the *Metropolitan*. After dinner, we lounged
in the Park, and then took a walk, then home to dress
for Lady Cork's, where we met and chatted with all sorts
of old acquaintances, Lady Marybrough, Lady Darlington, Lady Augusta Paulet, Rogers the poet, Lady Davy,
Lady Caledon, &c.; the Duchess of Cleveland is a very
pleasant woman, full of spirit and spirits. It was
curious to see that handsome head encircled with
diamonds, which first attracted notice under a basket
of onions and salad. She was a garden girl, attending
the London markets. What a romance was hers!

Rogers said, that Moore's book *The Gentleman in
Search of a Religion*, was a failure, and that Moore was
much disappointed, though he did not expect a very
brilliant success.

Yesterday Bellini and Gabussi came, and sang and
played like angels. Lucien Bonaparte came in as they
were singing —

> "O bella Italia che porte tre color.
> Sei bianca e rosa e Verde com 'un fiore!"

Lucien exhibited a supressed emotion that was very
touching. How honest and clever he is! He said,
what I have often preached, "nations that *deserve* to
be free, *are* free!" He blamed Lafayette in the late
events of France — elect a Bourbon to the throne —
and talk of the voice of the people in this election!
The people who forget and who bled, were *consulted*,
but betrayed. We talked of Ireland. I said, "The
Irish have no idea of liberty, they want a king of their
own. Come and present yourself, and I will promise
you a crown." He laughed, but said, "Point de
couronne, point de couronne."

I said "Voilà donc encore une couronne que vous refusez!"

It is well known that he did refuse a crown at the hands of his brother. He and his brother Joseph have only just enough to live upon; Lucien is lodging in a little bit of a house in Devonshire Street (No. 50); Joseph has a *toute petite campagne*, where he lives with his daughter, whom he insists on calling la Princesse Charlotte.

Lady Cork has just written to beg I will name a day to meet the ex-majesties of Spain at dinner! I have been obliged to refuse, as we are off to Belgium this month. What strange things do come to pass in this tragical fever called life!

I am always studying eminent persons. Women above all — eminent no matter for what, De Staël, or Taglioni, *c'est égal*. Talking with Pasta the other day, I cross-questioned her about her diet. I said, "I remember, one night, being with you in your dressing-room when you had just come off the stage in your highest wrought scene, (the quartetta 'Come o Nimé,') your woman had a bit of cold roast beef ready to put into your mouth, and some porter."

"Ah si," was her reply, "mais je ne prends plus la viande — et pour le porter, I take it half-and-half." This bit of London slang, from the lips of Medea, and in her sweet broken English, had the oddest effect imaginable.

Saturday. — Yesterday was a curious day. I went with dear Lady Charleville and Mrs. Marley to see some original pictures of Nell Gwynne, at the Duke of St. Albans. The Duchess received us in a superb morning room; her dress was ridiculously fine for the

morning — rich white silk trimmed with white lace; a
quantity of gold chains, bracelets, &c. She had black
ringlets, surmounted by a black lace veil, which fell
over on one side. She is a coarse, full-blown, dark-
complexioned woman, about fifty. The last time I
saw her, was as Miss Mellon, in the *Honey Moon*, when
I came over to London to sell my *Wild Irish Girl*.
She was then a model of beauty, symmetry, and grace.
As I stared at her now, surrounded by ducal coronets,
even on her footstools, the pretty poem of *Le Tu, et
le Vous*, of Voltaire, came into my head. She accompanied us to her dressing-room, where she showed us
two pictures of Nell Gwynne, not original; the one, a
beautiful woman wearing a jewelled carcanet, by Sir
P. Lely, a copy of an original in the possession of
Mr. Calcraft, the Duchess believed; the other, was a
miserable thing in the dressing-room.

The Temple and the Idol, were the most interesting things to me; the magnificence and taste of all the
mirrors, gilding, pictures, furniture — the profusion of
flowers, and, above all, the attending priestesses, the
abigails, all over-dressed and ugly, such as any young
Duke might be trusted with. The robust Duchess
complained all the time of ill health, and said she
would hand us over to her housekeeper after she had
shown us over the ground-floor.

In the Duke's sitting-room, she pointed out a picture of herself as Miss Mellon, in Mrs. Page — "Very
beautiful, done," said she, "for my dear Mr. Coutts,
and the Duke will hang it up, you see, as a match for
his father, the late Duke, and here is a bust of Mr.
Coutts; you will see a statue of him up stairs," and
so we did, at the head of the drawing-room — an awful

figure! We were shown by the housekeeper into her
Grace's second dining-room, almost as magnificent as
her first. She said her Grace dressed here in the morning and below in the evening, to save her the trouble
of going up stairs. I was thinking of the Polly Pea-
chum Duchess of Bolton, and Nell Gwynne, and her
descendant marrying another Nell Gwynne. The
whole of this day was amusing. I dined at Lord
Charleville's, the company, the old Tory Duchess of
Richmond, enjoying the honours founded by Mademoiselle de Querouille (Duchess of Portsmouth), Sir
Charles Wetherell, lovely Lady Antrim, young Lord
Tullamore and his beautiful wife. After dinner went
to a dance with my girls.

August 15, *Monday.* — Yesterday was curious and
interesting; people coming to take leave of us. We
had at the same moment, Moore, Madame Pasta, Bellini,
Gabussi. And now for writing letters, apologies, &c.,
and off to-morrow for the Rhine.

Monday night. — The eve of our departure for the
Rhine. All packed up and ready for the Tower stairs
except my stomach. Oh, the horrible sea, and steam-
packet!

Tuesday morning, 6 *o'clock.* — Half inclined not to
go. London, hot rooms, and late hours have nearly
killed me, and yet there is but one place in the world,
and that is — dear London!

Everybody has been up the Rhine; and everything
worthy of note about Antwerp, Liege, and Cologne,
has been written, and may be read in the guide book;
but Brussels, at that time, fresh from its revolutions,
has a charm that cannot be repeated. We may, there-

fore, give a few patches from the diary kept during
her sojourn in Brussels after they had finished their
tour.

September 7th. — After our charming tour through
Belgium, here we are settled for some little time. We
had scarcely arrived when the French ambassador and
his lovely young wife (the *La Tour Maubourgs*) and
her charming sister and brother-in-law, Count and
Countess D'Oraison came in what they called *con-
spiration*, to lay violent hands and detain us here, and
we, nothing loath, have consented — my two girls in
the third heaven!

Received visits from Monsieur and Madame Engler.
The Frekes, Seymours, Dr. Bowring and Count
Hompèche. The latter dined at the *table d'hote* with
us, and sat beside me, and had we not fun! An English family at the *table d'hote impayable*. Mr. J—
turned up his nose at the French wines, "sour stuff,
monsieurs," and called for brandy and water. "I'll
lay you a cheney tea pot," said he, "they have no
melted butter for the salmon."

Thursday — Dined yesterday at the Engler's, a magnificent dinner, and music in the evening, met and
chatted a good deal with the minister of the interior,
Monsieur Rogier, sensible, modest, and high-minded.
He is to come and see us to-morrow.

Thursday 15. — What a *levée* to-day of all nations!

Foreigners complain here that there is no society,
each *menage* suffices to itself, and when amusement is
to be sought, it is bought ready made. The lower
orders fly to their cabarets in the environs, the middle
class have their *cafés* and *estaminets*, and the highest

rank go to their box at the opera; and this with the
diversity of a ball in the season and the court ceremonies makes up the whole of their social existence,
(very like our own), but there is no house open to
receive either morning or evening visits, as there are
in Paris. There is no intellectual society as in England;
there is no material for it. The women are sedentary
and silent, domestic and *devote*, and resemble the mass
of our female English society, but without their habits
of intellectual cultivation, which brings ease, grace, and
courtesy along with it.

September 17. — We shall have to leave this hotel,
as it is *all taken* for the great *fêtes*.

September 18. — Hardly got into our pretty apartments in the Rue de la Regence (with our books,
flowers, piano, drawings, &c., &c.), when enter Lady
Clare, and Lady Isabella Fitzgibbons, and Sir Robert
Adair. What a pleasant chat of times and people,
past and present! How they recall the bright days of
the Priory to me!

September 18. — We dined yesterday at the Palace;
great simplicity, with just as much splendour as any
nobleman of good taste and wealth might indulge in,
but nothing more. The Queen — young, fair, simple,
and more than courteous — reminds me of our English
girls of rank: a little shy and very graceful, but nothing
of the *morgue* of our belles of quality. I looked about
me for a ribbon. I spied a gentleman in black, with
the broadest blue scarf from shoulder to flank. I
thought he represented some ancient order of chivalry,
pas du tout. It was an *English knight* of the Guelphic
Order. The Grand Maréchal, a very agreeable Count,
asked me what Order that was. I could not help

saying, *L'ordre de tout bête.* Strange to say here was
a royal company of forty persons; there was not one
Prince amongst them. There was all the intellect
and manhood of the present administration. The
Belgian Lafayette, Baron De Hoogoorst, the brave, the
patriotic commander of the National Guard: there was
Charles Rogier, the Minister of the Interior, who, in
the most awful moment of political fermentation at the
time of the revolution, flung himself into the very gap
of anarchy, and established that character of dauntless
devotedness to a great cause which may be deemed
the chivalry of politics; Monsieur Le Beau, Ministre
de Justice, the prose, as Rogier is the poetry of the
revolution; Monsieur Northomel, Secretary-General des
Affaires Etrangers, with countenance full of intellectual
fire, *pensante et instruit;* not one dandy or dunce amongst
them. Could one say as much for a diplomatic table
of London? In short, I was better pleased with this
royal dinner than with anything royal I have ever yet
assisted at. "Il faut avoir que votre Roi est le plus
grand Roi du mond," said I to my neighbour; "S'il
n'est pas, il le doit être," said he.

September 20. — What an odd coincidence. We
had last night nearly the whole of the last Provisional
Government of the Belgian Revolution, with the addition of Colonel Prozinski, Mr. White, author of *The
King's Own,* the two De Brouckers, Henri et Charles,
Quételet, the Royal Astronomer, Jullien, the Orator of
the Opposition, Sir Robert Adair, our Ambassador,
and the dear, charming, La Tour Maubourgs. The
evening was amusing. I had also Van Hallan, the accomplished author of an historical tract of the *Trouble
Belgique* in 1718; he is the type of the character and

national feelings of the Belgian youth, and one among
the many illustrations of the beneficial change in the
character of a people effected by the removal of oppres-
sive and anti-national institutions.

September 26. — A week of carnival festivities.
The Concert d'Harmonie à la Place Royal, by six
hundred musicians, consisting of the corps of the army,
with an audience of nearly ten thousand persons in
front of the beautiful Hotel de Ville, — really one of
the most imposing sights I have ever seen. In front
was inclosed a space for the Ministers, the Deputies,
and the Senate. The windows and balconies belonging
to the houses and hotels all round filled with elegantly-
dressed women. To the right, in a balcony window,
sat the King and Queen and officers of state. The
royal party were received by the music of the "Mar-
seillaise," mingled with the "Brabaçon." There was
no loud enthusiasm, for these people now repose upon
their past emotions, and their recollection of their past
hard-won liberties is now enjoyed by them in sober
satisfaction, and the full consciousness of their happiness suffices them. The beautiful music elicited
more applause than any other occurrence of the day.
Alas! the rain fell in torrents before it was over, and
Bruxelles presented a canopy of umbrellas which had
the most extraordinary effect.

September 28. — The races went on yesterday in
spite of the rain; rather a laughable business, men and
horses stuck in the mud, and one poor horse broke his
back, and the jockey, I fear, much hurt. These are
happy times when events are greater than the men
that are placed at their head. It is something to represent the first state that has thrown off its slavery

The immense masses of opinion now afloat upon the surface of the political society of Belgium forced into collusion by the ferment and kicking against each other. It requires a cool head and a firm hand to wield the sceptre, and Leopold seems to have both, and has a fine career before him. On the king's visit to Verviers, he said to the bourgmestre, "Qu'il protegerait toujours l'industrie." "Sire," replied the burgomaster, "il n'y en est pas besoin ça va bien comme ça." The king laughed much at the *naïveté* of this good fellow, and this is the essence of all the philosophy of commerce — *laissez nous faire.*

October. — Just returned to London, and St. James' Street, after the most delightful tour up the Rhine that ever was made. A day or two for seeing friends, and a few visits, and then — off for wretched Dublin!

Lady Morgan, who had been very kind to Madame Belzoni, as to all classes of foreigners, received from her at this time a curious present.

Madame Belzoni to Lady Morgan.

September 25th, 1833.

DEAR LADY MORGAN,

On my arrival at Jerusalem, 1808, the Temple of Solomon was then under repair, and nearly finished. The Turks, whenever they require any work of importance done, send out an order to arrest such Christian workmen as may be required for the undertaking, paying them with the greatest liberality; so much so, that they frequently return to their homes with a little fortune. Living in the same quarter, I naturally went

10*

with them. Among those whom I was acquainted with,
were an old man and woman, whose son was employed
as Scrivener at the temple, a place of some importance.
For his particular privilege and emolument, an old
door of cedar was given him; this door had been placed
on the same site that tradition reputes that our blessed
Saviour used to pass through.

The Turks hold in the greatest veneration all places
that are sacred to our Saviour, *excepting the Sepulchre*;
considering *Christ* as a spirit, consequently a spirit
could not be crucified, and that it was the body of
Judas that had been taken into the *Sepulchre*, of course
they ridicule the Christians for worshipping there. I
am ashamed of this *preamble* about nothing, but the
insignificancy of the article required it. The accom-
panying cross was made out of *that door*, and it received the benediction in the holy *Sepulchre*, under my
own sight. Will Lady Morgan accept my *offering of
thanks*, poor as it is.

S. BELZONI.

PS. — The basket plate was made above the first
cataract of the Nile, *Nubia.* Fruit of the *date tree, the
inside is dissolved, and made into bowls.*

The spoon that I bought in grand *Cairo*, 1837,
which the grand Turk's people eat their rice with.

Forgive, dear Lady Morgan, the insignificant offerings of a *human heart.* I have often longed to see you
— that wish is at last gratified. In 1822, I passed
the Simplon, two days after you had passed, and was
much mortified at having missed seeing one who had
charmed me so often.

Again, we return to the diary: —

December 24. — We returned to Ireland the middle
of October, after our most delightful, gratifying, and
interesting visit to the Continent, but I had not the
heart to resume the thread of my chronicles till this
day, and now only because the year is winding up,
and I am going away for a time. During my charming June and July in London, I kept a very rough
outline of what I was about, and whom I saw (and
whom I did *not* see who was worth seeing)! My
principal impressions are in my head, for I had no
intention of ever writing a journey again till I was
urged to do it by all parties and classes in Brussels.
On my return to this dreary city, my house full of
dirty, idle, loitering workmen, I set to work myself,
hurried them through theirs, and got ill, and went to
recover with my dear friends at Malahide, whose
castle is always open to us. On my return, settled
in to write, in spite of some pleasant intentions. We
have dined with the Littletons; Mr. Littleton, his
lovely wife and daughters. He is in politics honest,
frank, and straightforward, but new. I have had
various and curious conversations with him, I wish I
had written them down.

Contrary to our intentions, we accepted an invitation from Sir Thomas and Lady Chapman, for the sake
of my dear girls, who were included. A most joyous
and agreeable fortnight. Think of their being *afraid*
of asking *me* to their superb castle, lest I should be
ennuyée with their society, and doing the honours by
me as if I were a little queen! Talking with Lady
Chapman the other day, on the radical liberalism of

her three sons and two nephews (the Tighes), I said,
laughingly, "With a Tory father, a Tory uncle, an
aristocratic mother, how comes it that all your young
men, bred up in absolution, should be such liberals!
who converted them?" She smiled, and said, "Why,
then, to tell the truth, it was your Ladyship." "I?
Why, I have talked so little to them since they grew
up." "You have talked enough, and written more than
enough to make them what they are!" It is thus we
women, the secret tribunal of society, can mine and
countermine.

We returned to town on Saturday, 21st, and dined
with Mr. Wallace, my old lover, M.P. for Carlow. I sat
at dinner between the Provost and the Secretary of
State, Mr. Littleton. I attacked the Provost's college
wall on one side (as we are struggling to have it down
to open narrow Nassau Street), and *other* walls on the
other side. I took the opportunity of bringing forward
the honest and the clever, who never make their way;
I always do this when I get beside the great and influ-
ential. I spoke of Dr. Macarthy, the honest and philosophical, and I put a spoke in the wheel of the College
of Surgeons, the jobbing, exclusive, monopolising College
of Surgeons. When we got upon O'Connell, I said,
"Listen to a foolish woman's prophecy. O'Connell is
veering towards you, because, just now he is losing
hold on the people, and the rent for the time has failed.
If you meet him a step he will entangle you, perhaps
betray you; at all events, he will make a merit of it in
the eyes of his dupes."

MR. LITTLETON. "But do you not think he will be
worth having?"

"Yes; if you can catch him and *keep* him, but he

has an Irish *physical* talent none of you can cope with,
subtlety. The eel is a lump of lead compared with
O'Connell, he has no one fixed principle; the end, with
him, consecrates the means, and *that* end is — O'Connell, the beginning and end of all things." Mr. Littleton
was silent, and then asked me if I were pleased with
the batch of commissionerships he had given away. I
said "yes, if they are to get nothing." He said, "Nothing but the honour; they are all rich men."

Christmas Eve. — Eating, drinking, flirting, and
reading. I must register an odd thought. The Irish
destiny is between Bedlam and a jail; but I won't
pursue it. So ends my journal of 1833. How
much I have felt, suffered, enjoyed, seen, and heard in
that year!!

CHAPTER IX.

THE BEGUINE — 1834.

THE diary for 1834 begins early in January.

PORTRAN, *January 5th.* — Here we are with our
friend the honourable, uncompromising M.P. for Dublin,
George Evans, the butt and victim of all O'Connell's
hatred, malice, and calumny, because he will not crawl
after him, and resists his repeal. Mrs. Evans is the
sister of Sir Henry Parnell, and daughter to the late
Irish Chancellor of the Exchequer; she is a first-rate
woman, but, perhaps, too ambitious about her husband's
parliamentary career. They are both excellent, and I

always enjoy my sea-girt dwelling; in spite of the wind
howling without, all within is peace, comfort, and good
cheer; by-the-bye, *à propos* to the latter, they possess
the first cook in Europe.

KILDARE STREET, *January 9th.* — Came into town
to dine at Lord Wellesley's. Had some chat with the
Viceroy, the Vice Queen; the Duke of Leinster, and
the Littletons were of the party. I was congratulated
on the approaching marriage of my dear niece, Sydney,
which gives us all great satisfaction.

After this came other dinners and parties, too numerous to specify.

February 14th. — I had a little musical soirée last
night. The last time my three girls may, perhaps, ever
sing together, for Sydney is to be married next week,
and then off to England. Vaccai sang with them; he is
a charming composer.

February 17th. — I am so busy with other people's
affairs, Miss O'Keefe, Madame Belzoni, Vaccai, — writing my new book, and Sydney's marriage, and letters
and felicitations, that I have not a moment to give to
journalising. Lord Cloncurry has lent Sydney Lawrence his villa of Maritimo till they go to England.

February 21st. — I am like Lady Teazle, "drawing patterns for ruffles; I shall never have materials to
make up," for here are two fine receipts just as I have
given up giving dinners! The reason I am up to my
eyes in fuss, is that I am so occupied with Sydney's
marriage, and my new work on Belgium, of which I
can make nothing; the fault is in me, and not in my
subject, which is fine. I am living without servants;
oh, would that I could live for ever without those
impersonations of whiskey, the Irish servants; *ce cha-*

pitre là would take a volume, the whole history of the country is concerned in it, — priests and bad government!

Poor Miss O'Keefe! her father's book has just come in; what feebleness, but what amiable feeling! She quotes my account of him, which I sent to all the papers, to try and get a subscription, but all in vain.

I have had to begin my *Belgium* all over again on a new plan. I have now made up my mind to make a Belgian novel of my materials, instead of a history; my heroine shall be a *Béguine.*

The feebleness of present men and present times is fully illustrated by the fuss and agitation in which Lords and Commons are thrown by discovering men to be rogues whom nobody ever suspected of being honest.

February 28. — Just had a visit from old, queer, Weld Hartstrong — a flirtation of near twenty years' standing; *ma foi*, Time has left him as quizzical as Nature intended him to be! His uncle, Sir Harry Hartstronge, was the Protestant gentleman who knocked the Catholic petition over the bar of the House of Commons some forty years back. This little Parliamentary anecdote would be a *floorer* to Mr. O'Connell's raving for the repeal — such was the Irish House of Commons! Would any one dare to do this in the Imperial Parliament? My friend, Weld Hartstronge, is author of a large portion of those books "that ne'er were read;" but he is a worthy man, a great antiquary, and my walking Encyclopædia.

May 24. — Half an hour back, writing hard at my *Béguine*, the bright sunshine drew me with my watering-pot to the balcony; a thundering knock at the door drove me in — somebody had entered the study. I went down. It was Cuthbert of Altadore.

"I am come," said he, "to tell you—that the news has arrived of — in short — Lafayette is dead!!"

Alas! our last, best tie to France is broken; only aged 76; he would have had some bright years yet before him but for that *one* false step — the restoration of the Bourbons; his death-blow came from that.

May 25. — My dear Francis Crossley arrived from India, *viâ* China; the same friend he ever was — kind, gentle, and devoted. He dines with us to-morrow, and all my own dear family.

June 20. — Malahide Castle; busy all day writing my *Béguine*. Delicious air breathing on me, and beautiful scenery. Just finished a scene — the basse Ville de Bruxelles, the *atélier* of a poor young female artiste. I took the idea from my visit to Fannie Corr, the young Belgian artist. Rogier, the Minister of the Interior, carried me off one morning to see an old *délabrée* house — pretty much as I have described it — and as we waited for the young struggling *artiste* in her studio, I was struck by its dreariness and picturesque desolation.

My dearest Morgan works with me at this arduous novel — copies and corrects whilst I throw off the proof impressions; but I would rather he walked on the seashore, which now gleams so brightly before me; but he won't. Alas! inertness is his malady.

I have received a letter about the copyright of my ballad of *Kate Kearney*. Somebody wants to publish it afresh. She certainly would be an old woman by this time, if women and heroines had not an escape from old age in immortality.

The Duke of Wellington has been made Chancellor of Oxford. Our Archbishop of Dublin demanded an audience of Lord Wellesley. "I come to demand a troop of horse, my Lord." "For whom?" "For myself." "Oh, I see!"

Sir Charles Morgan was the physician to the Marshalsea, an office which Government had the intention of abolishing at this time. Sir Charles and Lady Morgan naturally expected the compensation usually granted to those who hold a Government appointment believed to be permanent. Their intimacy with persons high in rank and office, was of little practical value to them. As Lady Morgan said herself, they never asked for anything and never received anything.

Mr. Lyttleton, Secretary to the Treasury, wrote to Lady Morgan on the subject.

H. Lyttleton to Lady Morgan.

TREASURY,
December, 7, 1834.

MY DEAR LADY MORGAN,

I cannot conceive it possible that the change in the Government can in any manner affect Sir Charles Morgan's claim for compensation for the loss of his office. His having bought it cannot be considered by the Treasury. But his removal will afford the Government an opportunity of making a very economical arrangement in the Medical Department of the Marshalsea, which will far more than cover any compensation he would expect. His loss, therefore, ought to be liberally considered.

I have not an accurate recollection of the state in which the correspondence with the Treasury on this subject was left to me. When the new Government is organised, I advise Sir Charles to write to Sir W. Gosset to urge dispatch in the settlement of his compensation. The Treasury is slow; is difficult to manage; it is like the hole of a till — it takes in money easily, but requires long fingers to draw it out again.

What do you mean by abusing us miserable servants out of place? When I was in the service of His Majesty, you never asked me for any of the good things from his table. Sir Charles was not considered a candidate for a seat in any of the Commissions, or I should willingly have submitted his claim to the favourable consideration of the Lord-Lieutenant, when a fair opportunity of serving him might have offered.

I never could make out what was meant by the often-repeated charge of the Irish Government forgetting its friends. A Mr. Glasscock, a Tory, was deprived of his office of patentee of first fruits by the Church Act of 1832. Lord Grey, in the House of Lords, promised him the compensation of the first vacant equivalent office. Can you tell me of any other Tory promoted during my short reign? It is possible there might have been one or two Tories in Whig guise who crept into favour, and imposed on the Government. But I believe we were tolerably wary. I admit we did not go far enough in depriving enemies in power of ill-gotten pelf. We left whips in the hands of our enemies; and they used them to scourge us with, knowing we dared not take them from them.

You are very partial, but not unjust to Mrs. Lyttle-

ton, who always makes sunshine wherever she goes.
We are here till Parliament meets, when we shall
hope to renew our acquaintance with you in town.
We are, meantime, all impatience to see your new
work,

I remain, dear Lady Morgan,
Very sincerely yours,
H. LYTTLETON.

Towards the close of 1834, Lady Morgan finished
her Belgian novel called the *Princess, or the Béguine.*
It was published by Mr. Bentley, of New Burlington
Street. She did not gain so much by it as by her former
novels. The sum she received was £ 350 for the first
edition. It is an admirable novel. Its main intention
was to interest the public in the new kingdom of Belgium, and to give a knowledge of the question and of
the conditions that had led to it. She began the work as
a history; but finding it dull to write, and still more
dull to read, she threw up that design and began it
again as a novel, which was as bright and sparkling as
any of its Irish predecessors. The pictures of English
fashionable life, as it existed at that period, are vivid,
and wonderfully graphic. The characters are all drawn
from the life, and would be easily recognisable by anyone conversant with the men and women of the time;
but though the characters are portraits, the circumstances and incidents are fictitious, sketched in to suit
the story. The descriptions of the city of Brussels —
its antiquities, pictures, historical recollections — are
brilliant and masterly, but they interrupt the story.
The chief personages of the revolution are historical
portraits of great force and spirit. The politics of the

time — the state of public feeling — the real condition
of things in the kingdom of Brussels — are given with
the same enthusiasm and vigour which she had thrown
into her Irish stories. She used up some of the materials she had collected for a life of Rubens, and they
are worked in with much skill. Those desiring a
picturesque guide to Brussels should read *The Béguine;*
and it is a novel as entertaining as though it had been
written for no other purpose than to adorn the idleness
and beguile the *ennui* of *des gens peu amusables.* Lady
Morgan always kept to the same type of character for
heroines, the heroine being one who has, by the skilful
exercise of common sense, risen to a high position in
the world.

CHAPTER X.

CHELTENHAM AND LONDON — 1835.

AT the beginning of 1835, Sir Charles and Lady
Morgan and one of their nieces went to Cheltenham,
where they remained some time. The record of her
sojourn there is slight; but the following extracts from
her diary, and a few letters, indicate the chief events
of this period.

January 8. — This place is the grand asylum of
mediocrity — the Paradise of old women — the Olympus
of old men — the resort of the refuse of all societies:
viz., the dull, the old, sickly, or tiresome; and yet it
has its aristocracy!

Well, with all this, we have found a few with whom

it is pleasant to live, and with them we live a great deal. The dear, old, agreeable, and cordial Corry's — James Corry, once the Coryphæus of the Kilkenny theatricals. They have given up Ireland, like others, and come to live in a pretty cottage here; our other most agreeable, but new acquaintances, the family at Beaufort House, Sir George and Lady Whitmore, and their most agreeable family, are quite after my own heart. *She*, unique in her way, has lived thirty years in Italy — a divine musician, and full of genius; her son Edmond, a charming little lazzaroni of sixteen, and my *devoué cavalier* — my darling Olivia such a favourite with them all.

January 10. — Moore, talking to Corry on the Whigs having done nothing for him, said of Lord Holland, Lansdowne, and Lord John Russell, "I had no reason to expect it; I live upon equal terms with Lansdowne, and when he is at Bowood I dine there constantly; now there is Macaulay, Lansdowne gave him a place of two or three thousand pounds a year, and never asked him to dinner once. These great men seek people in different ways, and for different purposes. I am quite contented."

And so he is. This is so Irish, and so much an affair of temperament, that there is no arguing about it. Moore is an epitome of genuine Irish character, feeling, fancy, genius, and personal vanity overwhelming all — I know him well.

Last night we had some charming music at the Whitmore's — my little Olivia sang divinely; but the dowagers and their turbans were too much for me.

Lady Charleville has one of the finest minds that ever took a wrong direction. The ingenuity with which

she argues on false principles, the eloquence with which
she does the honours of error, are curious; but if you
force her to step out of the track in which her position
has placed her, as a great lady, reared in the bosom of
high Toryism, she is amazed, bewildered, but admires
the new doctrines she fears, and it is thus she listens
to and bears with me.

A letter from Sir Henry Hardinge to my husband
about the compensation for his office. Nothing definite.

Sir H. Hardinge to Sir C. Morgan.

CASTLE, DUBLIN,
February 10, 1835.

DEAR SIR CHARLES,

I have had some correspondence with the Treasury
on your subject, and was in hopes to have induced
them to have made a more desirable arrangement.
They adhere, however, to that of their predecessors,
and when I return to London, which I do this day,
you shall hear from me officially; the exact amount
of the retiring pension not having been as yet com-
municated. The division shall be expedited without
delay.

I hope Lady Morgan enjoys the fine air of Cheltenham, and that her unrivalled talents are employed in
amusing and instructing all classes and ages.

I am going to see Lady Clarke. I beg to offer my
best regards to Lady Morgan, and am, my dear Sir
Charles,

Yours very truly,
H. HARDINGE.

On leaving Cheltenham, Sir Charles and Lady Morgan proceeded to London, where they were joined by their niece, Josephine. Their first locality was in St. James's Place. Afterwards, they removed to 49, Grosvenor Place, of which she says: "delicious lodgings — just after my own heart; an old house, built a hundred years ago — a balcony, a verandah. I had great difficulty in getting Morgan out of St. James's Place, where I was dying. He considers this delightful site banishment." They entered on their new quarters on the 1st of March, and she already began to contemplate writing a history of Pimlico. The diary continues: —

This pretty district, the principality of his highness the Duke of Westminster, is just the *locale* that suits me, hanging on the verge of the world's bustle, not in it. The district of fashion, with all the advantages of seclusion; a garden before, though a royal one, and space and fresh air everywhere. In short, I am charmingly lodged. Yesterday, Morgan and I dined with Lord and Lady Charleville; left my dear Olivia at home. Lady Charleville growing finer by time, — noble, better and pleasanter. Lord Charleville a fearful monument of vitality, surviving all but its infirmities. His son, Lord Tullamore, a Lord in Waiting, a Tory, a dandy, an exclusive. He talked to me of *the class and order* to which he belonged! I told him the Irish story of the *Baynishes of Cork*, which set them all in fits of laughter, and even the servants were obliged to rush out of the room to hide their faces: so much for the *class* and *order* to which *I* belong.

March 2. — Received, to-day, a most gracious and

grateful letter from Monsieur Northomel (Secretary of
State for Belgium), conveying his thanks and those of
his friends, for my Belgium novel; and says, all the
journals are loud in its praise. Another, from the
Minister of the Interior to the same effect. I am so
glad they like my little *Béguine.*

Last night I met Moore at Lady Stepney's — looking old and ill — much out of spirits, and, he says,
weary of London after a few days' residence. He had
come to publish his *History of Ireland*, but Longman
and Co. found it was not half bulky enough, so he was
sent back to enlarge it. He would not sing. I delivered a message to him from Lady Charleville. "Tell
him he must, as an historian, rectify an error in the
life of Lord Edward Fitzgerald." He praises Lord
Camden (then Viceroy) for giving Lady Louisa Conolly
permission to see the dying Lord Edward; and he ac-
cuses Lord Clare of cruelty for refusing her permission
to do so. The case was the reverse. Lady Louisa
threw herself at Lord Camden's feet, and *he* refused
her petition. Then she flew, in her despair, to Lord
Clare, who said, "I cannot — dare not — give you a
written permission, but I will go with you to the prison myself." They went together, at night. When
they came to the door of the miserable room, Lord
Clare said, "I cannot leave you alone with the prisoner,
but I will send away the jailor and leave the door
open, and watch before it myself. I shall hear nothing." Moore seemed much annoyed when I told him
this. "I have been bored to death," he said, "by
friends of Lord Clare, about this, already; but I saw
the letter — had it in my hand — in which Lord Clare
refused Lady Louisa peremptorily. I have already

mentioned the anecdote alluded to by Lady Charleville
in my book, but people do not read it. It is not worth
while writing for such a public. I am amazed how I
have made my way. People read with their prejudices,
not with their intellects."

Last night, after our dinner at Lady Charleville's
we proceeded to Mrs. Skinner's, Portland Place — *ou
par example*, Parnassus and Port Royal — the Sorbonne
and the Antiquarian society — a quadrille. I was the
lioness of the night, *malgré moi!* and there I sat,
couched in a sort of a bay window, and there was presented to me all manner of notabilities, and scores of
people from all corners of the earth. Amongst others,
Mrs. Somerville, the mathematician, all celestial and
descended from her solar system, the learned commen-
tator of La Place! and Miss Herschel, member of the
Royal Society. Mrs. Somerville struck me to be a
simple little woman, middle aged. Had she not been
presented to me by name and reputation, I should say
one of the respectable twaddling chaperones one meets
with at every ball, dressed in a snug mulberry velvet
gown and little cap with a red flower. I asked her how
she could descend from the stars to mix amongst us?
She said she was obliged to go out with her daughter
(who was dancing with my niece in the same quadrille).
From the glimpse of her last night, I should say there
was no imagination, no deep moral philosophy, though
a deal of scientific lore and a great deal of *bonhomie.*
She had long wished to know me, and I replied, with
great truth, I had long revered her, without presuming
to appreciate her! So we agreed to know each other
better, and we are to go and see each other. She and
Dr. Somerville live at Chertsey. What a woman! com-

pared to the flum-flamree novel trash writers of the present day!

Then up comes Bob Montgomery, the poet — he bows to the ground, a handsome little black man. I asked him if he was *Satan* Montgomery? and he said he was, so we began to be very facetious, and we laughed as if the devil was in *us*, till he was obliged to make place for Sir Alexander Creighton! physician to the late Emperor of Russia, author of a treatise on *Insanity*, a most playful and agreeable old gentleman; we knocked up a friendship for life, and should have gone on gossiping nonsense, but for Godwin, to whom Sir Alexander resigned his place. Alas, for Godwin! *Caleb Williams* Godwin, with whom I almost began my literary life at a dinner at Sir R. Phillips's, my first publisher! He talked of Curran, Grattan, Hamilton Rowan, whom he had known in Ireland — wit, eloquence, chivalry! — now all dust! Then we got on the subject of his poor son-in-law, Shelley, and his daughter, whom I shall go and see as soon as she comes to town.

Dinner at Mr. Dilke's — sat near Allan Cunningham — immense fun — Willis, the American poet, and other celebrities.

After our pleasant dinner went on to another congress at Portland place, where we met all the arts and sciences, and where we spent the night on the *stairs*, with the grand Turk (I forget his name) and his suite — I had a deal of fun with them, making *Mr. Urquhart*, the Turkish traveller, our *mutual* interpreter. They are coming to see me. Urquhart's *tie* in Russia, and the necessity of combining against her; but he is a clever creature!

Dined yesterday at Mr. Courtney's, M. P., the great epicure, — an exquisite dinner, — but Courtney so occupied with his dishes, he never spoke to his guests. I sat beside one of the greatest wits of the day, Sidney Smith! what a charmer! so natural, so little of a *wit titré*, so *bon enfant*, that the delicacy of his wit appears the natural result of a fine organization, and of a happy mind ready to enjoy and to receive as much pleasure from others as he confers upon those with whom he converses. He comes to see me to-morrow.

Yesterday, had a long visit and sofa conversation with Lucien Bonaparte, — his Italian ideas, no monarchy without an aristocracy. The reason France is all, *à tors et à travers*, is a wish to remove the peerage. He thinks with me, that Cardinal Richelieu was the founder of the revolutionary system. He said it was Richelieu who turned the cold, brave chivalry of France into the *valetaille d'anti chambre* of an effeminate despot. Speaking of the French, he said, "at the outburst of the Revolution of '88, there were a good many people in France with common sense. The Emperor used to say to me that the French were essentially a monarchical people, and we used to deny this; but everything he ever said has come out true since."

April 3. — My journal is gone to the dogs, *je n'en peut plus.* I am so fussed and fidgetted by my dear charming world, that I cannot write. I forget days and dates. Ouf! Last night at Lady Stepney's — met the Milmans, Lady Charlotte Bury, Mrs. Norton, Rogers, Sidney Smith, and other wits and authors. Amongst others, poor dear Jane Porter; she told me she was taken for me the other night, and talked to *as such* by

a party of Americans! She is tall, lank and lean, and
lackadaisical, dressed in the deepest black, with rather
a battered black gauze hat, and an air of a regular
Melpomene. I am the reverse of all this, *et sans vanité*,
the best dressed woman wherever I go. Last night I
wore a blue satin, trimmed fully with magnificent point
lace and stomacher, *à la Sevigné*, light blue velvet hat
and feather, with an *aigrette* of sapphires and diamonds!
Voila! The party at the Murchison's — Lord Jeffrey,
the *Edinburgh Review* — Lockhart, of the *Quarterly;*
Hallam, *Middle Ages*; Milman, the poet; Mrs. Somerville; &c., &c. Lord Jeffrey came up to me, and we
had such a flirtation. When he comes to Ireland, we
are to go to Donny-brook Fair together; in short,
having cut me down with his tomahawk *as a reviewer*,
he smothers me with roses *as a man;* and so he comes
to see me. I always say of my enemies before we
meet, "Let me at them."

Mrs. Smith, Moore's first love, and the subject of
his graceful song,

> "I'll ask the Sylph that round thee flies,"

was a friend of Mrs. Hemans, the touching mention of
whose last illness and death will interest the reader
both for the poetess and her friend.

Mrs. Smith to Lady Morgan.

UPPER FITZROY STREET, DUBLIN,
March 21, 1835.

MY DEAR LADY MORGAN,
  It was no common pleasure to receive a letter from
you, and I beg you to believe that I know how to

value such a favour, given in the midst of all your
bustle and gaiety.

I heard with pleasure of your triumphs at Cheltenham; but I knew you would not settle there. It is very
well for a few weeks; but I see that dear London will
get possession of you at last. It is a dismal thought
that you are to leave us, and you are really too scepti-
cal as to the number of those who will feel your absence from Dublin a serious loss.

Of course you have heard of Mrs. Hemans' illness.
She has long been given over. It is three weeks since
her physicians owned they had no hopes, and now a
few days will rob the world of one who will not be
easily matched. She was *past remedy* when Dr. Graves
gave her into the hands of Dr. Croker. The latter has,
I believe, done all that could be done; but the constitution was gone. Her fortitude of mind and sweetness
of temper shine out to the last. She is quite resigned,
and will not allow a mournful look or tone at her bed-
side. Her sister, Mrs. Hughes, is with her, and her
brother, Major Brown, and it is a comfort to know that
she has every kind of care.

Sad, most sad has been her history! Those who
love her, ought to rejoice when she is at peace; a lofty
mind, ever soaring above the realities of life, essentially
poetical, and *never otherwise;* ardent, sentient, enthusiastic, and all this contained in a frame of the most
fragile delicacy. What chance had she here in Dublin,
and with an utter disrelish for the kind of society that
was attainable? When she was in the county of Wicklow
last August, her anxiety to remain there was like the
thirst of fever. Poor thing, I wish I had never known
her.

Robert has been hunting the whole winter, till he
is more like a horse than a man. I am hoarse with
praying him to marry and be respectable; but he grows
more hardened daily.

If you have heard that we are to have drawing-
rooms in the *daytime*, as in London, I am sure you
have laughed at the idea of it. Our whole turn out!
our equipages, our poverty, alas! need the friendly
cloak of night.

Ever sincerely yours,
MARIA SMITH.

May. — The other night at Lady Clare's; found
myself seated by Poggo di Borgo (the object of thirty
years' despotism). He has a pension settled on him
by the Tory government, and still paid him by the
Whigs — a disgrace to England. All the three daughters of Tom Sheridan have pensions settled on them.
Lord Seymour has resigned Lady Seymour's.

Babbage's party last night very pleasant; got into
mon petit coin — had a minister, a philosopher, a reviewer, a politician, and a dandy, successively *sur la
sellette.* Vanderweyer charming, *spirituel* and *observing.*
He inspires one with views and opinions similar to his
own, and we agree upon most things. I told him I
had received a letter from one mutual good friend,
Rogier, in the morning, full of cordiality and warm
feeling — reminding me of the old happy days of '33.

July 21. — Last days in London.

With a heavy heart, as with a presentiment of the
misery that awaited me. Even before leaving London,
at seven in the morning, my dearest Morgan looked
ill, and complained. At the end of the first stage he

was taken ill — this was Barnet, and before we reached
the second stage it was an interval of agony to both.
He became very faint; I fanned and bathed his face
with eau de cologne — it was very hot — and becoming fainter, he fell lifeless into my arms. As we
were galloping down hill at the time, the carriage could
not stop. At last we drew up at a little pot-house inn,
the Black Bull, London Colney, where he was taken
out of the carriage helpless, and thrown on a wretched
bed.

No medical aid nearer than St. Alban's, four miles
off; thither I sent. What an interval! His extremities
cold; his hands blue; congestion coming on; I, helpless, hopeless, watching all this!

The arrival of surgeon Lipscomb — his active practice — covering him with hot tiles, mustard, blisters,
bleeding him profusely, in a word saved his life — and
mine. If there is desolation on earth, and misery in
its supreme helplessness, it is the situation in which I
was placed. I dare not think of it.

I discovered I was in the neighbourhood of Royal
Porters! and making my dreary position known to
Colonel and Mrs. White, they came to invite us to the
great house; but this was impossible, so they supplied
us with fresh flowers, fruit, and wine, and with the
delight of my dear husband's hourly recovering under
my eyes, I began to think the Black Bull a very
liveable, enjoyable place.

I filled the little Sunday parlour with flowers, and
heard the whole history of Mrs. Black Bull, the hostess,
and of her son, the butcher; and in the evening, when
Morgan slept, I took my seat on a bench before the
door with "boots" (Sam Edgell) and "mine host," with

such stories of highways and byeways! — a new view
to me of humanity and society.

Wayworn travellers · stopping and economizing a
few halfpence in the matter of refreshment — and the
poor weary women — and the pleasure I felt in turning a pint of small beer into a pint of good ale, which
was thought so noble on my part — and the joke cracked
by Sam, with the natty, returning postilion — for little
Sam, a ricketty fellow of two feet and a half high, the
Asmodeous of the Black Bull, was evidently the wit
titré of London Colney! Then the lovely, quiet scene,
the pond and the stream, the parson's house; the cattle
coming home, and the shower of red sunset showing
over all! A gentleman in black passed us twice, and
stared, and at last took off his hat. Our landlady said,
"'Tis our rector, who sent your ladyship the sal vola-
tile and offers of services."

The great skill and vigilance of Dr. Lipscomb
brought back my husband and life to me. In London
he might have died for want of that close attention
paid him by this country doctor. We have had more
opportunity of becoming acquainted lately with this
order of medical men. What talent in obscurity!
What worth unknown! while charlatanism is fed and
flourishes in this world, beyond all talent and all
worth.

July 25. — While seated on the stone bench of the
Black Bull, the rector approached me with a look of
curiosity and doubt, and said he had heard of Sir
Charles' illness, and he had come to offer his services
to us both. He told me he was a Divine of two plu-
ralities, the rector of London Colney, and something
else that I forget, and while we sat gossiping before

our cabaret, he said he could scarcely believe that the
companion of Sam and of the master of the Black Bull
was Lady Morgan of whom he had heard so much, &c.
As the dew and darkness were falling, we adjourned
to the little sanded floor parlour and a pair of tallow
candles, and talked of books and the fashions of the
neighbourhood of London Colney. In short, my parson was a parson of gentility, and an agreeable man of
the world.

August 1. — DUBLIN. — After an anxious and
fatiguing journey, and having been on the point of
losing all that was most dear to me, and necessary to
the future remnant of my life — my husband, after having
witnessed the distress of my sweet Sydney in the dreadful illness and threatened death of her almost bride-
groom husband, I have at last reached wretched Dublin,
the capital of wretched Ireland.   I found our house in
a wretched condition, half-painted, half-repaired, and
full of dawdling drinking workmen, so we were obliged
to take up our abode with my sister and Sir Arthur
Clarke.   Morgan laid up with a second attack; I,
obliged to trudge over, at eight in the morning and
remain till two with the workmen, who made a strike
and left their employer, all because he employed a man
whom they did not like.

August 9. — Tom Moore, the poet, arrived yesterday, so Clarke went to ask him to dinner to-day.
Clarke met him in the street going to mass, near the
Metropolitan Chapel, and accompanied him; he accepted the invitation, but conditionally — *à l'ordinaire*
— if some great person, who he was pretty sure would
or had asked him, did not renew his claim. This is
his old way of accepting invitations. His old friend —

his and mine — Edward Moore, of Cleveland Row, told me a pleasant story of Tom having made *three* of those conditional promises in one day, and got through two of them. Clarke was struck with the earnestness with which he performed all the acts of grace during that picturesque service; nobody, however, knew him, or noticed him. Clarke told the beadle it was the great Thomas Moore, upon which he went to the organ-loft, and announced in a loud voice — Sir Thomas Moore!

As the great man (who turned out to be old Jockey Hume of the Treasury, whose brother Tom came over with t'other Tom) did not send the invitation expected, Moore dined with us. We were only *en famille* with the addition of Mr. Reynolds Solly. Moore looks very old and bald, but still retains his cock-sparrow air. He was very pleasant; but rather egotistical and shallow, justifying all we ever thought of his little mind and brilliant imagination. He declaimed against the spread of knowledge and the diffusion of cheap literature, as destructive to wit and talent of the highest order; pronounced that the throwing open of high and royal society would leave no play for all those epigrammatic touches and charming literary effusions (in which he by-the-bye excels); above all, he said the unclassical and uneducated people meddling with literature (Gad-a-mercy fellow!), and the *dilettanteisms* of the age were destroying genius. I said, "But if the greater number are to be the happier, the wiser, and the better for this spread of knowledge, the goal of all human effort and labour is obtained?" with many other things that seemed to strike him as new.

After dinner, he sighed and said, "I walked through

the streets of Dublin all day, and not a human being
knew me. I suppose they will, before the week is
over." He exclaimed bitterly against writing-women,
even against the beautiful Mrs. Norton. "In short,"
said he, "a writing-woman is one unsexed;" but suddenly recollecting himself, and pointing at me, said to
my sister, "except her," (me) whom, in all his works,
he had passed over in silence.

August 12. — In the midst of all my workmen,
philosophers from the British Association have made
incursions — Babbage, Lardner, Whewell, Sedgwick,
and about a dozen other Oxford and Cambridge Fellows
— and Wilkie, too; so I throw open the house to them,
tale quale, to-morrow evening. But I am worn out,
miserable about Morgan, and Sydney being away from
us all.

August 14. — My *soirée* very fine, learned, scientific, and *tiresome!* Fifty philosophers passed through
my little *salon* last night.

My sister, Lady Clarke made a song about the
philosophers, which she sang to them with great effect.

FUN AND PHILOSOPHY.

BY LADY CLARKE.

Air, *"All we want is to settle the play."*

I.

Heigh for ould Ireland! oh would you require a land
Where men by nature are all quite the thing,
Where pure inspiration has taught the whole nation
To fight, love and reason, talk politics, sing;
'Tis Pat's mathematical, chemical, tactical,
Knowing and practical, fanciful, gay,
Fun and philosophy, sapping and sophistry,
There's nothing in life that is out of his way.

II.

He makes light of optics, and sees through dioptrics,
　He's a dab at projectiles — ne'er misses his man;
He's complete in attraction, and quick at re-action,
　By the doctrine of chances he squares every plan;
In hydraulics so frisky, the whole Bay of Biscay,
　If it flowed but with whiskey, he'd stow it away.
　　Fun and philosophy, supping and sophistry,
　　There's nothing in life that is out of his way.

III.

So to him cross over savant and philosopher,
　Thinking, God help them! to bother us all;
But they'll find that for knowledge, 'tis at our own College,
　Themselves must inquire for — beds, dinner or ball;
There are lectures to tire, and good lodgings to hire,
　To all who require, and have money to pay:
　　While fun and philosophy, supping and sophistry,
　　Ladies and lecturing fill up the day.

IV.

Here's our *déjeuner*, put down your shilling, pray,
　See all the curious bastes, *after* their feed;
Lovely lips, Moore has said, must evermore be fed,
　So this is but suiting the word to the deed;
Perhaps you'll be thinking that eating and drinking,
　While wisdom sits blinking, is rather too gay;
　　But fun and philosophy, supping and sophistry,
　　Are all very sensible things in their way.

V.

So at the Rotundo, we all sorts of fun do,
　Hard hearts and pig-iron we melt in one flame;
For if love blows the bellows, our tough College Fellows
　Will thaw into rapture at each lovely dame.
There too, sans apology, tea, tarts, tautology,
　Are given with zoology to grave and gay;
　　Thus fun and philosophy, supping and sophistry,
　　Send all to England home happy and gay.

Mrs. Smith (Moore's old flame, and the subject of
his poem, "I'll ask the sylph that round you flies,")
came to me on Friday, and said Moore wanted to get
up a play for himself, and Calcraft, the manager, said
that I ought to bustle about it and go. Then comes

the strangest advertisement, viz., "That whoever wished
to see the illustrious bard, &c., &c., might do so at the
theatre on such an evening!"

August 16. — The theatre was crammed last night.
The Great Unknown, and *The Gentleman in Search of
a Religion*, and — *popularity*, was called forth by the
galleries, with "Come out here, little Tom! Show
your Irish face, my boy; and don't be ashamed now!"
Tom descended from the manager's-box to the stage-
box, and there made a speech, and was encored and
bravoed. '

Sunday, Moore dined in Kildare Street, and spoke
in raptures of his reception at the theatre. We had,
also, Mr. Coombe, of Edinbro' (the phrenologist).

Wednesday last we lighted on Hayward, translator
of *Faust*, in Sackville Street. We asked him to dine
with us the day after. Just as we were sitting down,
en tiers, enter Professor Whewell, of Cambridge, so
we seized on him, and we had a rather awkward but
pleasant little dinner party. Awkward, because our
Irish cook was drunk, our English butler insolent, and
the dinner bad.

September 8. — What times! what a country is Ireland! The O'Connell "rint" already accumulated for
this year, is thirteen thousand four hundred and fifty
pounds — a census of the gullibility of the poor Irish,
and of the incapacity and roguery of the Tory party
and their House of Lords — the true partisans of O'Connell and the founders of his fame and fortune.

September 9. — So the Lords have rejected even
the moderate amendments of the Church Bill; and
wretched Ireland, or rather the independence of England, and her efforts for Ireland, are baffled in all their

expectations; not a grievance removed, not an abuse
abolished, not a step taken for the improvement of
education or the peace of the country — the "Church
Establishment," the filthy corporations, the Orange
powers, sheriffs, magistrates, jury, placemen, and even
habitués of the Court — all the elements of misrule, are
retained in their primitive force.   Ascendancy still
flourishing, Catholicism undermining, and the nation
prostrate to both!   The turbulence of the Irish is
coupled with their stupid acquiescence in every wrong,
and oppression and intolerance.   For six hundred years
they have borne a greater sum of oppression, injustice
and wrong than any other people in the world.   Their
submission is their ignorance.   There is a long and
very new chapter on this to be written — and then —!

Since my return I have been given up to my usual
domestic duties.   Morgan begins the day with his face
buried in the newspaper while at breakfast, then sets
in to read and write, if he can, the whole of the rest
of the day, in a close room by a hot fire. I try to
get him out at two o'clock, and then there is a painful
struggle; if I succeed, I can see he is impatient to
come home, and then, after dinner, he reads till bed-
time, and so reads and writes to the end of the chapter.
My most painful efforts to draw him off these destructive habits are met with violent resistance and temper.

A more blameless life was never led; some great
occasion would soon rouse him; he is always ready to
meet an event with energy, he has no external world;
his world is within, and were it not for his fidgetty
wife, he would never look out of it.   He is inherently
shy, timid, proud, anti-social, and neither acts nor
writes in reference to society or its opinions, but al-

ways to its interests. He does this on a principle in
his nature, a love of liberty and of ease in his own
person, and desiring the same for his species.

September 18. — We are going to-day to Portrana
(the Evans') thank God!

Two hard-headed English lawyers, Jos. Evans and
Mr. Blackburn, M.P. I was baited by the first for the
amusement of the second. Mr. Evans himself always
attacks me with some bitterness about my fashionable
friends and my aristocratic tastes. They have all got
something, these Irish Liberals — one brother a place
of one thousand five hundred a-year, the other his
election for Dublin, and Blackburn a commission. We,
who live with aristocrats, that is people of good taste
who happen to bear some rank, have got nothing,
asked for nothing, and never can get anything.

Whilst here, Morgan, who is ill and weak, would
take no exercise, so my sole object in coming here
was disappointed.

October 2. — A charming note from Lord Morpeth,
asking us to dinner, and begging me to bring "one of
my harmonious nieces." I know there will be a storm
in great George Street at the "harmonious nieces," as
their mother does not like to let them from her side.
After some debate and a lively resistance, I carried my
point (as I usually do). The invitation of a secretary
of state cannot be expected every day by *des petites
demoiselles.*

October 6. — Dinner at Lord Morpeth's — what a
charming host! The absence of all the official *morgue*
by which we have so long been oppressed, was delightful. The new officers of the Crown amuse me very
much by being the least amusing men possible — iron-

bound men, all their muscles rigid, like men who,
living out of society, have lost the play and movement
of gesture which men of the world exhibit from long
practice; but what uncompromising minds and characters! What honest men! How much and how long
they have been wanted, and here they are, thank God,
after five hundred years of struggle!

October 11. — Just heard of the deaths of Bellini
and of Don Telesfora de Trueba — these two fine
emanations of talent — extinguished, and oh, the block-
heads who go on living and boring for ever! I think
it was in the summer of 1833, on our way to Belgium,
that Captain Marryatt brought Don Telesfora to us in
St. James's Place. He was one of the refugee victims
of Ferdinand "the Beloved," whose tyranny deprived
Spain of the services of this able and estimable man.
On the death of the king he returned, and was elected
member of the Chamber of Procuradores and secretary
of the Cortes. His literary and conversational talents
were of a very distinguished order, but what was perfectly miraculous, was his speaking and writing of
English; he wrote his *Sandoval* and other works in
English; contributed much to the *Metropolitan.* Such
bright glances of mind flash across one in life to light
up its ordinary horizon of dulness, and then vanish for
ever.

CHAPTER XI.

LAST RETURN TO KILDARE STREET — 1836.

January 1836. — What a melancholy winding-up of the year 1835, and commencement of the year 1836. I went ill to Malahide Castle for Christmas-day — tried to bully a sore throat and head-ache, but finally knocked down and took to my bed, which I only left at the end of eight days, to be wrapped in hot blankets and conveyed to my own bed in Kildare Street. The united skill and hourly attendance of my dear husband and good Doctor O'Grady, shirked old death, and saved me from a delirious fever. How my head worked! what books I wrote! what plans I laid for the good of those I loved! what regrets that I had not settled my worldly affairs as I wished! But did I recant one opinion? Not one! I thought I should die, and yet I repeatedly said to myself, had I the sorry battle of life to fight over again, I should just take my old ground!

January 20. — The Registration Society is going on famously, all the young liberals of the highest rank have joined. They say it is entirely got up by "Lady Morgan's School of young men." The high compliment!

January 30. — I have met with a loss that breaks my heart; I have lost the locket with lord Byron's hair, sent me by Countess Guiccioli, enclosed in a curious reliquary. The small gold chain which I wore

12*

round my neck, and from which it hung, broke; I must have dropped it walking down Kildare Street this morning, to warm myself after a cold drive. I am the most unlucky woman in England.

February 1. — The Tories, at last, have placed O'Connell at the head of ascendancy in England; of this, his speech at Birmingham the other day, is a proof. It represents the spirit and opinion of England.

O'Connell is one of the instances of men who have been the offspring of events. From event to event he has climbed. He has grasped his opportunities; where will he end?

February 5. — Read last night Mrs. Lee's *Life of Cuvier*. It gives me no just idea of the man, and still less of his reputation in France — where he was considered a great naturalist and bad philosopher. He was a man of the highest scientific genius and of the highest personal character; but vain, ambitious, tergiversating, serving all the powers that could serve him; equally subservient to Louis XVIII. as to Napoleon; and prouder of his station, honours, and title, than of his immortal scientific reputation.

March 20. — Death of my old friend Sir William Gell. Poor Gell! it seems but yesterday that I saw him walking up Berkeley Square, the mirror of fine men upon town. He had written a *Topography of Troy* as early as 1804. How often we met in my gay days in London, again at his residence at Rome, and a great deal at Naples, at the Margravine of Anspach's, and many other places. He died at Naples, on the 4th February, 1836, worn out by twenty years' gout.

April 1. — Busy to-day with my *Woman and her Master*, making extracts for it.

April 2. — I have been reading Von Raumer's *Letters on England*. Clever, but German; a laborious but inconclusive book — full of brilliant incoherences. The product of a bold mind grappling with strong truths; but not following them to their consequences.

A letter to-day from Lady Cork, announcing the death of her macaw, the original of my article in the *Book of the Boudoir*.

Lady Cork to Lady Morgan.

6, NEW BURLINGTON STREET,
April 3, 1836.

DEAR LADY MORGAN,

Your old friend departed this life a few days ago; he is buried in my garden, and his merits well deserve an epitaph from your pen. He committed but one crime, and only made a bit of an assault on George the Fourth's stocking. That was an offence merely, the *crime* was running away with a piece out of Lady Darlington's leg. I have been ill with the *tic*, but am better now, and just going out of town for the holidays. Your admirer, Lady Hatherton, has just returned from Paris. Are you coming to England — and when? I am more stupid, than ever — only pick a little bit of dinner and drink a little drop of tea. I have neither vocals nor wit going on, *chez moi*. Don't forget that I am ninety years old, and was, and am, and shall be to the end,

Your ever affectionate,
M. CORK AND ORRERY.

A charming note from Lord Morpeth.

NUNEHAM,
April 5th, 1836.

MY DEAR LADY MORGAN,

How am I to thank you enough for your most amiable letter, which has just come to divert the not-unoccupied repose of my holidays?

> "In vain to deserts my retreat is made,
> The *tithes* attend me to the silent shade."

And so far, not inappropriately, as I am the guest of the Archbishop of York, and within seven miles of Oxford. But then there is another awful phantom, styled poor laws,

> "Whose gloomy presence saddens all the scene,
> Shades every flower, and darkens every green."

I am showing symptoms of bolting from the stout turnpike, where I ought to travel into pleasant pastures. I am convinced that Dublin has been very gay, though you will not allow it. I am very sorry to miss the occasion of renewing my acquaintance with Mrs. Laurence.

I cannot but be glad that Sir Charles has worked so hard for the lobster and anchovy sauces; I wish that his country might continue to appropriate some still more persevering labour from him. I shall feel the grey towers of Malahide a great and real loss. But we will have a look and luncheon there some morning.

Your most loyal servant,

MORPETH.

April 11. — Working all day and all night; spirits at a low ebb.

LAST RETURN TO KILDARE STREET — 1836.   183

April 13. — Another, too, gone! Poor Godwin
died on the 7th, at the Exchequer Office, Whitehall
Yard, aged eighty-one. I saw the last of him in his
den at the Star Chamber, *last year.*

April 18. — I am getting down my old harp, which
I had exiled to a lumber-room, and will have it put in
order. I will then get up a song or two.

April 24. — Unable to use my eyes, in any way,
since the 19th. I write these few lines unknown to
Morgan. Indebted all this time to the charity of
strangers for the distraction of a little conversation,
all other resources bereft me. Lady Beecher has
been very kind in coming to me; the once celebrated
Miss O'Neil — the "Juliet" of admiring thousands.
When she was a poor, obscure young actress, I saw
her by chance as Belinda, in "*All in the Wrong,*" and
afterwards in a suit of armour, dressed as an Amazon,
as the heroine in *Timour the Tartar.* I sought her out,
and asked her to a party the next evening, and pre-
dicted her future triumph. Shortly after I followed
her triumphant success in London. She is passing
through Dublin on her way to see her old mother.
She comes every day to see me while she stays here.
The poetry of her own voice remains; it is still Juliet's
voice in the balcony; but all else that was poetical in
her beauty has gone. She is now a thin, elegant-
looking lady; but no beauty, except that she has the
indestructible beauty of goodness.

May 20, *London.* — Arrived in London quite safely,
and we settled in pleasant lodgings in Stafford Row,
Buckingham Gate.

Poor Lady Glengall died on Monday, seventy years
of age. She was the daughter of *the celebrated* Mrs

Jeffries (Groves of Blarney) of county Cork. She was
the Lady Cahir of my youth.

May 22. — We are charmingly lodged, and in a
quarter I like above all others. Yesterday, dined with
some of my literary friends at Mr. Dilke's.   Kind,
gay, and pleasant. After dinner, I got up and danced
a *reel* with the *grave editor*, "to my girls playing," and
then we walked home, and sauntered till midnight,
and by moonlight, under the trees of my pretty Grosvenor Place; how pleased I am with it, what true delight to live with trees!

May 27. — Got a cheerful letter from my beloved
Sydney, so up early and at work for *Woman and her
Master.*

I have made acquaintance with the Lockharts, he
editor of the *Quarterly*, and she Sir W. Scott's daughter; we were mutually charmed with each other, and
have sworn an eternal friendship.

Ambition, and vanity, and *social tastes*, have led
me much into that chaos of folly and insincerity called
the world; but domestic life is my vocation — unfortunately, my high organisation, and my husband's
character of mind, our love of art, and all that is best
worth knowing, renders *la vie domestique* impossible.
Yesterday, I went with Lady Dudley Stuart, and Urquhart (the Turkish traveller) to visit Wilkie, and see
his pictures — a charming Flemish painted-like house,
Knightsbridge, in a garden, and a pretty, "neat-handed
Phillis," opened the door. The great picture was the
"Columbus in the Convent," which is to be removed
to-day to Somerset House. Fine heads for expression,
and a fine conception; but in execution slap-dash —
no finish, but good effect at a distance. A picture of

the Duke of Wellington, much flattered; Lady Salisbury who was standing before it, remarked, "he is much changed *now*," (the tiresome *Liberals* would change everything.)

Wilkie is simple and enthusiastic — he is the *Teniers* of England — domestic interiors. He told us an amusing story of the Turkish ambassador sending him, on his arrival, a *cake* for his breakfast, *à la Turque.*

CHAPTER XII.

FAREWELL TO IRELAND — 1837.

THE year 1837 was marked by a handsome recognition of Lady Morgan's literary merits, and by the grant of a pension of three hundred a year. She used to tell the story that one morning, on coming down to breakfast, she found her letters as usual laid beside her plate. Sir Charles, seeing her much occupied with one of them, said impatiently, "Sydney, I wish you would eat your breakfast, and never mind your d—d dandies," (it was his usual alliterative for the tribe of men who came about his wife). She said nothing, but handed him the letter and enclosures, which were as follows. Nothing could be more gracious or more gracefully done. The announcement from Lord Melbourne, the William Lamb of other days, being sent through Lord Morpeth, the friend whose kind regard lasted to the end of Lady Morgan's life, gave it additional value.

Lord Morpeth to Lady Morgan.

GROSVENOR PLACE,
May 8th, 1837.

MY DEAR LADY MORGAN,

I thought the enclosed note came very *à propos*
after my agreeable visit to you yesterday. I hope the
contents will be acceptable to you, as I am sure they
are creditable to Lord Melbourne for offering to your
merits, literary and patriotic, the highest scale of acknowledgment which our *material* times permit. I
ought to state that Lord Mulgrave has been a joint
solicitor to Lord Melbourne, with myself.

Very sincerely yours,
MORPETH.

Enclosed, was the note, as follows: —

Lord Melbourne to Lord Morpeth.

SOUTH STREET,
May 7th, 1837.

MY DEAR MORPETH,

I have settled that Lady Morgan shall have a pension of three hundred, as you wished.

Yours faithfully,
MELBOURNE.

May 8. — The very first intimation I received *of
my pension!* Lord Morpeth never alluded to it on his
visit the day before.

There is a break in the diary for five or six
months. Among Lady Morgan's papers is Lord Melbourne's graceful reply to her letter of acknowledgment.

The allusion to the "pressure of suffering" refers to her failing eyesight, which at that period threatened total blindness.

DOWNING STREET,
May 11th, 1837.

MY DEAR LADY MORGAN,

I have derived great satisfaction from your letters; I am very glad to find that what has been done is agreeable to your feelings, and I can assure you that I have had much pleasure in doing that which may in some degree alleviate the pressure of the infirmity under which, I very deeply lament to hear that you are suffering. It is also a gratifying reflection that no doubt can exist but that your talents and exertions afford ample grounds for the advice which I have humbly given to His Majesty upon the present occasion.

Believe me, my dear Lady Morgan,

Yours faithfully,

MELBOURNE.

In the absence of a diary for this summer, the following extracts from a letter may be given: —

"I must tell you I am perfectly enamoured of my present residence, and am determined on writing a PIMLICO; it ought to be a most interesting bit of topography, and I am urged to it by Mr. Lemon, my landlord, who is first clerk in the Rolls Office — a most intelligent and learned man. We are within reach of every one we wish most to see of interest. We had a long and cordial visit from Lord Adolphus Fitzclarence, who has invited us to dine with him, at St. James's Palace; he is very like his royal father, with all the *naïveté* of his mother in her dramatic characters. Lady Aldborough wanted to take Morgan to see a famous mesmerist — a magnetic séance which set him into a rage, as humbug always does. Lady Arthur Lennox was here, also, to recommend me a bit of a house which she thinks will suit me; but the flower of all flowers in my garland of friendship, is Mrs. Dawson Damer. You know she is the adopted child of the Prince and Mrs. Fitzherbert, whose property she has inherited, and *such* property! I spent two hours with her, yesterday, in her house in Tilney Street, *tête-à-tète* — the house, observe, of Mrs. Fitzherbert! What a *causerie!* No one now talks like her; and she is so handsome, so elegant, and genial. She told me that she was at the Duchess of Gloucester's, the other night — a child's ball. The young Queen was there, looking quite a child herself. When her uncle, the Duke of Sussex, was leaving the room, she ran after him and said, "Won't you give me a kiss before you go?" and then whispered in his ear, "you have forgotten to wish mamma good night." What a charming trait; it is a pity to make a queen of this creature, with these warm affections!

Tilney House is full of reminiscences of its celebrated but, I suspect, unhappy late mistress — the true, legal wife of that type of heartless *roués*, George IV. Mrs. Dawson Damer said she had got up a table expressly for me — it was covered with beautiful relics. In a coffer filled with pledges of love and gallantry from the Prince in the hey-day of his passion — a Pandora's box *without* Hope at the bottom! The most precious were a number of their own portraits, set in all sorts of sizes and costumes, and oh *what costumes!*

Toupées, chinons, flottans, tippy-bobby hats, balloon
handkerchiefs, and relics of all the atrocious bad taste
of succeeding years, from the days of Florizel and Per-
ditta, to the "fat, fair and *fifty*" of the neglected favourite, a series of disfigurements rendering their personal beauty absurd. The Prince's face was insignificant,
through all his ages and disguises, a fair, fat, flashy
young gentleman, his mother's snubby features spoiling
his pleasant smile; in short, he was the old queen
bleached white! By-the-bye, the last time I saw him
was in a doorway at Lady Cork's which he filled, to
the utter annoyance of Lady Cork, who was obliged to
open another doorway, contrary to her arrangements.
The pictures of the Prince and Mrs. Fitzgerald were
all splendidly set in brilliants, with hearts and ciphers,
crowned with royal coronets and true lovers' knots.
The initials G. P. were never omitted.

There were two lockets of very curious description,
minutely small portraits of the Prince and the lady;
they were each covered with a *crystal*, and this crystal
was a diamond cut in two! They were less than the
size of a halfpenny, set in small brilliants. Each wore
the portrait of the other next their heart — at the
depth of their love.

On the death of George IV., Mrs. Fitzherbert sent
to William IV., to request back some of her pictures,
gems, and letters, left in the late King's hands.

William IV., always the kind and constant friend
of Mrs. Fitzherbert, sent her everything that he could
find in the cabinet of his brother, and a beautiful
picture in oil of Mrs. Fitzherbert; but the diamond-
enshrined miniature was not forthcoming. After some
time, however, she received a letter from the Duke of

Wellington, who wrote to say, having heard that such a locket had been enquired for, he would be happy to place it in her hands, as it was in his possession. He added, that in his quality of the King's executor, he had gone into his room immediately after his decease, and perceiving a red cord round his neck, under his shirt, discovered the locket containing the miniature.

The correspondence of the Prince and Mrs. Fitzherbert, most voluminous, and doubtless full of interesting political and social incidents, which have escaped history, were burned by Mrs. Fitzherbert's trustees — one of these was Sir C. Seymour, Mrs. Dawson Damer's brother; the other was Colonel Gurwood, who was one of her best and most intimate friends. I think she added that the Duke of Wellington and Lord Albemarle were present, and that the room where this *auto-da-fé* took place smelled of burnt sealing-wax for weeks afterwards! Mrs. Fitzherbert had labelled all the letters she wished to be destroyed — a few, however, escaped — a few in Mrs. Dawson Damer's casket, Mrs. Fitzherbert had ordered to be preserved.

Mrs. Fitzherbert was *never* in love with the Prince, and much of her virtuous resistance may be ascribed to her indifference. The Dowager Lady Jersey was the true object of his passion, or if not the object, at least the disport of his weak mind, and certainly the cause of his infidelity to his mistress and his cruelty to his wife. When that most fashionable of French novels, *Les Liaisons Dangereux*, came out, it became the subject of much fashionable criticism, and one evening, in the circle at Devonshire House, it was disputed whether the character of Madame la Presidente was not an outrage upon probability and female

humanity. The late Duke of Devonshire observed,
that he thought he knew *one* such woman; but refused
to name her. The next moment every one present
confessed they had known *one* such woman, also; but
refused to denounce their fair friend. Curiosity became vehement, and Lord John Townsend proposed
that each person present should write their secret on a
slip of paper, and throw the slips into a veiled vase,
and he would draw them out slip by slip, and read
them for the benefit of the society present under the
solemn seal of silence, — when, to the surprise and
amusement of the distinguished society, every little
rouleau, as its contents were announced, bore the
inscription of "the Countess of Jersey!" When
the anecdote was told to the author, he exclaimed,
"*Heureux pays! ou l'on ne peut trouver qu'une seule Presidente!*" I saw the last picture of poor Mrs. Fitzherbert ever taken; it was done on the day of her
death, and yet was lovely, though she died in her
eightieth year. It was curious (but not an unusual
thing) that her face had fallen into its original form;
its fine osteology was perfect; the few furrows that
time had traced upon its round muscles had disap-
peared — it presented a fine and firm oval face —
the beautiful mouth — a high and rather Roman nose.
The simple dress of death (not the most unbecoming
she ever wore) added to the solemn beauty of her appearance.

Mrs. Fitzherbert died in the beginning of 1837,
and Mrs. Dawson Damer's expressive countenance
changed often as she spoke, and tears fell from her
eyes as she deposited the relics of her adopted mother

in the casket whence she had drawn them. She was
still in mourning for her.

We had a very amusing, and to me, very interesting dinner at Lord Adolphus Fitzclarence's, in the *old*
St. James's Palace, comprising the Marquis of Belfast,
Sir George and Lady Wombwell, the handsome Mr.
Stanley (alias Cupid), Josephine, and ourselves, — a
round table dinner. Lord Adolphus took me into his
boudoir in the evening; we were alone, and he showed
me a miniature set in brilliants. "The king!" I said.
"Yes, my father," said he, taking another picture out
of the casket, "and," added he, with emotion, "this
was — my mother." After a pause, I said, "It is a
great likeness, as I last saw her." "Where was that?"
"In Dublin." "On the stage?" "Yes, in the *Country
Girl*, the most wondrous representation of life and
nature I ever beheld! I saw her, also, when she was
on a visit at Sir Jonah Barrington's. She sent to my
father to go and visit her, he did so; she called him
the most amiable of all her managers." After a pause,
he said, "Sir Charles and you will accompany me to
Chantrey's to-morrow, to see her beautiful monument,
which they have refused to admit into St. Paul's,
though Mrs. Woffington's monument is still expected
there! I said I could not express how much I honoured
his sincere feelings to the most attentive of mothers,
whose fault was, that she loved not wisely, but too
well.

We found Chantry, as frank, simple, and cordial,
as when some seventeen years back, we trotted *en
groupe* with Moore, Playfair, and Lord John Russell
through the streets of Florence, and paused to worship

the memory of *Jean de Bologne*, the key note of our
conversation whenever we met. Well, the Gordon
monument is a beautiful *work of art*, I had almost said
of nature; but no time to write more. I have to dress
for Lady Charleville's dinner, and here is the carriage,
and Morgan roaring like a bull.

In the autumn of 1837, Sir Charles and Lady
Morgan carried into effect their intention of leaving
Ireland, and taking up their residence permanently in
London.

Dublin had long become distasteful to Lady Morgan, for Dublin is, after all, a provincial city, and the
society lacked the brightness and freedom of a great
capital. Except a separation from her sister and her
sister's family, there was not much to regret. Sir
Charles Morgan's desire to settle in London had only
been yielded to his wife's wish to live in Dublin; now
they were agreed to seek a new home. They first
freighted a small vessel with all their household goods,
and then came over themselves to England.

The following extracts from Lady Morgan's journals
will tell the reader the incidents of the removal and
settlement in their new abode: —

> "Oh Ireland, to you
> I have long bid a last and a painful adieu."

You have always slighted, and often persecuted me,
yet I worked in your cause, humbly, but earnestly.
Catholic Emancipation is carried! It was an indispensable act — of what results, you fickle Irish will
prove in the end. To predicate would be presumptuous, even in those who know you best. Creatures
of temper and temperament, true Celts, as Cæsar found

your race in Gaul, and as I leave you, after a lapse of two thousand years.

I shall meet in England the effects of the glorious Reform, after seven years' experiments; that is the event that opens the free port of constitutional liberty, so long struggled for by the Saxon in England.

We bid our last adieu to Ireland, October 20, 1837, accompanied by my niece Josephine; we proceeded to Leamington, where Mr. and Mrs. Laurence joined us; they left us on the 25th, and José with them; we were very sad after the departure of our young people.

October 28. — Received the intelligence of poor Mr. Laurence's sudden death! My poor Sydney! We left instantly to go to her.

December 23. — Lord Morpeth sent us, with one of his kind notes, two tickets of admission to the body of the House of Lords to see the Queen open Parliament and return thanks to her faithful Commons, &c. I went with Lady Georgina Wortley and my dear Mrs. Dawson Damer. We were placed close to the bar of the House of Commons, being rather late. It is a gorgeous, imposing, but rather theatrical *spectacle*. The young Queen's *aplomb* was truly wonderful; her voice clear and sonorous — whoever "taught the young *girl* to read," did every justice to the development of her vocal organ, and her small person seemed to dilate under the pressure of her conscious greatness; for the Queen of England is, at this moment, certainly the greatest sovereign in the world, because she is the chief of a free people — what charmed me most, however, was her inexpressibly girlish laugh. When the House of Commons rushed in with all their rude, rough, schoolboy boisterousness, Philip Courtnay, and some of my Irish members, were so close to me, that I could not help turning to them and muttering, "My faithful Commons, *why* are you so vulgar?" When the royal *cortège* had moved off, and we paused at the head of the stairs whilst my husband was looking for our carriages, dear Lord Melbourne came up and shook me heartily by the hand, and said he was glad to see me there; Lord Brougham also joined us, and two or three other agreeable men.

Our lodging in Pimlico, 6A, Stafford Row, is opposite a wing of Buckingham Palace, and commands a view of its gardens. What an historical, what a charming site. I shall make myself mistress of it before I have done with it.

I have finally given up all hopes of getting ***** * * * * * pretty house at Buckingham Gate; after a most capricious negotiation on his part, redeemed, however, by many charming notes and letters from a charming man, which are always worth something. I think I have found the clue of his

> "Letting I dare not wait upon — I would,"

"like the poor cat in the adage." It happened thus: — I have been in the habit of popping, at all hours, into the house, which I considered all but my own, and the other day I found a fine embroidered pocket-handkerchief on the table and a tiny pair of gloves. I saw at once that the gloves had carried it, and that the handkerchief would never be flung at my feet, and that there was a tenant who was resolved not to quit, and whose lease, perchance, would not be renewable

13*

for ever; and so we have given up, and are again on
the search for a house.

December 25, 1837 — My birthday. London, 6,
Stafford Row, opposite the King of Buckingham's
house. I open this new journal at the close of the
year 1837, a year to me full of events of good and ill
together, to commemorate most gratefully *my partial
restoration to sight*, so far as to enable me to write an
hour a day without pain or annoyance, and I trust to
recommence a work undertaken in the sincere spirit
of philanthropy and the inextinguishable desire to do
good — *Woman and her Master.* I have this day put
aside the long green sheets of paper on which I have
been scrawling *Woman and her Master*, which that dear
thoughtful Morgan got for me in Dublin.

December 26. — I am really beginning my regene-
ration and new life as a denizen of London. Everybody congratulating us: old friends are true, new ones
all agreeable.

Lady Normandy has most kindly offered to present
me at the Queen's first drawing-room.

CHAPTER XIII.

SETTLEMENT IN LONDON — 1838.

THE first entry in the journal for 1838, refers to a
work which caused a great scandal and excitement at
the time, though now it has fallen into the heap of
things forgotten — *The Diary of the Court and Times
of George IV.*

6, STAFFORD ROW, PIMLICO.

January 3. — The murder is out! There is the
Diary in everybody's hands, and since the publication
of the *New Atlantis*, by Mrs. Manley, in the reign of
Queen Anne — a scandal, a libel on the queen, people
and court of that day; such a book has not been seen,
written, nor read.

January 8. — For the last month nothing has been
thought of or talked of but the *Diary*, and now Animal
Magnetism has taken its place, and all the titled credu-
lity in London have been putting their fatuity to the
test of exhibiting themselves under the hands of Baron
du Potet. I was busy writing my article on Pimlico,
when Lady Arthur Lennox came to know what were
my intentions. I told her of my search after a house
in the new quarter of Belgrave Square, I wanted one
which should be cheap and charming. She advised
me to look in a new street containing only two or three
houses as yet, built by the great builder Cubitt.

January 9. — I am just returned with Sydney and
José from looking at such a charming maisonette in

William Street, which will meet our taste, and not exceed our means; no houses opposite, and all looks rather wild and rude (a thing that would be a field if it could), and a low wall round it; but then there is to be a pretty square, and then, no doubt the street will soon be built. The street terminates in Knightsbridge, of which *locale* I had a curious account from Dr. Milman, prebend of Westminster, which he has extracted from the rolls.

At the bottom of William Street, bounding the park, is a little bridge over the great sewer of this quarter, behind which stands the hideous gate of the beautiful Hyde Park. The tops of two poplar trees are all we can see of it. This bridge was the spot where the Knights of St. John of Jerusalem used to assemble on a certain day in October to give convoy to the monks of Westminster Abbey, on their return from their quest for provisions, &c., for the convent, and to conduct them through the perilous jungles of what is *now* Piccadilly, through which they were obliged to pass on their way to the Abbey, according to an ancient tenure. Next to this gate stands the Cannon Brewery, with its eternal smoke. On the other side of the Knightsbridge Gate stands a little hostelric called the "White Hart," now a shabby public house; though it was here that the Duke of Buckingham, in James the Second's time, came to sleep the night before his appointed duel with Lord Rochester, because it was out of London.

I saw Mr. Cubitt yesterday, a good, little, complying man; he has yielded to all my suggestions; will knock down walls between the rooms, build balconies, and a terrace, and is to give me a tree to plant in my bit of

a garden (four feet by two) though I heard him say
to Sir Charles, "She shall have it, but it will not grow
in so confined a place."

Mr. Cubitt was quite mistaken, the tree was planted
(a plane tree), it grew and throve from the first day, it
is now a fine piece of timber, standing higher than the
chimneys.

To the diaries again:

January 11. — The fatal and almost pathetic con-
flagration of the Royal Exchange and its neighbourhood has swallowed up the discussions on all minor
subjects. A note from my poor dear Sydney, who was
an eye witness of the scene, sets my heart at case as
regards any harm having extended to her. It is one
of the great fires that are historical.

Mrs. Lawrence to Lady Morgan.

January 11, 1838.

What a sight I came in for last night, my dear
Little Mamma. The burning down of the *Royal Exchange!!* I write you a few lines this morning to put
your mind at ease respecting me. Being so close to
it, we were, as you may suppose, kept in a state of
great excitement and alarm. It was splendidly awful
to see the beautiful dome all in a blaze, and tumbling
piece by piece into the flames below, and the bells
chiming their last in the midst of the fire, and strange
to say, the last tune they chimed was at twelve o'clock,
and *that* tune was "There is na luck about the House."

It quite affected me to hear it, and it had a *choking*
effect upon us all, for the bells literally dropped one
by one as they were playing the tune.   All that
now remains of this once great work of Sir Thomas
Gresham's, are the pillars!   What ages it took to
build that which a few hours has consumed!   The
gentlemen here rendered all the assistance they could,
and when they came home at six o'clock this morning,
the frost was so hard, that their clothes were literally
frozen upon them, and they waited to melt them before they could take them off.   We ladies have never
been in bed, and have been kept very busy making
hot tea all the morning for the frozen men who have
dropped in.   The house has been thronged all the
morning with Lloyd's people.   I shall be with you to-
morrow, dearest; so more anon.

                                                    S. L.

   January 14. — Colburn, my persecutor, has become
my slave and blackamoor!   He has written Morgan a
letter, offering to suppress the libellous passage about
me in the Diary (a funny term for being represented
as an ugly monster!).   I have refused his offer, and
given him a *coup de patte* for lending himself to such
nastiness!   Here is his letter, and the rough draft of
my answer.

Mr. Colburn to Sir C. Morgan.

MY DEAR SIR,
   I was very much disconcerted on having pointed
out to me a day or two ago, a passage in the diary
about Queen Caroline, which refers in a very bad

spirit to Lady Morgan. Unfortunately, the work was never properly examined by me, having been hastily published the moment it was finished at press.

On enquiring how it was that the passage came to be overlooked by the reviser, I am told it was thought that the note at the foot of the page was considered as a perfect refutation of the unjust and ill-natured remarks. I need not say that if I had been made aware of them, and had had time to give them proper consideration, I should certainly not have allowed them to appear, and I will now cancel them with great pleasure, if you wish it, being anxious to do everything that is honourable towards Lady Morgan, with whom it gives me great pleasure to be again on the most friendly terms.

With my best compliments and apologies to Lady Morgan and yourself, I beg to remain,

Dear Sir,

Yours very faithfully,

H. COLBURN.

PS. I had not either the least knowledge that such a person as Lady Holland was alluded to in the book, and few others would have been aware of it, had not Colonel Webster made it public, and acted against my advice, very urgently given, of submitting first to Lord Holland the letter he sent to the *Literary Gazette*.   H. C.

Lady Morgan to Henry Colburn.

STAFFORD ROW,
Tuesday, 16th January, 1838.

DEAR SIR,

I beg to thank you myself for volunteering in a

letter to Sir Charles the offer of suppressing a passage
in the Diary of Queen Caroline, which you say, "refers
in a very bad spirit to Lady Morgan." I never in my
life interfered with the printed expression of an opinion
relative to myself, personal or literary; of this you are
well aware, and whether you repeat through future
editions, or suppress in the next, a passage which you
say ought never to have appeared, I leave to your own
taste, feeling, and discretion. On your confession that
"unfortunately the work was never properly examined
by you, and was hastily published," &c., I beg to remark, that such conduct in a publisher will be taken
by the public as anything but an apology for the consequences, and to remind you that in the course of the
many years you published for me, I have repeatedly
urged for the interests of literature, and your own,
that you should confine your publications to works
which should, in a moral as well as in a literary sense,
reflect credit on and give consideration to the publisher.
Among the many temporary causes which in the present
moment have tended to degrade British literature, is
the promptitude of publishers to produce such works
as the one you have just brought out. You say, that
"on inquiring how it was *that the passage came to be
overlooked by the reviser, I am told that it was thought
that the note at the foot of the page was considered as a
perfect refutation of the unjust and ill-natured remarks.*"
That note, like all the other apologetical notes in the
book, only proves that the author was fully cognisant
of the malice and impropriety of the text. In return
for the many kind expressions in your letter with
respect to myself, I beg to reiterate an advice so often
given: in a literary, as well as in a social sense,

confine your dealings to honest men and women; when you did so, you were among the first of European publishers.

I am, dear sir,
Yours, &c.,
SYDNEY MORGAN.

CHAPTER XIV.

ALBERT GATE — 1838.

ON the 17th of January, 1838, we, viz., my beloved husband and myself, accompanied by our dear niece, Josephine Clarke, and our trusty servants from Ireland, John and Mary Forman, took possession of our dear, *very dear* house, No. 11, William Street. Belgrave Square is the only place of any note, *i. e.*, of gentility near us. I take great interest in this new and pretty *quartier*; but I must have a new Gate where the Fox and Bull pot-house now stands; there is a rural air over the whole that is pretty; but a gate we must have into the park at the top of William Street, for pretty it will be when it is finished, though I shall regret having houses opposite to me in place of the green swards. We have a branch-Gunter, the confectioner, near us, and I have paid my score to that illustrious house, by giving him a receipt for a *plombière*, which I had from Carême in 1829.

March 5. — Colburn followed up his efforts at reconciliation, by presenting Lady Morgan with a beautiful mirror for her new drawing-room, which was

graciously accepted; and the old terms of friendly good-
will were restored, after eight years' interruption.

March 11, *William Street.* — I see it is quite absurd
to attempt keeping a diary here within the sound of
workmen and mills; I give it up. I have been so busy,
with my good *Woman and her Master*, lying in abeyance — heaps of letters to write — having to receive
all day and go out every evening. When I had nothing
to write about, then I had time to journalise. Now,
when every day would supply a volume, I have not a
moment to write a line!

Lady Morgan always got up the history and
traditions of whatever place she visited. She wrote
some charming papers upon the history of Pimlico,
which were published in the *Athenæum.* They excited
interest in the neighbourhood, as appears from the following note, selected from many others.

Lady Carlisle to Lady Morgan.

April 26th, 1838.

Lady Carlisle presents her compliments to Lady
Morgan, and must tell her how much pleased and
gratified she was by the interesting paper she was so
obliging as to send her. She thinks the inhabitants of
Pimlico ought to give her a vote of thanks for making
their situation classic ground by the associations of her
mind and genius.

May 14. — My first shaking of the Albert Gate!
What a charming *quartier!* what capabilities! I have
been talking it over with Cubitt, the *Pontifex maximus*
of this new estate. What I want is a Gate, where the

old sewer tap now moulders and flanks a ditch of filth
and infection; a sort of little rustic bridge should be
over it, which would not be without its picturesque
effect.   Cubitt wants it too, but despairs of getting it.
That terrible brewery points its *cannon* against all improvement! even whilst we spoke, a volume of smoke
rolled out from its chimney, making its curling way
direct for the Duke's windows.   "That smoke will
serve us yet," I said; "it will ruin the Apsley House
picture gallery, if the Cannon Brewery be not removed,
the Duke must know of it."   "I will buy out the
Cannon Brewery," said Cubitt.   He is a great little
man!

May 29. — Last night we were at Lady Stepney's
great rout.   I was presented to the Duke of Cambridge all over again, who shook hands and said he
remembered me.   I had much to do to persuade Miss
José to sing for his Royal Highness, and though she
sang *pretty bad*, yet he praised her beyond beyond, and
said her voice and school were equally fine.   I have
had a great many people come to call on me.
The Queen's coronation is put off till August next;
not to cut short the season, she does not go to Ireland.
I have just returned from the Queen of *Modistes*,
Madame Dévey, getting a hat for Lady Clanricarde's
concert.   Never were hats worn so *small*, but pretty
and new.   Everything is *black*, lace or silk, and all
caps or *fraises* under bonnets, *black*, ditto gloves and
fichus, loose sleeves and large, from shoulder to elbow.
The Queen wore them at the Duchess of Somerset's.
     Yesterday we were at Lord Ducie's, where the
Chanoiness Talbot had just arrived per diligence from

the top of the Pyramid, and was the fun of the party.
Every one was in their Devonshire House full dress
and she in a black frieze gown, leather brogues, and a
green pocket-handkerchief on her head, and *no* gloves
on her naked stout arm. She will not be here long.
Rogers was here all yesterday; he has sent José all
his works as a present.

London looks like the last scene in a pantomime,
all transformed for the Coronation. Every house, from
Hyde Park Corner to the Abbey, cased up with
wooden platforms, canopied balconies. The Duke of
Devonshire's house, and the great houses in Piccadilly,
which have courts before them, have superb boxes
erected as in a theatre, all draped and gilt. The
whole front of the Orduance, where we are to have a
grand *déjeûner*, is fitted up as an amphitheatre, deco-
rated with the Queen's arms and crown. The streets
all barricaded, and on *the* day, no carriage is to pass
after eight in the morning.

August 26. — Here is a letter which I have just
sent to Lord Duncannon. Another touch at my gate.

Lady Morgan to Lord Duncannon.

11, WILLIAM STREET,
August 26th, 1838.

Lady Morgan presents her compliments to Lord
Duncannon, presuming upon the kindness with which
his Lordship received the petition for the opening of
an ancient gate in Hyde Park, Knightsbridge. She
takes the liberty of enclosing a plan of the district to
which this ingress to Hyde Park would be of such an

incalculable advantage, together with an explanatory
letter from Mr. Cubitt, the founder of this new capital
of the west, who is willing to incur the expense of the
alteration.   Should the lords of the woods and forests
not dismiss that petition (as frivolous and vexatious),
the spirit of which is to preserve the health and beauty
of thousands of fair pedestrians, now denied the advantages of their neighbourhood by the noxious atmosphere they must pass through to attain it, Lord Duncannon will receive the gratitude of many a fair generation yet unborn, and merit a statue, which, compared
with the bronze gentleman in the park, and the wooden
one, who *tête-à-têtes* him on the other side of the way,
will be as an "hyperion" to two "satyrs."

Lord Duncannon's Answer to Lady Morgan.

OFFICE OF WOODS AND FORESTS,
August 28th, 1638.

Lord Duncannon presents his compliments to Lady
Morgan, and regrets that he cannot recommend to her
Royal Highness, the Ranger, to comply with the wishes
expressed by her ladyship and the other persons in the
neighbourhood of Belgrave Square.   Buildings are
growing up in all directions adjacent to Hyde Park,
and there is no doubt that similar applications will be
made for a similar accommodation.   At present, there
are six public entrances into Hyde Park, besides five
or six foot gates, and when the contiguity of Hyde
Park Corner is considered, in reference to the present
application, it would not appear desirable to establish
another thoroughfare so near to the former one. Under
the circumstances, Lord Duncannon regrets that he is

under the necessity of declining to forward the proposal.

Well! we have got our answer; but we are not beaten. Cubitt has actually bid for the Cannon Brewery, and will buy out all the old houses, including the dear old "White Hart." We are going to get up a memorial to the Queen, signed by all the respectable inhabitants of Cubittopolis, with the Duke at the head of it. We have got the Duchess of Kent to give her name also.

A letter from General Sir John Burgoyne, whose alarms on the subject of the defences of England have made his name familiar to all. It relates to an article in the *Athenæum* upon one of his reports on railways.

General Sir John Burgoyne to Sir Charles Morgan.

DUBLIN,
October 2nd, 1838.

MY DEAR SIR CHARLES,

I am much obliged to you for sending me the *Athenæum*, but I had been on the look out on each of the last three Saturdays, and at last found the article and read it with much interest. I am particularly pleased with the dissertation on commissions, which is most just, and is a subject on which the world (that is the British imperial world) rejoice to be enlightened; for a pack of interested jobbers have been calling mad dog till they have almost persuaded John Bull out of his senses, that is, out of his commissions. It is something on a par with the London thieves, who made a bold effort to cry down the police, when they were first instituted. Because a commission cannot perform a miracle, such as making Ireland in a moment rich and happy (and a greater miracle than that was never yet achieved), they abuse it; but there are none, I believe, that have been appointed, but have produced at least a great amount of most useful information, that in one way or another has been of the greatest service.

Your remarks on the report in general are very good. I have been arrested by various persons, with — *"Have you seen a very moderate and sensible article on your Railway Report in the Athenæum &c."*

Lord Cloncurry tells me that the Duke of Leinster is about to agitate for our course of railways; he has read the report attentively, and approves of it much; is about to signify to the government (with others) a hope that some measures in conformity with our recommendations, may be taken. The *Government* can do nothing of this kind without being pressed and the Duke of Leinster is the best possible man for the purpose. He is a man of strong sense, anxious for the good of Ireland, and works for no *party*. His *personal* interests, I imagine, ought to lead him to favour the Kilkenny and the Great Central Irish, &c., that our plan condemns; therefore, his opinions should carry weight. The journalists ought also to use a little of the pressure from without on the government and on parliament for this object.

Dear Sir Charles, I am just going to Paris, to bring home my wife.

Yours faithfully,
J. F. BURGOYNE.

December 23. — We went last night to a literary *soirée* given by Messrs. Henry Chorley and Henry Reeve, authors and sub-editors. Count Alfred de Vigny was presented to me, and I said all sorts of things *en graciosité* on his "*Cinq Mars;*" he talks well, and is high bred. I joked a little about the present state of literature in France, and its melodramatic character, *du plus beau noir.* He said "Oui, mais croyez moi milady le fonds du caractère Francais est la tristesse." I gave a little *soirée* for him, very pleasant. He said, in answer to my observation on the bright, gay literature of the eighteenth century in France, "La jeune France prend pour model Byron, et puis Napoleon." This was too pleasant. The one an Englishman, and the other an Italian. Voltaire called the French, "*les singes tigres.*" It was the *doctrinaires* who upset the throne of Louis Phillippe, and now they are "*les singes Anglais,*" and very agreeable monkeys they are.

CHAPTER XV.

LONDON LIFE — 1839.

THE reader, who has had so many letters from Madame Patterson Bonaparte, may like to see that her husband, King Jerome, in his later time, found himself living on very familiar terms in Lady Morgan's London circle.

Jerome Bonaparte had been, from the beginning, the plague of his family. Thoughtless, idle, vain,

extravagant, and inconsiderate, the one idea which his
mind was capable of containing, was a supreme conception of his own value, or, as his biographer politely
expresses it, "le trait dominant de son caractère était
le sentiment profond de sa dignité personelle." He
tried the patience of his august brother as no one,
except his wife, Josephine, had ever ventured to do.
Being the youngest of the family, he was a spoiled
child, and developed into a prodigal son, with an unlimited faculty for spending money, getting into debt
and mischief, varied by an occasional duel, the ferocity
of which was only equalled by the absurdity. Like
other scapegraces, he was sent to sea to get him out of
the way, and in the hope that his troublesome wilful-
ness might take the shape of a genius for adventure
and command; but he had no genius except for pleasing himself. Jerome was a caricature of his great
brother. He possessed the true Bonapartean imperious
will; but it was never exercised except in following his
own inclination, in spite of remonstrance. He was the
torment of his commanders, and refused to be amenable
to discipline. He would neither join his ship, if he
chanced to be amusing himself on shore, nor learn his
duties as a sailor. At Martinique, he had an attack of
yellow fever, which so disgusted him with the service
that he expressed a wish to throw it up altogether;
this his Admiral refused to allow, and ordered him to
rejoin his vessel; but just then, Jerome chanced to be
amusing himself on shore at Martinique, where the
Governor invited him to dinner, and received him with
garrison turned out, under arms, and he refused to obey.
Jerome was a *parvenu* to the backbone; and his
vulgarity was ingrained. The Admiral, Villaret Joyeuse,

14*

exasperated by his stupidity, and fearing that if war broke out between England and France, some mischief might befall Jerome, who, as Napoleon's brother, had an importance quite distinct from himself, ordered him to return to France. Jerome loitered and made excuses till the opportunity of a safe return was gone, and then the Admiral, anxious to be rid of him, gave him permission to go to America. Jerome went, glad at the prospect of being out of the reach of his Admiral and of his brother. He landed with three companions, whom he called "his suite," at Norfolk, in Virginia, where he gave himself the airs of a Prince in disguise. He went to Washington, and announced to Pichon, the French Consul, that he must supply him with funds and find means to convey him and his suite to France, which, as war was by this time declared, and English vessels were on the watch, outside the bar, for every French ship leaving America, was no easy matter.

At first, there was an affectation of incognito observed; but Jerome, with his vainglorious folly, was quite unable to keep it up, and all the United States were made aware that the brother of the First Consul of France had come among them. They proceeded to offer the homage so dear to Jerome's heart; and he was flattered and fêted to the top of his bent. He proceeded to Baltimore, and was received with enthusiasm. For the first time in his life he was entirely his own master, and he gave himself up to the pleasures of the position. Pichon had not much money to give him, but all Baltimore asked for the honour of giving him unlimited credit. At Baltimore, he met Miss Elizabeth Patterson,—whom all contemporary testimony declares to have been extremely beautiful, agreeable, witty,

clever, and ambitious. Her father was a rich merchant,
well known and respected. All her family belonged to
the American aristocracy of the upper ten thousand. In
birth, parentage, and education, she was Jerome's equal.
In intellect and character, she was much his superior,
but Jerome's brother was rising to the ranks of royalty,
and carrying his family with him. Jerome fell violently
in love with Miss Patterson, and proposed marriage.
She accepted an offer which made her the envy of all
the women of Baltimore. Jerome was in the zenith of
a vulgar success; he was young, lively, and tolerably
good looking. Mr. Patterson, the father, in consideration of the connection, overlooked Jerome's want of
actual fortune, and gave his consent.

Pichon was frightened out of his senses at what the
First Consul would say, and made formal representations, both to Mr. Patterson and the French consul at
Baltimore, declaring that he was under the age at
which a lawful marriage could be contracted. Jerome
feigned to comply; but not the less, on the 25th of
December, 1803, he was married to Miss Patterson by
Bishop Carrol, the Roman Catholic bishop of Baltimore. The marriage was regular and legal in every
particular, and so far as rites and ceremonies could
make her so, Miss Patterson became the lawful wife of
Jerome Bonaparte, — qualified to share in all the honours of his rising star. Jerome coupled this announcement to Pichon with orders to supply him with funds;
and then proceeded on his wedding tour.

They passed a few months in the midst of all the
social gaieties and splendours that American society
could bestow. On the 18th of May news came that the
First Consul had been declared Emperor. Jerome had

not yet received his brother's answer to the announcement of his marriage. He had not, however, to wait much longer for it. In June, 1804, the answer came. Napoleon declined to recognise the marriage, taking his stand on a recent French law of February, 1803, which prohibited all French subjects, under the age of twenty-five, to contract marriage without the consent of parents or guardians. Pichon, and all French officials, were ordered to treat Madame Jerome Bonaparte as Jerome's mistress; French vessels were forbidden to afford her a passage to France; and if she attempted to enter France with Jerome, orders were given that she should be arrested and conveyed back to America.

Jerome himself was ordered to return home immediately. A pension was offered to Miss Patterson of sixty thousand francs a year on condition that she never assumed the name of Bonaparte, nor molested Jerome. Napoleon could not, however, alter the law of marriage as recognised by the Catholic church and by the consent of all Christendom. Except the local enactment, which only held good in France, Miss Patterson's marriage with Jerome was as valid as the sacraments of the church could make it. If Jerome could only be firm, the marriage must hold good whether the Emperor recognised it or not; but Jerome could not hold firm to anything but his own inclination. He was, in fact, a man — who could see nothing, feel nothing, care for nothing, except the whim of the moment.

He had had his whim out in marrying Miss Patterson, and now to go back to France and be the Emperor's brother, was the idea that possessed him. He was already beginning to feel his wife a clog and an encumbrance. He embarked with great secrecy on board an American merchantman bound for Portugal, accompanied by his wife and secretary. The vessel arrived quite safely at Lisbon; the French consul refused a passport to Madame Jerome, and wrote to Paris to announce their arrival. Jerome had already pretty well proved that no consideration stood in the way of pleasing himself; without any consideration of his duty as a husband, or the common feelings of humanity for a woman about to become the mother of his child, he abandoned her in a strange country, where she had neither friends nor relatives, and where, if she were not in want of the necessaries of life, it was no thanks to Jerome, who made no arrangement for her support. He left her, a beautiful woman of seventeen, entirely unprotected, and in a condition which rendered her return to her father's house physically impossible; he left her almost immediately on their arrival in Lisbon, professedly with the intention of throwing himself at the feet of the Emperor, and obtaining his pardon and recognition of the marriage, but the whole of his subsequent conduct showed that he had no intention of ever again encumbering himself with her. Jerome found his brother at Turin; he wrote a letter of abject submission, offering to recognise his marriage as absolutely null from the beginning, and his offspring illegitimate, submitting himself absolutely to his brother's pleasure. In return for this submission, Jerome was pardoned. Napoleon married him to a German princess, who was a great deal too good for him, and made him king of Westphalia, where he caricatured royalty until the fall of the empire. His royal wife died in Italy, and Jerome was now an elderly widower travelling in

England, and mixing in society with the chance of encountering his first wife in the doorway or on the staircase of a London party.

Jerome Bonaparte to Lady Morgan.

FENTON'S HOTEL,
May 22nd, 1839.

DEAR LADY MORGAN,

I regret very much that I cannot have the pleasure of passing this evening with you; the news of the death of my uncle, Cardinal Fesch, which has just reached here, would render my presence too unseasonable. I shall probably leave here on Friday, for the interior of England, and eventually for Ireland; would you be so kind as to send in the evening of to-morrow the letter you were good enough to offer me for Lady Clarke.

I am most truly yours,

JEROME BONAPARTE.

In the course of the same season, Lady Morgan received a note from Madame Patterson Bonaparte.

Madame Patterson Bonaparte to Lady Morgan.

PARIS, RUE D'ALGERS, NO. 4,
September 22nd, 1839.

DEAR LADY MORGAN,

You will be less surprised to know of my arrival in Europe than I am to find myself here. I never supposed that I had preserved sufficient energy or moral courage to put into effect my inclination to absent myself from the *Republique par excellence*. A residence of a few months in the *Etats Unis* would cure the most

ferocious Republican of the mania of Republics. We
have security neither for our lives nor our persons in
America. I have been two months nearly in France, a
period of time which has passed very dully; I have
found few of those persons whom I knew and saw
habitually five years ago. Death, time, and absence
have left me scarcely an acquaintance at Paris. If our
friends do not die, their sentiments change towards us
so much, that really I know not which is most distressing, to hear that they are gone to the other world, or
that they have forgotten us in this vale of tears, and
have become strangers to us. I have met few persons
who possess the stability of friendship that I find in
yourself. You are, in this particular, as in most others,
une personne distinguée. My son is gone from Geneva
to Italy, to visit his relatives, and to see after a legacy,
which the late Cardinal Fesch, his grand uncle, had the
goodness to leave to him. He wanted me to go to
Geneva to see him, but I could not attain the courage
to extend my long journey farther than Paris. Here I
am in solitary existence. In one of his letters he remarked that it had been your intention to write to me;
If you have had that goodness, your letter must have
reached Baltimore after my departure. I regret this
circumstance very much. I have seen Mr. Warder; his
regard for me has held out against time and circumstances; he is unchanged in kind feelings; but, poor
man, time has dealt hard with his exterior; he looks
as if he had begun to exist a century ago.

Madame Benjamin de Constant is an agreeable
person; has had the goodness to recollect me. I dined
yesterday at her house, *en petit comité.* I have myself
grown fat, old, and dull, — all good reasons for people

not to think me an intelligent hearer or listener. They mistake, however; I have exactly the talent to appreciate the high powers of all others, without being able to contribute much to the liveliness of conversation myself.

Have you no agreeable work to promise us?

The poor Duchess d'Abrantes, Madame Junot, made a sad end, the natural consequence of her prodigal expenditure. Her pecuniary difficulties, it is said, caused her death. I liked her very much, and I always felt pained at the misery which her want of judgment in the direction of her affairs had brought on her. I believe that her heart and feelings were generous and warm.

I wonder that you did not select Paris in preference to London, for a permanent *séjour*. I should much prefer living at Florence, but there lives there one individual whom I wish not to meet again. Whether persons have been the voluntary or the unreflecting cause of having spoiled a destiny, I would sooner avoid their presence. I know not whether the princess Charlotte, the late daughter of Joseph Bonaparte, was fortunate enough to be personally of your acquaintance. I did not myself know her, but I have heard from those who did, that she possessed some mental superiority; and a great many noble qualities.

I hope that Sir Charles Morgan still recollects me, and preserves for myself the friendship he formerly entertained for me.

Adieu, my dear Lady Morgan,

Believe me, ever your sincere and

Affectionate friend,

E. PATTERSON.

It was during this year that Lady Morgan completed the first portion of her important work, *Woman and her Master*. It was published by Colburn. The sum she received for it does not appear. It is only a first instalment of a very extensive project. The design is nothing less than to demonstrate that in all ages, women, in spite of the systematic depression and subordination in which they have been kept, and in spite of all difficulties, have not only *never* been subordinated, but have, on the contrary, been always the depositories of the vital and leading IDEA of the time; that the spiritual life in women has always been more pure and vigorous than in men; that women have a more subtle and delicate instinct for whatsoever is "pure, lovely, and of good report," and that, alike among the most degraded savage tribes (those in Australia and New Guinea), as among the Hebrew of old, women were held the oracles, and proved themselves to be of "finer clay" than their so-called "master," man. This doctrine Lady Morgan illustrates by historical examples, which exhibit industry and research. Of course there is much eloquent and special pleading and declamation, but the work is wonderfully clever, and the lady having all the talk to herself, she rides on to the end upon a gently undulating wave of triumph, which, to disturb, would be to break the charm of the book. There is nothing American or strong-minded in *Woman and her Master*. It is a contrast to the *Rights of Woman* tone, in which the question is generally discussed; on the contrary, nothing can be more pretty and persuasive; no man in the world could find in his heart to interrupt the pleasant flow of narrative and assertion by a question,

much less by a contradiction. There are some true observations; the work evinces a great deal of laborious
and industrious reading, and the style is not so much
disfigured by a polyglott of languages, as is usually
the case. It is evident, from the beginning, that her
ladyship is riding her "hobby," which, well bred and
well broken, obeys her hand, shows the smoothest
action and carries her along like a Pegasus. The work
was never completed; her eyesight failed; and, when
restored, was still precarious; but she had collected an
ample store of materials to finish her task, had her
health and eyesight remained in their natural force.
Some portions of the second part were left by her
almost ready for the press.

We return to the diary, in which there is a brief
reference to this book.

June 9, 1840. — The first time I have written in
this journal during the year 1840. *En attendant*, I
have finished and published the first and second volume
of my *Woman and her Master*.

Just read the account of the funeral of Mary,
Dowager Countess of Cork and Orrery; she died in
harness, full of bitterness and good dinners.

The following note from Mrs. Otway Cave is about
the Braye peerage. Lady Braye, as she ultimately
became, was one of the closest of Lady Morgan's
friends.   ˙

Mrs. Otway Cave to Lady Morgan.

THOMAS'S HOTEL,
Wednesday Evening, August 14th.

MY DEAR LADY MORGAN,

I am going to be very troublesome, but I am quite sure you will be kind and indulgent. The case is this: — The Lord Chancellor has fixed *to-morrow* afternoon, at half-past three o'clock, to give judgment as to my claim to the Braye Peerage, and it is *my* business to obtain a sufficient number of peers to form the committee; numbers of whom, as you know are gone out of town, and I have a thousand fears, lest we should fail in obtaining the right number, for a female, and an *aged* one like myself, must of course find it a difficult task, without the aid of kind friends. The purport, therefore, of this application, my dear Madam, is to request you would do me the favour to ask any peers, who are friends of yours (and *very* many, I know, are on your list), to be at the House of Lords to-morrow, rather before three o'clock, as *that* is the hour which the Lord Chancellor has fixed to give the final judgment. If you can, without inconvenience, do me this favour, I need not say what an essential service you would render me, and my servant shall call at your house to-morrow morning, at any hour you may kindly appoint, in case you may write any notes for him to convey; and, perhaps, you would be so good as to give him the directions to each. I am quite distressed to give you such trouble, but will not detain you with more of this.

Remaining with best compliments to Sir Charles,
Your much obliged,
SARAH OTWAY CAVE.

PS. — I would have *called* to petition you in person, but my carriage has been in a distant quarter all the day, and I could not leave the house.

I shall hope to call very soon, after the present fatigue is over.

The judgment was given in Mrs. Otway Cave's favour, and she became Baroness Braye in her own right. Lady Braye died February 21st, 1862. She and her daughter, Lady Beauchamp, were among Lady Morgan's warmest friends.

The next letter will interest readers who knew the fine though undeveloped genius of George Darley.

George Darley to Lady Morgan.

CLARENCE CLUB,
January 23, 1841.

DEAR LADY MORGAN,

I felt very much flattered by your warm praises of *Thomas à Beckett*, and the more so, as its rough nature is opposed to the present refined and polished mode of poetry. Most persons prefer a Paris or a Perseus by Canova, to a Knight-Templar on a tombstone, and looking as if he had been sculptured with a pickaxe, not a chisel. But I suppose you have a heart big enough for both styles, a heart on both sides, while most critics have only the sinister one, or none at all. Your suggestion about "a series of historical dramas," such as *Beckett*, encouraged me in that design, and hence *Ethelstan*. I hope not to have presented this subject in all the mere ruggedness and rust of antiquity, yet to have preserved some of its simple relish and raciness.

If my recurrence to such olden times be objected, you
will say for me, (as your countryman, proud of the
name) that King Ethelstan is, to us living now, a far
more poetical personage than the Emperor Napoleon,
and that history often teaches us nearer the farther it
removes, like "dear home," which is seldom so very
dear until it is rather distant. There are a thousand
better reasons for loving the antique than the antiquarian one; but you are familiar with them all, and
to my distaste for the present style of poetry, I confess
myself the bee in the honey-bottle — quite sweet-sick,
and although my palate is not altogether asinine and
made for thistles, yet it does prefer even the *amari
aliquid* to chewing an eternal cud of rose-leaves.

Dear Lady Morgan, excuse the liberty of this long
answer to your note; but as I am, in a worse sense
than the weird woman, one of the "imperfect speakers,"
[he had an impediment in his speech] it forces me to
spend all my tediousness in writing. Sir Charles will
perhaps take the trouble of decyphering these hiero-
glyphical characters for your convenience.

With best respects to him and your ladyship, I remain what all the world is towards you, and to what
I need not say besides,

Your much favored,
GEORGE DARLEY.

John Poole, the dramatist, and author of *Paul Pry*,
had made the acquaintance of Sir Charles and Lady
Morgan. From the letters of this singular and farcical
genius, the following note may be given: —

John Poole to Lady Morgan.

BRIGHTON, 40 BLACK LION STREET,
March 26, 1841.

DEAR LADY MORGAN,

I wish I could come and see whether you are better.
I hope you are. *Are you?* Mr. Herring was here a
few days ago — very funny; but I could learn nothing
from him distinct about you.

So here I am still, seeing everybody out. None of
your acquaintances here, I believe, but Edwin Landseer, who is gone, and Colonel Webster, whom I don't
know, so *faites vous en une idée!* The fish are all in
the water, because there is nobody here to want them
out; the flies stand sulkily waiting to be caught, and
nobody to catch them; the goats' occupation's gone —
two, with their pretty baby-carts at their tails, are at
this moment fast asleep under my window, and likely
to remain so till next September — because there are
not sufficient *carriage*-children to wake them; the
theatre is closed, because, as nobody went to it when
the town was full, it would be very stupid indeed of
them to expect people to go to it now that the town is
empty. The only happy person in the place I believe
to be Garcia, who is in the seventh heaven at Sir
Charles's notice of him in the Brighton article. *A
propos* of theatre — our *tragedy* will be in the *Miscel-
lany* next month. Bentley has had it for a long time
under a restriction that he should not publish it till
then, I expecting to have finished what I am about
for his dear friend that time; but, alas! though every
day adds a little bit to the heap, it is *so* little!

When I come to town I hope to find some or all

of your charming nieces with you. Has some lucky
Irishman caught Miss Josephine yet? Oh, how I do
wish I were *two or three* years younger and thirty
thousand pounds richer!

That being all, with kind regards to Sir Charles,
who, I take it for granted is well,

Believe me, dear Lady Morgan,
Your ladyship's, very sincerely,
JOHN POOLE.

Sir Charles and Lady Morgan this year made another visit to Germany; they went to Kissingen for
Lady Morgan's health. She did not keep a journal
while in that country; but the following letters to Lady
Talbot gave some account of her progress: —

Lady Morgan to Lady Talbot de Malahide.

BADEN,
September 30, 1841.

MY DEAR LADY TALBOT,

In the course of our delightful and prosperous tour
in this region of plenty and *bonhomie* I have often
thought of writing to you; but, strange to say, having
come to the very *heart* of Germany, as a retreat from
bustle of all sorts, I have been living in a continual
fuss and movement, and, except to my family, to tell
them I am "alive and kicking," I have never put
pen to paper since I left London. I requested Lady
Clarke to send you a fragment of my scrawl as a remembrance. I have derived infinite benefit from the
waters of Kissingen, and I was delighted with the
society I found there, and gratified *up to my bent,* by

the manner of our reception everywhere. The kindness of the Esterhazys and several other distinguished Austrians, was extreme; and that we are not now on our way to Vienna and divers chateaux in Germany and Hungary, is not from the want of invitations. We fell in with many friends of *Madame la Chanoinesse Talbot*, and heard many characteristic anecdotes of her, that I shall reserve for our next meeting. Amongst others, the beautiful Countess Assemay, Count Malgan (the Russian ambassador), the family of the Von Walthers, charmers, and who spoke of the Chanoinesse with great kindness; but all seem surprised how anyone distinguished with the illustrious name of Talbot should accept of a German title! for in Germany, ancient descent, not title, is the illustration most prized. I suppose Josephine has told you how courteous the amiable Queen of Wurtumberg was to us, and what a pretty royal rural *fête* we assisted at. In short, we left pretty, salutary Kissingen with infinite regret. We made our journey here by a long *detour*, in an open carriage. We stopped at Wurzberg and Heidelberg for a couple of days; and the palace of the first, and the ruined castle of the second, are well worth the fatigue of the whole journey; and oh, such a land of abundance as we passed through! There is nothing I ever saw comparable to the Valley of the Necker, and the scenery from Heidelberg to Baden. I shall never forgive myself for having lived so long without having visited this paradise. I cannot tell you how it seized on my imagination — such a combination of all that is civilised and romantic, enjoyable and sublime. The Grand Duchess has rendered it delightful to us in a social point of view, by the distinction of her attentions. The day after our arrival she sent (through the Baden minister) to invite us to go to her in the morning, so we went to the *vieux chateaux*, and were presented by *la grande maitresse*, who left us to the enjoyment of a most agreeable and intellectual conversation, with one of the most *spirituelle* and gracious persons imaginable. The next evening we were invited to her concert, and presented to the Prince and Princess Vasa. The Countess Merlin sang, and still charmingly.

Last night we were at the most original entertainment ever given since the days of Charlemagne! by the Princessa Vasa, for it was amongst the ruins of the old castle (Alte Schloss) at the top of that steep rugged mountain, which I need not describe to you. I got very nervous about going, as the descent at night was no joke! We assembled at five in the centre of the ruins, all in grand toilette — the men all *chapeau bas!* The grand spectacle was the sun setting — and the moon rising over such scenes! Here there was a collection — three tables. I was summoned to her Royal Highness, where, by-the-bye, Lord Douglas and myself were the only British. As the night advanced, the rest of the ruins were suddenly illuminated, as if by magic, and we ascended to a Gothic chamber, superbly furnished *en rococo*, where there was a concert, and a ball terminated the whole. The old dungeons rang with the echoes of the most delightful bands of music all night. To-night is the Grand Duke's *fête*, to which we are invited. And now I think I have tired you out, and shall beg of you to give my people a peep of this letter, which

15*

will save me going over this ground to them. So
God bless you.

　　With kind respects to Lord Talbot,

　　　　　　Yours,

　　　　　　　　SYDNEY MORGAN.

In the autumn, Sir Charles and Lady Morgan returned to England by way of the Rhine, Brussels, and
Ostend. By the end of September, they were again
in William Street. Of their pleasant journey, no literary use was made by Lady Morgan. She spoke, for
years to come, with ardour of the beauty of German
scenery and the cordiality of German manners; but
she had long ago given up the thought of making a
book on that country, to range with her *Italy* and
France. Another race of writers, younger and less
scrupulous than herself, had rushed into the field
which her genius had first laid open to feminine ad-
venturers.

Even in the lighter sphere of fiction, the public
mind had somewhat changed, as Lady Morgan thought,
for the worse. The days of sentimental and patriotic
novels had passed away, — Ireland had no serious
wrongs to redress; and the story, with a purpose graver
than the amusement of a passing hour, no longer
warned, or even found, a public. In place of laughing
and musing over adventures like those of *O'Donnel,* the
world was sneering and mangling over the character of
The Dowager, by Mrs. Gore.

In this once popular novel, Mrs. Gore was supposed
to have sketched with a free and wicked hand that
ancient dame, Mary, Countess of Cork and Orrery,
who had just died, as Lady Morgan said, "full of

bitterness and good dinners." Much scandal thereupon ensued. Mrs. Gore abstained from making any reply at the time to those who accused her of traducing private character in her book; but to Lady Morgan, personally, she made a clean confession of her offence, so far as she had been guilty of offence.

Here is her note: —

Mrs. Gore to Lady Morgan.

DEAR LADY MORGAN,

You are very kind to like my new book. Till you praised it, I was in despair. It *sells*, and I was convinced of its utter worthlessness; for surely nothing can equal the degradation of the public taste in such matters! The subject and title were of Bentley's choosing; and my part distinctly was to *avoid* hooking "M.C.O." into the book. In certain *mannerisms* the *Dowager* may resemble her; but not in essentials. She was *better* or *worse*. I never heard of her troubling herself about her opposite neighbours, except so far as by sending her dog to walk in their gardens, when under a course of Epsom salts.

I am grieved (*à propos* to being sick) to hear that you have been so great a sufferer. No person who writes books has the least claim to a digestion; and I wonder you should ever have thought of such a thing!

My French books will disappoint you. Paris has been a land of Canaan to me, and the milk and honey will necessarily find their way to my pen, and prevent the possibility of adding shades to the picture. I love them all so well as to see everything *en couleur de rose*.

The English (except you, who are frank and generous, but then you are not English) are not half so good to me; and I therefore permit myself to see them as nature made them and art has spoiled them.

My daughter is going to Brighton in the course of the week, and will throw herself at your feet. I hope she will send me better news of you.

Sincere regards to yourself and Sir Charles, from
Yours faithfully and obliged,
C. F. GORE.

CHAPTER XVI.

ALBERT GATE CONCEDED — 1842.

IN 1842, the *Book without a Name*, by Sir Charles and Lady Morgan, appeared, published by Colburn. It was a collection of sketches and articles which had been contributed by them from time to time to the *Metropolitan*, *New Monthly*, and the *Athenæum*. It was not then so common to collect fugitive articles as it is now. These articles had obtained a good deal of notice when they originally appeared, and Mr. Colburn found his account in their republication. *The Memoir of the Macaw of a Lady of Quality*, to which reference has been made, will be found in these pages. We resume the diary as it occurs in a letter from Lady Morgan to her niece: —

April 12, 1842. — Talk to me of *your* gardens! I have at this moment, perfuming my rooms, twelve

hyacinths, mignionette, sweet briar, and verbenas; follow
me that in *your* garden!

My right eye is very weak and painful, causing me
to spare it as much as possible. You have got the
Athey., and books to keep you *au courant.* We had
Captain Marryatt to dine with us on Saturday, a pleasant, cosy little day, and I bore it very well, although
Morgan exclaimed against my *lights*, and wanted to
extinguish them; but I would rather give up my *rouge*
than my lamps, *et c'est beaucoup dire.*

I can do nothing for your young friend, P——;
never encourage young people to suppose they are to
throw themselves on their friends; they should be early
taught to have no dependence but upon their own
exertions. At fourteen, I worked for myself, and dis-
dained living on any fine relations, the Croftons, and
if I was left destitute to-morrow, I should begin and
write again, as of old. How often have I preached
this to you all?

Well, I am working at my *Gate;* the Cannon
Brewery is *blown down*, and the Counter intrigue
blown up. We have got the Duchess of Kent on our
side, and that there is a likelihood of our having the
Queen, whom we have petitioned. Lord Duncannon is
dead against us, but I do not despair, for it will be a
great *public* benefit.

April 17. — Hurrah! have got my Gate, just as
we got Catholic Emancipation, by worrying for it!

It was said of somebody that he could be eloquent
on a broom-stick. Sidney Smith could be lively about
the gout, and Horace Smith about everything. A note

from each may be given, — the first, for its graceful turn; the second, for its puns and conceit.

Sidney Smith to Lady Morgan.

56, GREEN STREET, GROSVENOR SQUARE,
November 14, 1842.

MY DEAR MADAM,

Among incitements so numerous that it would weary you to mention them, there are two obstacles, a late dinner, to which I am engaged, and uncertain health. I had last week an attack of gout, which is receding from me (as a bailiff from the house of an half-pay captain) dissatisfied and terrified by the powers of colchicum; but I swear by that beautiful name we both bear, that I will come if it is possible.

Ever, dear Lady Morgan,
Truly yours,
SIDNEY SMITH.

Horatio Smith to Sir Charles Morgan.

BRAMBLETYE HOUSE, BRIGHTON,
December 30th, 1842.

MY DEAR SIR CHARLES,

(Which, of course, includes Lady Morgan, you two being one) the same to you, and many of them (I mean happy returns, &c., &c.) Right glad am I to hear that Lady Morgan has thrown off her coughs and colds.

We are as dull here as you can be in London, with nothing half so good to enliven us as Lady Morgan's *improvement* on Webster's *Cracked Rib.* Your riddles are excellent, and so is your doggrel, which I must leave Eliza to answer. We must borrow Borrow's book, which seems to be the best thing recently published.

As to my Adam Brown, I know nothing about him, except that Colburn seems rather ashamed to bring him out. I don't mean to write any more, being quite worn out; so I resign Adam to his fate without any compunctious visitings of nature. I have had as much success as I deserved, and much more than I expected, and more money too, which was ever my sole inspiration.

Make sugar of paper! then there is a hope that poor authors may make *plums*, and critics become *candied*, and writers of tragedies may be more successful in the *writing mood*, and the worst productions be constantly in the mouths of the public, and all the evils of literature be twined into *bonbons!* I always said and felt that to restore the taste for tragedy, she must be taken from the stilts, and brought down to common life and common language. Everything is a round robin, rudeness, simplicity, perfection, decay, simplicity, rudeness. You *must* have novelty, and after you have reached perfection, you can only innovate by inferiority.

Never mind, it's a very pretty world, and I am perfectly well contented with it, especially now that my wife is better, and my three girls at home, and all of us as *cozy* as possible, trying which can talk the most nonsense, and laugh the loudest at a bad joke.

Our united regards and wishes for lots of happy new years are wafted to you and Lady Morgan from the family amanuensis.

Yours very faithfully,

HORATIO SMITH.

PS. — Should this papyro-saccharine process go
on, what capital kisses will be made from Little's poems
and sugar of *lead* from my works! You will see in
the Magazine a poem of mine which will remind you
of the fellow's *recantation* for calling another a swindler. "I called you a swindler, it is true; you're an
honest man, I'm a liar."

The diary resumed: —

11, WILLIAM STREET, *January 1st*, 1843. — I
enter on my third year's illness, which has interfered
with my enjoyment of life, my worldly interests (for I
cannot write without pain and palpitation), and all my
social pleasures. My dear family are all far away, and
I am deprived of my liberty at home and abroad, still,
two of the great blessings are left me, the society of
my most dear and true friend, my husband, in full
health and spirits, and my own consciousness that I
never lost an occasion of working or rendering a service during my long life, to the best of my ability; my
sight has wonderfully recovered since my other attack.

January 28. — "Charming well again!" and in my
pretty drawing-room. An old friend dropped in to-day,
and found Morgan and myself sitting over the fire and
laughing, *à gorge deployé*, at some nonsense, and he
said, "You ought to work it up for the *New Monthly.*"
And so we will; we are to call it the *Memoirs of Mar-
gery Daw*. A hit at a *fadaise*, which has come out
lately, about good little fools.

The following notes are from Lady Morgan's letters
to her niece: —

February 6th, 1843. — Your uncle has made a
very perfect recovery from a very alarming illness, but
is still rather more "pale, mild, and interesting" than
in my unromanticism, I am desirous to see him! *au
reste*, I, too, am beginning to turn the corner of my
three years' malady (though even writing such a scrap
as this brings on my old heart-beat), and so we have
launched once more our old bark the *Darby and Joan*,
on the broad seas of society; but with all the caution
and *inland* steering of old and shipwrecked mariners.
We did our Babbage last Saturday (his first of the
season), where were all the *habitués* of the good old
times, "your slave, but now your slave no longer,"
Rogers, gave me a crush of the hand as he passed me
in the crowd, and turned his eyes tenderly on me,
whilst I averted mine disdainfully; we looked an illustration of *Death and the Lady*, and I had a mind to
ask Landseer, who stood near me, to take it for his
next subject. Before I drop the *Yellow Poet*, I must
tell you that he is the slave and blackmoor of another
lady, who is now the receiver of all his pretty speeches,
and the idol of his *iced butter parties*, *que vous con-
naissez si bien*.

Diary again:

June. — Is it possible that I am again restored to
health and sight. My dear Morgan is well and hearty,
and Olivia better.

Soirées, operas, concerts, *à discretion*, which we (old
fools as we are) enjoy *à l'indiscretion!* Well, so here
I am, taking a new lease of life, available for any
length of time, with a peppercorn fine, which is about

the worth what we give in return. And here, if I open
my journal again, it shall be to write something new
and pleasant.

My life may be deemed a frivolity for one of my
age, but no, it is a philosophy, a profound and just
philosophy, founded upon the wisdom of the principle,
to *do* and enjoy all the good I *can*, while I submit to
the penalty of that mystery called life.

Some of the "young Englanders" have just been
here; they might as well have been New Zealanders,
for any advance they make in the art of thinking. But
they are *good boys*, of the school of Tommy Goodchild,
in the *Universal Spelling Book*, and they know it. All
little "Jack Horners" in their way,

> "Who put in his thumb,
> And pulled out a plumb,
> And said what a good boy am I!"

Their plumb is a *green*-gage, poor dears! I knew
the firstlings of this school of good boys, some thirty
years ago. Some of them are now cabinet ministers,
and others — nothing; and they are the best off, as
the world has not been put in the secret of their inap-
titude.

Sidney Smith has been in the Thames Tunnel, and
sent me his experiences: —

Sidney Smith to Lady Morgan.

56, GREEN STREET, GROSVENOR LANE,
June 5, 1843.

I had fully intended, my dear madam, to have been
of your party to-night; but I went to the Thames Tunnel, and have destroyed myself by walking under the

river, and descending and ascending one hundred and
twenty steps; there was a suffocating heat and a want
of ventilation for which I was not prepared. I am astonished the Thames submits to the insult; one day or
another it will come down upon the subaqueous intru-
ders with all the force of a basin of water flung from
the seventh story of a house in Edinburgh.

Yours, my dear madam,
Very sincerely,
SIDNEY SMITH.

PS. Mrs. Sidney (ill with the influenza) desires me
to say that she depends upon Sir C. Morgan and you
for Thursday; I beg you will keep away from the
Tunnel in the interim.

June 30th. — One of the most wretched days of
my life — bad letter from Ireland.

"Yet love hopes on, when reason would despair."

My dear, dear Olivia; my hereafter in this world
— gentle, spiritual, intellectual, full of the finest affections — unselfish beyond all comparison! My beloved
Morgan said to me, as I wept over Dr. Carmichael's
letter — "Oh, Sydney, if you grieve thus for a *niece,*
whom you never see much of, what is to become of
you if *I* were to go?" This dreadful idea consoled
me. How strange — my present loss appeared less;
my beloved husband took me off to Richmond, and I
came back in better spirits, and again full of hope —
and Morgan beside me.

In Richmond Park we sat under an old tree, within
view of the Mount where Henry VIII. stood when a
cannon announced to him the decapitation of Anne
Boleyn.

CHAPTER XVII.

DEATH OF SIR CHARLES MORGAN — 1843.

THE sorrow felt by Lady Morgan for the death of her niece, was soon to be merged in a deeper grief. The suggestion thrown out by Sir Charles to moderate her grief about her niece was suddenly realised. That expedition to Richmond was the very last they had together. They had seldom been separated during their long married life; but the final separation came when least expected. Lady Morgan had often complained of Sir Charles Morgan's disinclination to take exercise, and of his love of remaining all day at home, engrossed in reading and writing, never feeling the need of fresh air. It would seem that this was connected with his state of health, though she did not then suspect it. He was ill only a fortnight; he had an attack of heart-disease, sank into a state of stupor and died before those round him had begun to fear danger.

It was the second great sorrow of her life. The death of her father, a few months after her marriage, was her first grief; the death of her husband was a far heavier affliction. As years went on, she felt his loss more and more. She had loved him thoroughly; her respect for him was equal to her affection; his influence over her and his wise judgment had greatly contributed to her brilliant success. He had been her best friend, her guide and counsellor in all things, and her constant companion, sharing all her employments and pursuits. He used to correct her writings, and curtail them of the redundancies and extravagances in which she took delight. He had no petty jealousy in his nature — he admired her genius and rejoiced in her success as much at the end of his life as he had done when he first knew her. The love-letters which the reader has seen in the second volume were redeemed; every promise and every profession was fulfilled. It had been a thoroughly happy marriage.

It was not in Lady Morgan's nature to cherish grief; she could not bear to be unhappy; she resolutely put sorrow away from her throughout her life. It is not the noblest way of treating sorrow, nor the most profitable; but it was her nature to refuse to entertain it, and she could not do otherwise. But if she endeavoured to bury her misery out of sight, she did not forget the dead. One who knew her very intimately in the later years of her life, bears testimony to the fresh tenderness with which she, from time to time, spoke of her husband, as though she had lost him but yesterday; but it was never for more than a moment; she always broke off abruptly, saying, "I must not think of that," and turned to something else.

The death of Sir Charles cast a gloom over the whole circle of their friends; he was a man singularly beloved by all who knew him both in public and in private life; he was of a sweet, affectionate, noble nature; he was thoroughly true and honest, and to be depended upon in every relation of life. "He was," says one who knew him well, "a man of a refined and philosophic mind, of varied accomplishments — a scholar and a gentleman in the largest sense of those comprehensive words."

It is long before there is any further entry in Lady Morgan's diary. She was as much crushed down by her great sorrow as she could be crushed by anything. The innumerable letters of sympathy which she received, the public testimonials to the worth and memory of her husband soothed her feelings; but she was in deep and bitter affliction. The first entry in her diary after her widowhood is —

Oh, my husband! I cannot endure this — I was quite unprepared for this. So ends my life.

November, 1843. — Plus ne m'est rien, rien ne m'est plus.

The winter fire kindles alone for me now. The chair, the table, the lamp, the very books and paper-cutter, all *these* are here, this November — gloomy, wretched November!! How I used to long for November — social, home-girt November; now I spend it in wandering through this deserted house. Is it possible? "Ce que je serai dorénavant ce ne sera plus qu'une demi être! — ce ne sera plus moi — je m'échappe tous les jours." When I first transcribed that monologue did I ever dream the dreadful dream that it would serve for me!

The next entry in her journal is many months later; but it is given here not to break the thread of the subject: —

April, 1844. — Time applied to grief is a worldly common place — time has its due influence over visible grief, that which is expressed by visible emotions — it softens sighs and dries tears! but *le fonds* remains the

same! Time gives you back to the exercise of your
faculties and your habits; but the loss of that which
is, or *was*, part of yourself, remains for ever. This
melancholy Sunday morning, April! The first word
written in this once gay record of pleasant sensations!

There is a long blank, and then the following entry,
headed —

"A period without date."

In the most awful moment of my life, I was not
without aid and solace; my sister was with me, my
brother-in-law, and my niece Sydney Jones and her
husband came to me immediately, and I was removed
from my own house to lodgings, whilst all the wretched
business that necessarily followed my most miserable
loss was arranged. After that, I accompanied my sister
to Brighton, where I was received by the dear, kind
family of Horace Smith, with affection and sympathy.
My dearest sister being obliged to return to her family
in Ireland (she had been with me ever since the death
of her own dear child Olivia — Mrs. Savage); Lord
and Lady Beauchamp, who were then at Brighton, insisted on my going to them at their delightful seat, so
I went, and, removed from all local association, without domestic cares (or joys), surrounded by pleasant
distractions and excessive kindness, I recovered my
health and *constitutional* cheerfulness much more rapidly
than I should otherwise have done. My return to my
own lonely house was woeful. The night I arrived,
my servant Delahaye attended me at my solitary dinner; I bade him recount to me the *Battle of Waterloo.*
He was an old soldier of the 18th, and fought there.

July 28. — Everybody makes a point of having me out, and I am beginning to be familiarised with my terrible loss. I go in and out of drawing-rooms, and "sit at good men's tables," and submit to the influence of the *laughing-gas of society.* I was told, only the other day, "I was *so* brilliant at somebody's dinner;" all this is very contemptible, but it is inevitable.

I *could* read now, if I had sight — once, and *so lately,* I never missed my eyes! One thing cheers me — my beloved sister comes to me soon, and will meet under my roof her beloved children and *mine* — the *all* that is left me now.

London is the best place in the world for the happy and the unhappy, there is a floating capital of sympathy for every human good or evil; I am nobody, and yet what kindness I am daily receiving!

If I were not incapacitated by a weak sight and a heavy heart, and above all, by the eternal "*qui bono?*" that now impedes every flow of thought, and checks every tendency to action, what amusing memoranda would I not set down from the ceaseless anecdotes dropped by the congress of visitors, foreign and home, that daily fill my little *salon.* Poor, dear, kind Sir Mathew Tierny has just been here; his loss, like my own, is irreparable, and of the same nature.

CHAPTER XVIII.

FIRST YEARS OF WIDOWHOOD.

LADY MORGAN resolutely entered on life again, determined not to be more unhappy than she could possibly help. The sense of her loneliness, her inward sorrow was never entirely absent from her thoughts; but she endeavoured to stifle it, and in some measure succeeded — at least, when she was in society.

July, 1844. — Another gone — poor Campbell! Oh for the day that I first saw him led in by Sir Thomas Lawrence, up the great dining-room of the Priory (Stanmore), in the middle of one of the great Saturday dinners! I was seated between Lord Aberdeen and Manners Sutton — the latter gave Campbell his seat beside me — opposite to us was Lord Erskine, and the Duchess of Gordon. Campbell was awkward, but went on taking his soup as if he was eating a haggis in the Highlands; but when he put his knife in the salt-cellar to help himself to salt, every eyeglass was up, and the *first* poet of the age was voted the vulgarest of men. His *coup de grace*, however, was in the evening, when he took the *unapproachable* Marquis of Abercorn by the buttonhole that joined his star! Oh, my stars! I thought we should all die of it, knowing the *extreme* fastidiousness of the possessor of the star. Next morning he went about asking every one if they could "take him into town with a wee bit of a port-

16*

manteau?" Lady Asgill (the most charming of coquets)
gave a place in her carriage to the man who, by a
line, could give her immortality.

My kind old friend, Horace Twiss (by-the-bye what
a pair of coxcombs he and I were when we first met
in the salons of Cork and Charleville), has just sent
me, most kindly, his *Life of Eldon*, and with a flattering word of presentation to boot. It is an honest book,
for the author believes every word he advances, in
form of faith or opinion, and it is the work of a gentleman and a scholar, and of a good artist, too, for he
knows his craft. His personal partiality for Eldon,
though *apparent*, is never officious. He is above his
subject — a narrow-minded, timid, and unenlightened
man. Horace Twiss's text is clear and brief, and in
the best taste and style.

In the autumn Lady Morgan paid a visit to Bou-
logne; her account of it to her niece, Mrs. Geale, shows
that, although she kept down all manifestations of de-
pressions and sorrow, she felt her changed and lonely
situation very acutely. It alludes to the precarious
state of Lady Clarke's health, which gave fears for
another grief in prospect. She says: —

You have long since heard of my melancholy illness — utterly alone, and in a foreign hotel; and I really
believe that if Sir Joseph Lafann had not arrived I
should have been at peace by this. What a curious
proof of the incoherency of all things — to have lived
for my family, and to have died without *one* of its
members near! But above all, I missed *the one* who
had been so long the comfort and saviour of my life!

Still I acknowledge, with gratitude, the most kind and
charitable attentions of the humane and kind strangers
I have found here — among them, Lady Banks and
her sweet, good girls; Lady Dundonald, the Cochranes,
Storys, and many others. Lord Wellesley calls often
at my door, offers me his carriage, and has ordered his
gamekeeper to supply me. Still I am longing to get
back to England, and was to have sailed yesterday,
only Sir Joseph thought me too weak to run the risk
of sea-sickness.

The health of Lady Clarke had been failing for
some time, her state was causing deep anxiety. In the
following extract from a letter, describing a mesmeric
sitting, Lady Morgan shows how she was endeavouring
to cheat herself into hope, and to keep the impending
sorrow out of sight.

If you could recover your sleep without opiates
you would soon be quite well. Mesmerism does this.
I am going to Doctor Ashburner's to-day, to witness an
exhibition *solely* on your account (for you know my
organ of anti-humbugism). I shall be able to tell you
more to-morrow on this head.

Monday. — Now, here is a full and true account.
"Well, my dear, our party consisted of the Marchioness of Hastings (a very fine woman, and going to
be married to Captain Hastings, Henry, her cousin),
both the Henrys and Colonel Lumley — *all believers*,
—and *two sceptics*, Lady Morgan and the Rev. Charles
Darley, who gave themselves great airs. Lord Anglesey was invited, and tried to come, but could not
get out of an engagement. We were all vastly clever

at dinner, when at the dessert enter a lovely little girl about twelve years old, in cloak and bonnet, which being doffed, she was brought forward as 'little Jane,' and presented to Lady Hastings (the queen mesmeriser of London). 'Little Jane' looked modest, simple, and childish, until Lady Hastings, drawing her closely to her, fixed her fine eyes on hers, and in a few minutes the child fell back as in a swoon. Dr. Ashburner caught her, and then she stood fast asleep at the table, her eyes shut, but looking flushed and fussy, and talking under the influence of any organ on which Lady Hastings pressed her fingers. The first was music, and she sang all sorts of scraps of songs sweetly, but incorrectly! but when Clifford Henry joined her in *My Father's Marble Hall*, she flew into a rage and said, 'you put me out of tune.' Then came the organ of affection, and she nearly suffocated Lady Hastings with caresses, and threw herself into the Doctor's arms, and ran round the table and poked every one together, and was, upon the whole, so tender that the Rev. Charles Darley and I got alarmed. The next organ touched was self-esteem, acted to the life, and when I said, 'Oh, Jane, you are a little rogue,' she flew into a rage with me, and said, 'You mean I am a thief, that is very wicked of you,' and away she went, and sat in a *niche* under the side-board, in great dudgeon and dignity. As to the organ of *imitation*, it was to the life; she personified Tom Thumb, several London cries, and danced a polka, and so ended act the first.

She was then de-mesmerised, and was again modest and childlike, and said she hoped she had not done anything rude, or sang an improper song; 'I hope I shall soon be married.' The two sceptics decided it was *acting* equal to Mrs. Jordan's. When the men came up, after dinner, act the second: I assisted to paste black sticking plaster over her eyes, so her seeing was impossible. The Doctor standing behind her, held his folded hands over her eyes, and Darley and I held a book open to her page after page; she read all, but complained of the small print. Sceptics startled; she sang scraps of songs. She frequently said to me, 'that lady is a sceptic.'

Act third. Lady Hastings insisted on Clifford Henry being mesmerised, and this was no joke, but a perfect exhibition of poor humanity exposed to an influence over which it had no control, and which subjected it to external impressions which left it but a complicated piece of machinery.

I now tell you all *I saw*, but as to my *faith*, it rests much where my ignorant interests left it some years ago. That the powers of magnetism and electricity are great, and may be beneficially applied in medical practice, I believe there is no doubt, and that they have induced sleep without the previous use of opiates, and by what I saw, muscular power increased to a miraculous extent. The whole of the doctrine is to be found in the *Philosophy of Life*, a work yet destined to give immortality to its author, whose misfortune was to have lived in advance of his age. To *this truth* all my convictions subscribe; and now, dear Olivia, I have done for you and your amusement what I would not do for myself. God help you, my dear Olivia, and be of good heart, all will go well."

The next entry in the journal is a sad one. The sorrow she had feared had fallen upon her.

Sunday, April 27. — The re-opening of my *Dooms-day Book*, after a struggle of nearly two years; submitting to the grave law of necessity by which all known things are governed, I have endeavoured to make head against that prostrating melancholy which poisons and embitters life, but does not destroy it, and to live in that world I could not leave by any voluntary act (for mine is not a suicidal temperament). Now I am again crushed by the *last* of the two greatest calamities that could befal me in this life. My noble-minded and affectionate sister, my first friend and earliest companion, with whom I had struggled through a precarious youth. My beloved Olivia is no more! I open this page in my *Doomsday Book* to note this; but I cannot go on, three of the dearest and the best in *two* years; it is *too* terrible.

April 29. — All is now over in Dublin, and the mourners are returned to their homes, *with time to weep*. Oh! I *cannot weep*, and have none to weep with, for I am alone. All my old friends and new acquaintances have been to my door to offer their sympathy, but I am beyond the reach, *the reach of solace now*, I almost think this last blow has struck most home.

So I reel on! the world is my gin or opium, I take it for a few hours per diem, excitement, intoxication, absence! I return to my desolate home, "and awaken to all the horrors of sobriety." My impressionableness of spirits, my debility of body, my sight dim from nervousness, my heart palpitating at the least movement; and yet I am accounted the "agreeable rattle of the great ladies' coterie," and I talk *pas mal* to many clever men all day. This is surely mechanism, for it

is done without effort on the voluntary system, and
yet, when alone, books, pictures, flowers, everything
has the touch of death on it, and that *park* so near
me, of which my beloved Morgan used to say, "It is
ours more than the queen's, we use it daily and enjoy
it nightly!" — that park that I worked so hard to get
an entrance into, I never walk in, it seems to me
covered with black crape.

CHAPTER XIX.

RETIRED FROM WORK.

In the year 1846 Colburn brought out a cheap
edition of the *Wild Irish Girl*. Lady Morgan sent a
copy of this new edition of her first work to Mr.
Macaulay, who at once wrote to thank her.

T. B. Macaulay to Lady Morgan.

ALBANY,
August 15th, 1846.

DEAR LADY MORGAN,
    I have received a copy of the *Wild Irish Girl*, of
which the value is increased by a line which tells me
that the author has been kind enough to think of me.
I shall always value the book for its own sake, and
for the sake of the giver.
            Believe me,
                Dear Lady Morgan,
                    Your faithful servant,
                        T. B. MACAULAY.

We return to the diary: —

November 4. — I am thankful to say that all my
roamings are over for this year, and that I am safe at
home in dear William Street, in sight of all that is
best. I got so ill at Worthing I was obliged to leave
the Duchess and her family party which, by-the-bye,
like most family parties (except it is one's own), was
dull. There was one member of this party with whom
I got on well, and who talks soundly upon all high
class subjects, but he talks like a ghost, only when
spoken to; and as no one ventured to draw him out
but myself, I had him all to myself. He appears cold
and self-reliant, stands apart from all contact with his
species. Apparently he was never in love, and his
family (who know him best) say never will marry.
When I left this ducal *ménage* and its aristocratic *morgue*,
I started off for my dearest Sydney's pretty little par-
sonage at Gelderton, in Suffolk, rather a different scene
to be sure; but its sunny and cheerful atmosphere made
everything bright and happy, and it was not till my
return to town with a severe *attack of rheumatism*, that
I found out their cottage was damp and low, and I
suspect disagrees with them, but they will not allow it.
I was obliged to send to my good friend Dr. Latham,
and have his advice and prescriptions, which set me up
again, and enabled me to go to Serge Hill, Herts, to
my dear old Solley's, where I was shown off to divers
Hertfordshire magnates, and made to trot out and show
my paces in the old style.

December 14. — I dare not trust myself to chronicle
my feelings as to passing years more! To forget is
my philosophy, to hope would be my insanity, to en-

dure (and that I *can*) is my system; but it is only a system, from which the dreary impulses of my state and condition revolt but too often. Still I am grateful for the good I yet enjoy — to be so is my religion.

Nothing is left me to love; but, also, nothing to fear.

December 25. — I am endeavouring to make head against the sad associations of this month, and to give evidence of my cheerful philosophy if not of my happiness. And so I end this old year quietly, somewhat anxiously, but with increasing social popularity.

January, 1847. — Another year! I cannot say I hailed it with a welcome or with a hope; but I endeavour to *cheer it in*, and gave a dinner for my most dear husband's family and friends, a large musical party in the evening — all the neighbours I could collect.

All my servants laid up with influenza.

I sent these rhymes, with a winter bouquet, to a friend: —

> Spring flowers,
> With spring showers,
> Like Love's promise,
> Pass, fleet away.
>
> While winter weaves
> His ivy leaves,
> For deathless wreaths
> For friendship's day.

August. — Death of the O'Connor Don. Another gone! my esteemed and tried friend, one of the honestest and best men Ireland ever had to boast of. It is but the other day since he was at one of my *soirées*, talking of old times. He was the lineal descendant of the supreme kings of Ireland. I saw the old crown of Irish gold at a jeweller's, in Dublin, when I was a little girl.

Lady Charleville, one of the very few old friends left to Lady Morgan, was growing very old and infirm, but she still retained the same warmth of regard for her as ever. Lady Charleville had also met with much sorrow, which she bore in a different way to Lady Morgan — she did not put it away from her.

Lady Charleville to Lady Morgan.

March 8, 1847.

I am very very sorry to be deprived so long of any enjoyment from your society, which I always cared for and valued when there seemed to be more of the same stamp current than in our latter days! Is it that as age advances we think complacently on those scenes we passed under the blaze of a meridian day with capabilities now blunted, and which neither can impart or receive pleasure with the same gusto as heretofore? Be that as it may, my dear Lady Morgan, I shall always rejoice in seeing you again, and be most anxious for the recovered health of Mr. and Mrs. Jones.

Yours affectionately,
C. M. CHARLEVILLE.

April 15. — I look into my old journals and find that my first lesson in *salad making* was given me by Lord Chancellor Manners — about the time my novel *O'Donnel* appeared. The day after getting my book, when he discovered its emancipating tendency, he ordered it to be burnt in the servants' hall, and then said to Lady Manners, (who told it to my sister) "Jenny, I wish I had not given her the secret of my salad." Ever after, he only *bowed* to me when we met at court, never spoke to me. Jenny was my old crony, friend and confidant up to that moment; but *O'Donnel* lost me my charming friend. She had been educated in a Catholic convent, was the child of Catholic parents, her mother born in low life, and she only became a Protestant on becoming a peeress. Her brother, Lord Glengall, was converted before.

A note from Sir William Napier, the great historian, though a trifle, is a trifle full of grace and character.

Sir W. Napier to Lady Morgan.

Scinde House, Clapham,
October 20, 1849.

Let me jump over all propriety — it is the only thing I can now jump over, but early practice and long, has kept me vigorous in that particular — let me jump over it, the tiresome obstacle, and address you at once as dear Lady Morgan.

What can I offer in excuse, what say for myself that I accept your promise of a visit by letter, instead of paying my homage in person? Rudeness I am guilty of "*Mais avec des circonstances extenuantes.*" I am seventy-two — that is no defence; but I am also like the prince in the Arabian tale of the coloured fishes, half flesh half marble, and I can scarcely move across a room; to get in and out of a carriage is almost as bad for me as it was for the genie to get in and out of the vessel sealed by Solomon, not that

Solomon ever put his seal on me. I am, however,
wise enough to be delighted at the prospect of seeing
Lady Morgan, and if she will allow me to say Thursday, as soon after two o'clock as she likes, luncheon
will be ready, and an humble admirer at her commands, meanwhile he remains,

Her devoted admirer,

W. NAPIER.

December 12. — What a *villegiatura* I have made
for the last three months — a honeymoon spent with
Lady Laura and Mr. Grattan, at their pretty villa at
Hampton Court, then for a fortnight at Lady Webster's,
Roehampton, and, *en passant*, I paid a visit at the
Grove, and found all the family at home except its
illustrious chief. Then to Dover with my poor Jones
for his health; but the place disagreed with me after
a fortnight, and so I left them and went to the
Deepdene, Mr. Hope's — all *en grand seigneur*, and
most of all the master. It is much to say that the
wealthiest man in England is also the highest bred,
the fine gentlemanism of good society when it was
best, with great natural kindness. The party gay and
charming.

Then from Deepdene I went to Llanover Court,
Monmouthshire (Sir Benjamin Hall's, now Lord Llanover's); staid there a week, and departed from it with
my dear Mrs. Murray, for a visit to her mother's,
Baroness Braye, at Malvern, and so on to the Duchess
of Cleveland's, Yorkshire; a fine party, who moved
and breathed by the *Lodge Peerage*, and then back
to town, where my dear niece and her husband was
waiting to receive me, the first time for years that I

was welcomed with cordial affection in my own lonely
dwelling.

December 22. — I am actually off for Brighton! on
a visit to my kind old friend Lady Webster, I little
thought I could visit this sad place again. All my
old friends have come about me. The dear, warm-
hearted and *clever* Horace Smith; the Duke of Devonshire reproached me for not having called on him
on my first arrival, and sent me an invitation to dine,
immediately he heard I was here. Alas, we first met,
a few days before he came of age, at the Priory,
Stanmore.

January 12, 1848. — Went to Elliot Warburton's
marriage with my friend Miss Groves — a marriage
made, I do believe, on my *little balcony*. All the muses
assisted at this literary nuptials — Monckton Milnes,
Hayward, Eothen Kinglake, — I was the only *she*
muse there. I offered two unfinished MSS. to any lady
who might adopt them for the nonce to qualify them
for being present.

Dined yesterday with Milner Gibson; amongst the
agreeables were Lord Dudley Stuart, that amiable
roué, Sir Henry Mildmay, and the most illustrious
Mr. Punch; *yes*, *really* and literally, *Punch;* Douglas
Jerrold — a very remarkable-looking man — diminutive,
plain, and evidently a valetudinarian; his manners
simple, mild and gentleman-like. We chatted across
the table, and agreed about the *national defences* and
the *national timidity* having brought on the coming
invasion. He said he would lower the prices of house-rent
at Brighton, if I would return there! I said I would;
and lo! there is an admirable and humorous paper on
"Brighton panic," in the *Punch* of this day.

February 12. — I have been very ill indeed for a month, and my poor Sydney has been in much sorrow; and I have been more miserable than I ever thought I should be again. After my three great calamities I did not suppose time *could* have another in store for me; but I have been threatened with the loss of all I have left me.

November 25. — The death of Lord Melbourne is one of the *triste* incidents of this *triste* month. How many passages of my own life are recalled by his death! How long I knew him, how much I owed him, what joyous days and nights I have passed in his charming society, from my girlhood to this moment! I called to inquire for him before I left town in October; he sent his valet down to request I would come up. He was sitting in his back drawing-room, amidst books and papers, *en robe de chambre;* he was quite himself, pleasant and chatty, and asked me what was the little packet I had in my hands. I said, invites for a little *soirée* the next evening, and I had not the courage to ask him. "Why not?" said he, passing his hand over his head in his old way; "I should like it much." "You don't mean that, Lord Melbourne," said I. "Yes I do, and if I feel up to it when the time comes, you will see me;" but when it came, he did not come, and sent me a verbal message. He was looking ill, and I did not *think* of asking him. Alas! I never saw him again!

CHAPTER XX.

THE LEAVES FALLING.

THE diary of the year 1849 begins thus: —

My first entry this year is to record a loss. Another old friend is gone, — Sir Robert Wilson. Sir Robert Wilson was born in 1777. He entered the army very early. He was much employed on diplomatic missions of delicacy and importance. In 1812, he was associated with Sir Raoul Liston on a mission to the Emperor Alexander, to prevail on him to make peace with Turkey, and *not* to enter into any negociations with Napoleon. He had seen a great deal of service; but the action with which his name will be for ever associated in the memory of Englishmen is the generous and gallant assistance he lent to effect the escape of Count Lavallette, generously perilling both his personal liberty and his position in life. It was an act of pure generosity, for he had never even seen the Count. It was in January, 1816. Lavallette had been condemned to be guillotined, and all the attempts to soften the stupid and callous heart of Louis XVIII. had failed. Lavallette's heroic wife had effected her husband's escape from the walls of the Conciergerie, and he had been concealed in Paris; but the police were on his track, and he must soon have been discovered if Sir Robert Wilson and two of his friends had not given their services to aid his escape over the

frontier into Belgium. Sir Robert Wilson conveyed
him in his own carriage in the uniform of a British
officer, as far as Mons.

The escape was entirely successful; but on Sir
Robert's return to Paris the police, seeing his coach
covered with mud, as though from a long journey, set
their spies upon his servant, and contrived to extract
from him that his master had been to Mons with an
officer of the guards who could not speak a word of
English. They bribed him to carry the correspondence
of Sir Robert to the prefect of police (for he was trusted
by his master to carry his letters.) The servant betrayed his trust, and the first letter they got hold of
was a long despatch to Earl Grey, containing full details of the escape. Sir Robert and his two friends
were immediately apprehended; but eventually they did
not fall victims to their generosity. Sir Robert, when
young, had been a very handsome man, with a fine
commanding presence.

A letter from Madame Bonaparte, chronicling the
changes that even dull times never fail to bring, and,
accordingly, her experience of republics.

Madame Patterson Bonaparte to Lady Morgan.

BALTIMORE,
March 14, 1849.

MY DEAR LADY MORGAN,

I was most agreeably surprised by your letter of
the 17th February. I had heard and believed that you
were living in Dublin. You may be quite convinced
that I consider it a *bonne fortune pour moi* that you in-
habit London. To enjoy again your agreeable society

will be my tardy compensation for the long, weary, unintellectual years inflicted on me in this my dull native country, to which I have never owed advantages, pleasures or happiness. I owe nothing to my country; no one expects me to be grateful for the evil chance of having been born here. I shall emancipate myself, *par le grace de Dieu*, about the middle of July next; and I will either write to you before I leave New York or immediately after my arrival at Liverpool. I had given up all correspondence with my friends in Europe, during my vegetation in this Baltimore. What could I write about, except the fluctuations in the security and consequent prices of American Stocks. There is nothing here worth attention or interest, save the money market. Society, conversation, friendship, belong to older countries, and are not yet cultivated in any part of the United States which I have visited. You ought to thank your stars for your European birth; you may believe me when I assure you that it is only distance from republics which lends enchantment to the view of them. I hope that about the middle of next July I shall begin to put the Atlantic between the advantages and honours of democracy and myself. France, *je l'espère dans son intérêt* is in a state of transition, and will not let her brilliant society be put under an extinguisher *nommée la République*. The Emperor hurled me back on what I most hated on earth — my Baltimore obscurity; even that shock could not divest me of the admiration I felt for his genius and glory. I have ever been an imperial Bonapartiste *quand même*, and I do feel enchanted at the homage paid by six millions of voices, to his memory in voting an imperial President; *le prestige du nom* has, therefore, elected the

17*

Prince, who has my best wishes, my most ardent hopes
for an empire. I never could endure universal suffrage
until it elected the nephew of an emperor for the chief
of a republic; and I shall be charmed with *universal*
suffrage *once* more if it insists upon their President of
France becoming a monarch. I am disinterested personally. It is not my desire ever to return to France.

My dear Lady Morgan, do you know that having
been cheated out of the fortune which I ought to have
inherited from my late rich and unjust parent, I have
only ten thousand dollars, or two thousand pounds
English, which conveniently I can disburse annually.
You talk of my "*princely* income," which convinces me
that you are ignorant of the paucity of my means. I
have all my life had poverty to contend with, pecuniary difficulties to torture and mortify me; and but
for my industry, and energy, and my determination to
conquer at least a decent sufficiency to live on in Europe, I might have remained as poor as you saw me
in the year 1816.

I shall have much to tell you. Lamartine, and
Chateaubriand are giving their memoirs to the public.
The first *de son vivant*. I am now reading *Les Mé-
moires d'outre tombe*. I have no doubt that your memoirs would be infinitely better, more piquant, and
more natural. When I knew Lamartine he was chargé-
d'affaires from Charles X. Florence was then a charming place; I met him every night at parties. How little
did I foresee that he was to become a poetical republican, and that dear Florence was to be *travestie en République! ni l'un ne l'autre ne gagnera par le troc*.
Hoping that England may remain steady and faithful
to monarchical principles, that at least some refined

society may be left in the world, I shall, *Dieu permet-tant*, have the satisfaction of seeing you in the course of next summer.

I am, as ever,

My dear Lady Morgan,

Your affectionate and obliged friend,

E. PATTERSON.

May. — The death of my husband's and my own dear old friend, Horace Smith, has not the least shocked me, being long expected. He was my blessed Morgan's intimate friend — an intimacy founded on the singleness of their character, their pure and honest lives, and the similarity of their political and social opinions and habits. Gay, tender, kind, hospitable, and intellectual. I have known him since the first day of my marriage.

Death of Lord Jeffrey. Jeffrey gone! Oh, for the last, gay, classic evening he spent with us at our *Taudis*, in Grosvenor Place! How many bright and brilliant women who were with us that evening are gone now!

December 30. — Confined to my room; my maid reading to me *Shirley*, by the author of *Jane Eyre*. It is high-flown, and the talent factitious. Great force of style, great feebleness of action, incoherent in its working out; but original in its thinking.

CHAPTER XXI.

LADY MORGAN AND CARDINAL WISEMAN.

IN the early part of 1850 there was rather a lively discussion about abolishing the office of Lord Lieutenant of Ireland. It excited more vehemence and party spirit than the question was intrinsically worth. English people were inclined to think, that one real queen was enough for the United Kingdom and the colonies besides; but the Irish clung tenaciously to having a viceroy of their own to preside over the festivities of the Castle, and to give a "court circle" to their capital, and they saw in the reported measure, only one insult more from England. Lady Morgan was appealed to by persons on both sides of the question for her opinion. Her political judgment was considered good; and her experience of the old vice-regal times had given her a knowledge which made her opinion worth listening to. She wrote one or two "letters" on the subject, which are not to be found now. The question fell into speedy abeyance; and the Lord Lieutenant is still "to the fore." Lady Morgan's opinion was to abolish the office. This note from Mr. Hallam refers to one of her articles.

Mr. Hallam to Lady Morgan.

April 14, Friday Morning.

MY DEAR LADY MORGAN,

Yours is a sharp pen, and I hope it will never be directed against me, of which, indeed, I have no fears

whatever. What you say of old viceroys is, I fear,
true enough. Yet, in those times it was impossible to
dispense with them — the necessity ought now to be
at an end; though I am not master enough of the state
of Ireland to *pronounce absolutely* against their con-
tinuance. But you can make any case a good one
with wit or raillery.

Truly yours,   H. HALLAM.

The following pleasant note from Douglas Jerrold
refers to a *coup de patte* in *Punch*, where Lady Morgan
took her share of life's game of give and take. Jerrold's note would be a compensation for a much more
disagreeable dispensation. The only thing Lady Morgan could *not* forgive, was neglect!

PUTNEY.
June 9.

DEAR LADY MORGAN,

I was very sorry that I had promised my friend —
and all the world's friend — Mr. Paxton, to dine with
him at a dinner where he presides to-day; and so I
further miss the opportunity of personally avowing to
you my opinion of that smallest of the small, and dullest of the dull onslaughts upon your party. I had not
read it until I received yours; and I think *Punch* does
not often make such a blunder, for which he owes you
penitential reparation; but when he *does* blunder, he
does it with a courageous stupidity. The editor is one
of the best hearted of men, and will, I know, be annoyed when brought face to face with the absurdity.

Believe me, dear Lady Morgan,
Your old and early reader,
And therefore most truly yours,
DOUGLAS JERROLD.

Another note from Douglas Jerrold.

Douglas Jerrold to Lady Morgan.

WEST LODGE, PUTNEY,
December, 20.

DEAR LADY MORGAN,

The devil — the devil take him — brings me your hospitable summons for last night — here in the wilderness this morning! Next time, pray *do* remember — PUTNEY! Gibbon's Putney — Fairfax's Putney — Cromwell's Putney — the Marchioness of Shrewsbury's Putney (where she held her horse whilst Buckingham made her a widow) — Putney, with a hundred other pleasant associations, — and the Putney of its humblest inhabitant, but

Yours faithfully,
DOUGLAS JERROLD.

This year was also enlivened by a controversy between Lady Morgan and Cardinal Wiseman. Let any one who knew Lady Morgan imagine if she did not enjoy a pen-to-pen encounter with a great churchman on a statement made in her long-ago work on Italy! 1850 was, as the reader may or may not recollect, the date of the Papal Aggression; when England, for the first time since the Reformation, was adorned by a Cardinal. Public feeling ran high, and any *pièce de circonstance* was sure of meeting with readers. Lady Morgan, in her work on Italy, had said, concerning that relic of ancient upholstery, so carefully preserved in the Vatican — the Chair of St. Peter — "that the sacrilegious curiosity of the French broke through all obstacles to their seeing the chair of St. Peter. They actually removed its superb casket, and discovered the relic. Upon its mouldering and dusty surface were traced carvings, which bore the appearance of letters. The chair was quickly brought into a better light, the dust and cob-webs removed, and the inscription (for inscription it was) faithfully copied. The writing is in Arabic characters, and is the well-known confession of the Mahometan faith: '*There is but one God, and Mahomet is his Prophet.*' It is supposed that this chair had been, among the spoils of the Crusaders, offered to the Church at a time when a taste for antiquarian lore and the deciphering of inscriptions was not yet in fashion. This story has since been hushed up, the chair replaced, and none but the unhallowed remember the fact, and none but the audacious repeat it. Yet such there are even at Rome."

This statement Dr. Wiseman had contradicted in a pamphlet written about 1833, and it might for ever have remained in the limbo assigned to pamphlets which reach their regulation term of a nine day's life, if he had not been made a cardinal, and the bran new light from his title shone into the literary corners of "dusty death."

Whether Lady Morgan had ever before seen or heard of the pamphlet in question is doubtful. She says herself, "I know not what rank your Eminence then held in that Church, of which you are now so brilliant an illustration, on your way to the '*all-hail hereafter.*' It is a singular fact that I never saw this able attack of your Eminence on my work until *lately;* and so the thunders of the Vatican rolled over me innoxious. I heard, indeed, that a very learned diatribe had been written against my description of St. Peter's

chair; but I carelessly dismissed the subject with the
observation of a French wit —

'Que les gens d'esprit sont bêtes.'"

At any rate, the present occasion was too appropriate
to resist; an Irishman could as soon have refrained
from hitting a head at Donnybrook Fair, as Lady
Morgan have abstained from a tilt with a Roman
Catholic Church dignitary who had attacked a work
of hers, no matter how many years before. She wrote,
accordingly, a very lively *brochure* in her best style,
entitled *Letter to Cardinal Wiseman, in answer to his
remarks on Lady Morgan's statements regarding St.
Peter's Chair.* It had a great success, both because it
was amusing and because it was well-timed; and it
had a run of criticisms in all the newspapers and journals of the day; — *il faisait le frais* of *Punch*, both in
prose, and verse, and illustration, for several weeks;
and it was to Lady Morgan a return of the *beaux jours*
of her literary celebrity.

December 25. — Christmas day — my birthday;
another and another still succeeds.

December 27. — Lots of notes and notices of my
Letter to Cardinal Wiseman! It has had the run of
all the newspapers. *La petite vielle femme vit encore.*

Lady Morgan, from age and weakness, was unable
to be present on the 1st of May, 1851, at the opening
of the Crystal palace in Hyde Park. But she paid a
visit to that wonderful edifice early in June, and described the scene in a letter to her niece, under date
of June 20.

I am leading a very gay life, for I think with so

solitary a home as mine is, social excitement is almost
necessary for me. I am, thank goodness, in better
health than I have been for a long time. I will turn
to *mon livre des bénéfices* and give you the cream of
the day as it passed me, leaving the skim milk in
oblivion. First, Lady Beauchamp's grand majority
rout (where I only staid half an hour) the heat and
crowd was too much for me; but I had a "word and
a blow," with fifty of my particular friends — old
Rogers in the thick of the fight. *Next on my list*, on
the 24th a dinner at Wentworth Dilke's; dinner excellent; company, the Earls of Carlisle and Granville,
and all Her Majesty's commissioners for the Exhibition, and many other eminent persons — a charming
dinner. I must tell you of my visit to the Crystal
Palace the other morning, where I have permission to
go early, as I cannot encounter the crowd. It is impossible to convey an idea of the beauty of this miraculous building, *as I saw it*, in the bright sunshine
and freshness of the morning, all silent and solitary!
The fountains, flowers, statues and gold and silver
draperies, and heaps of jewels, sparkling in the sun
— a scene of magic, that one dreams of, but never till
now was created. Whilst I was lost in wonder and
admiration, and fixed in silent adoration of a beautiful
statue, I heard a slight movement of feet, and sweet
voices approaching me, — when lo! the whole royal
party issued from an adjoining compartment; the
Queen leaning on the arm of the King of the Belgians,
in animated conversation, — Prince Albert looking
both pleased and proud of this great and noble work.
The children, with their governess, and the whole
charming procession, preceded by our friend, Went-

worth Dilke, *chapeau bas!* I never saw so happy a
party — certainly, *la Reine est la plus grande Reine
du monde*, as my dear Madame de Sevigné said of
Le Roi, when he asked her to dance. The whole
scene was a fairy tale in the Arabian Nights, and had
for me a charm that I cannot explain; for there was
before me, IN THAT MOMENT, all that was greatest and
best, *visible and invisible*, and the sublime sun shining
down his rays on this beautiful creation of man!

On my return from this palace of the genii, a
charming Bohemian lady, Madame Noel, took me to a
matinée, given for the benefit of the distressed Hun-
garians, for which I had passed tickets and subscribed;
but it was a hot crowd with cold draughts. Fanny
Kemble recited the divine Allegro and il Penseroso.
It went to my very soul, where every line was im-
pressed half a century back; but I returned tired and
weary. Alas! I feel

"I am wearing away to the land of the leal."

Still my spirits keep me afloat, and I am good for —

"A few gay soarings yet."

Poor Rogers! I sat an hour with him the other day;
he is the ghost of his former ghost; he talked with
compassion of Moore's state, who is now bed ridden,
and has lost his memory, — remembers nothing but
some of his own early songs, which he sings as he lies,
and which is heartrending to hear by those who are
around him.

Moore lingered on a few months longer, and then
passed away. Before this event happened, a cata-
strophe which still retains its fascination for the public —

the burning of the Amazon — robbed Lady Morgan
of a younger friend. This terrible disaster is the topic
of the next letter.

Mrs. Gore to Lady Morgan.

HAMBLE CLIFF, SOUTHAMPTON,
January 9.

MY DEAR LADY MORGAN,

I do not often bore you with letters, because I
know it troubles you to read and answer them; but I
cannot resist my inclination to write and ask you a
question or two about poor Eliot Warburton, who, I
remember was a friend of yours. I am happy to say
I never even saw him; or a double pang would be
added to my grief for the poor Amazon. I had
watched all her experimental cruises, with much interest, and saluted her as she passed my lawn in
triumphant beauty this day week! On the evening
we received the news of her disaster, I sent off an
express, nine miles, to get a second edition of the
Times for the names of the passengers, and while my
messenger was gone, solaced myself by reading *Darien.*
I had just reached the chapter (at one in the morning)
of which the motto is from Shelley,

The thirsty fire crept round his manly limbs,
His resolute eyes were scorched to blindness soon,
His death-pang rent my heart!

when the groom returned with the sad list containing
poor Eliot Warburton's fated name!

I cannot tell you how deeply I was shocked. What
I want you to tell me is, whether he has left a wife
and children (as well as talented brothers), and whether

there was any *occasion* for him to cross the sea? which is, at this moment, looking as bright and beautiful under my windows as in one of Stanfield's pictures, and as if incapable of mischief. My house has been full of juvenile visitors for the Christmas holidays. My son and daughter hunt three days a week — the latter you may infer to be well and happy, for she is often ten hours a day in the saddle, which is the home her soul delights in. I am afraid you are not as much delighted as myself that one is no longer obliged to travel so far as Persia to witness a perfect despotism — the best of all possible governments; the only one where one's head feels quite safe on its shoulders, — till the day on which it is struck off. How I should like to see the press in England equally gagged: *The Times* sent to the Stone-Jug, and little Hayward to Cayenne! I am expecting Mr. Roebuck here to-day, and feel it necessary to let my Toryism explode before he arrives. I am also much rejoiced to see the mouldy old Whig cabinet crumbling away like a stale cake. It has done so little to advance the cause of civilisation, that I am fain to believe we should be better off under the most stringent of conservatisms, provided they do not employ Dizzy, who is a radical at heart. I am very much disappointed in his memoirs of Lord George. I expected the book would amuse one by a world of absurdities; instead of which, it is as full of common sense and dulness as his best friends could wish.

A propos of friends, have you seen anything of Mr. Hope? Baillie Cochrane was here lately, who told me he had paid him a visit in the new house; that Mrs. Hope did the honours in the most ladylike manner, and was covered to the chin in crape for Lady Beresford. She spoke very pretty broken English, and has quite *forgotten* she was ever a French woman. The little daughter will be one of the richest heiresses in England, and I dare say we shall live to see her marry a duke.

Do not take the trouble of answering me yourself; let one of your servants be your amanuensis, I have no doubt they all write quite as well as our Hampshire squires. My children are out with the Hambledon hounds, or they would place themselves at your feet, as well, dear Lady Morgan,

Yours sincerely,

C. F. GORE.

CHAPTER XXII.

DEATH OF MOORE.

THE diary resumes with the notice of Moore's death:

February 28. — On coming down, an hour back, to the drawing-room, *The Times* was lying on my writing-desk; I lighted on the death of the poet Moore. It has struck me home; I did not think I should ever shed tears again; but I have. The funeral attended only by strangers, to the neighbouring churchyard! Surely they will do something to honour his memory in Ireland! I will write on the subject to Saunders' *News Letter* and other papers.

March. — I have written to Mr. M'Garel, sending my contribution to the fund for the benefit of the school of poor Irish children; and I took the opportunity of suggesting that some monumental testimony to Moore, Ireland's greatest poet, should be raised in St. Patrick's cathedral, Dublin; and that no occasion for proposing it could be more aptly made than the celebration of the festival of St. Patrick.

The question of raising a monument to Moore in Dublin was at once taken up, and Lady Morgan was involved in correspondence on the choice of site and other particulars.

Lady Morgan to Mr. Mulvany.

WILLIAM STREET,
March 27.

Lady Morgan presents her compliments to Mr. Mulvany, and, in answer to his flattering note, begs to say, that any project for honouring the memory of their illustrious countryman Moore, cannot fail to interest her feelings or her pride, both as a personal friend and as an Irish woman. With respect to Mr. Mulvany's allusion to Lady Morgan's suggestion of a monumental tablet in St. Patrick's Cathedral (the Westminster Abbey of Ireland) it was only incidentally made in a note to one of the best patrons of the benevolent St. Patrick's School Society in London. For the rest, Lady Morgan presumes to say, that in the choice of a site, and the selection of a monumental testimonial, climate and money are necessary subjects of consideration; to "consult the genius of the place in all," is an old maxim of taste, and to have *some* regard to *financial* means, is an indispensable restraint upon national enthusiasm in Ireland. Lady Morgan has *lived*

to see so many "*emerald crowns*," national monuments,
tributary cenotaphs, and other such offerings decreed
to national merit by Irish gratitude through vocal ac-
clamation and on paper, which "no storied urn or animated bust," ever afterwards realised, that she now
ventures to suggest the necessity of first consulting
the funds collected for a consummation so devoutly to
be wished, before any decision is made as to the quality
of the testimonial. Lady Morgan humbly gives her
opinion, as Mr. Mulvany asked it, and will be happy
to contribute her very limited influence to the promo-
tion of that object, admirable in itself, and doubly con-
secrated as being decided under the classical roof of
Charlemont House, where all that was ever done "*wisest
and best*," was debated and carried into effect by that
illustrious Irishman under whose banner Ireland was
first led forth against a foreign invader, and taught to
resist domestic despotism, the father of the always
patriotic nobleman who is about to honour the meeting
by his presence.

This letter received a lively response. It was copied
into all the Dublin papers; and a meeting was called
at Charlemont House. It was suggested that the site
of the proposed statue should be Leinster Lawn, facing
Merrion Square.

Lady Morgan also wrote to Mrs. Moore:

Lady Morgan to Mrs. Moore.

WILLIAM STREET, ALBERT GATE,
May 27th, 1852.

MY DEAR MRS. MOORE,

In looking over some letters the other day, of the

year '46, I found a note of dear Mr. Moore's, which I
have copied and sent you, knowing how useful and
precious *even the most trifling* memorandum becomes,
when collecting materials for the life of an illustrious
person.   I do not like to part with the *autograph;*
though, if I had strength or sight, I am sure I should
find many of his little notes written in "Auld Lang
Syne," when he lived in the same gay circle in Dublin, and afterwards met in England, France and Italy.
He was a good deal with us in Florence.

I assure you, my dear Mrs. Moore, I rejoice to hear,
and from yourself, that you are so well circumstanced,
in a worldly point of view; and the *Memoirs*, edited by
Lord John Russell, will, I am sure, prove a *mine.*
And should business, connected with that most interesting publication, bring you to town, I shall be delighted to see you, in any way *most desirable to you.*
My house is small, but I can offer you a tidy little
bedroom, though rather *loftily* situated.

Mr. Rogers called here yesterday, but I was un-
luckily out. The last time I saw him, though very
helpless, he was in good force and spirits, and *narrated*
with his *usual precision* and accuracy.

I am, my dear Mrs. Moore,
Most truly yours,
SYDNEY MORGAN.

October 1. — Returned to town from my country
excursions. I had just come off my journey and was
lying stretched on the sofa in the drawing-room, very
dead and shattered, when I heard a voice, sharp and
Yankee, bullying my maid in the hall, for a free ad-
mittance; having, said the owner, come from America,

to see me, and was going back the next day. He told me that he was cousin to the American minister, whom he familiarly called "'Tom." I never was so bored in my life. My face was dirty, my clothes dusty, my voice husky; I was sulky as a bear; and no doubt I shall see myself, *en longue et en large*, some of these fine days in some American journal, under the head of "An Hour at Lady Morgan's."

My house is greatly improved — looks beautiful in its fresh green paint, but I am more inclined to my inclined plane, a sofa at home, than to gaieties; I am so completely "used up," or, as Madame de Sevigné says — *Je suis affamée pour le silence* — for I am made to talk my life away at these charming country houses.

October 5. — Dined at Lady Talbot de Malahide's; met there the Rajah of Courg, an amiable barbarian, or rather a specimen of the early creation. He played on the fiddle, and gave us "Rule Britannia," to show his allegiance to England.

November 3. — I have missed my beautiful Irish seal with my Irish harp on it; I am astonished and do not know what to think. I have had it thirty years. It has been taken off my bunch of seals, which lies on my Pompadour.

November 4. — My whole nervous system has been upset, by the discovery that I have had a FELON living in my house for the last three weeks. Dr. Ferguson made the discovery. He came to tell me, last night, too late to stir in the business — and such a night as I passed! Locked up; my maid and myself, and had a bell at my window ready to ring it. The felon was my servant, McDonald. An accident revealed to him

18*

that measures were being taken to get rid of him. He gave my maid to understand as much, and suddenly took himself off without further trouble. Revelations have come to light which prove that he belonged to a party or gang who get into gentlemen's houses by false characters, to which they affix seals, stolen like mine. I dismiss this disagreeable subject with this remark, that it is impossible to describe the dangers and annoyances to which single women are exposed.

November 18. — The Duke's funeral. — A melodramatic exhibition in the very worst style, in which there was but one noble feature, — the peace, order, and respect, as well as the respectability of the people. We saw the procession from the windows of the Vice Chancellor's house, next door to Apsley House. We had a most sumptuous entertainment afterwards — not the display of "funeral baked meats," but a very *recherché* repast. All London was eating and carousing, and the whole thing was in the spirit of an Irish wake. I hope we shall have no more heroes to bury for a thousand years.

In the last days of November I was struck by the most serious illness I have ever had, but I have been carried through by skill, care, and affection. Dr. Ferguson attended me daily for nearly a month. He has been the successor to poor Dr. Chambers, to my gratitude and confidence. Both are noble specimens of the noblest profession.

August, 1853. — Went to Bognor for my *villegiatura*; a most disagreeable place.

Fiction has nothing more pathetic than that great melodramatic tragedy now performing on the shores of Ireland, — *The Celtic Exodus*. The Jews left a foreign country — a "house of bondage;" but the Celtic exodus is the departure of the Irish emigrants from the land of their love — their inheritance — and their traditions — of their passions and their prejudices; with all the details of wild grief and heart-rending incidents — their ignorance of the strangers they are going to seek — their tenderness for the objects they are leaving behind. Their departure exceeds in deep pathos all the poetical tragedy that has ever been presented on the stage, or national novelists have ever depicted in their volumes.

Left Bognor. Returned to London in September. A long night of blindness and suffering, from the first week in September to the month of March following, when the dawn of light, health, and comfort once more broke upon me.

CHAPTER XXIII.

FALL OF THE LEAVES.

THE entries in the journal and the letters grow scantier as we proceed. Lady Morgan's life had few changes or vicissitudes; friend after friend departed; but she steadily refused to mourn.

The first entry is: —

Poor Charles Kemble! I knew the whole dynasty of the Kembles, from King John downwards; Charles was the last and best of the whole stock — beautiful, graceful, gallant, and a very fine gentleman; such he was when I first knew him.

July. — Silvio Pellico is dead.

During our delightful residence on the Lake of Como, the Villa Fontana was frequented by some of the most illustrious men in Lombardy. Confalonieri, Count Porro, Count Pecchio, and the charming women of their family. Silvio Pellico was the delight of all; he was then all poetry. Many a moonlight night he passed with us in a gondola on the lake, while Pecchio sang to his guitar and the others joined in one of their sweet *canzone*. He was a great favourite with my dear Morgan.

The poor Pellico on his deliverance from prison entered into the *travaux forcés* of the old, bigoted Marchesa Baralo. His great merits, his glowing imagination were gone; the most elegant of poets, the most free-thinking of philosophers, became a melancholy monk, and earned shrift by the utter prostration of his intellect.

September 2. — Moore Park. A sort of hospital for odds and ends. Since I arrived here, a month this day, I have been charmed with everything, *en gros et en détail*. I have an obituary already. Abbott Lawrence, my most kind and hospitable host is gone. Poor old Colburn gone too — my brilliant advertiser and publisher of thirty years! one who could not take his tea without a stratagem. He was a strange *mélange* of meanness and munificence in his dealings. There was a desperate vengeance that had more of the jealousy of love than the resentment of business in his attempt to destroy my fame and fortune when I went to Messrs. Saunders and Otley with my second *France*. We had a last quarrel about the cheap edition of my novels two months ago. I read of his death in the papers. I wish that we had *parted friends*.

Another death! — General Pepe is dead at Turin, at the age of seventy-two — one of the noblest men in the contemporary history of modern Italy.

I am getting up memorials for a history of Moore Park and its many associations. Sir William Temple, Swift, Stella, &c. Shall I ever get it finished?

November. — In the beginning of September I went to Llanover on a visit to Sir Benjamin and Lady Hall. The gardens there are always in their full beauty in the autumn.

I went thence to Stamford Hall, Leicestershire, to pay one more visit to my dear and venerable friend, the Baroness Braye, and her charming daughter, Catherine, Countess of Beauchamp.

I arrived there very ill, with a severe attack of bronchitis. Nothing could exceed their kindness. I left Stamford Hall and my dear friends with the intention of proceeding to Combermere Abbey.

Lady Braye's last words to me were to intreat that I would keep away as long as I could from the fogs of London. But I found myself so unwell on the railway, that is, my eyes so painful, that I proceeded on to London, and found my house more comfortable and pretty than ever. No high stairs! no long galleries and their draughts! and in short, I was *at home*. And so ends my *villegiatura* of the autumn of 1855.

Lady Morgan remained at William Street for the Christmas holidays, surrounded by attached and admiring friends, and drawing to her pleasant drawing-room all the young men who were just gaining public notice by their talents or adventures. Among the correspondents who held to her most loyally was the Earl of Carlisle, then lord-lieutenant of Ireland. One of his letters runs: —

DUBLIN CASTLE,
January 31, 1856.

MY DEAR LADY MORGAN,

How kindly you have written to me. Malahide was indeed full to me of pleasant, though mixed, memories, and I am sure you will not think the vivid historian of its storied site was omitted from them. It appeared to me a great change from former times, when we rollicked on oysters, and barristers sang treasonable songs. Now, we talked of archæology, and looked at old porcelain. The portrait-gallery has received additions. I thought Dublin smiled very graciously on my levee and drawing-room, and my health has not, as yet, at all repined at my splendid captivity in the Castle, and we are to have Grecian theatricals, and an amateur opera, got up by Lady Downshire, and mainly indebted to Mrs. Geale.

Your imperial city is full of a more serious drama. I am sure you are too good a friend to the humanities of every kind not to be a sincere well-wisher to peace.

Macaulay is not in power at the Castle of Tyrconnel, as you may well guess. Have you good authority for the striking speech you recounted to me of the Duchess to James, after the Boyne?

Now, dear lady, I must leave you, for — the Lord Mayor!

Ever gratefully yours,

CARLISLE.

Lady Morgan, like a true Irish woman, clung to her family. The great relations of Clasagh na Valla, had a peculiar interest for her, not only on account of her own recollections of her visit to Longford House, before she had become famous, but also because she thought the Croftons a creditable family to belong to. She wrote to Sir Malby Crofton, challenging the renewal of her ancient acquaintance, and claiming her kinship — here is her letter.

Lady Morgan to Sir Malby Crofton.

11, WILLIAM STREET,
ALBERT GATE, BELGRAVIA,
March 5, 1856.

MY DEAR SIR MALBY,

Maclean, the publisher of a portrait of mine, showed me lately a list of the subscribers' names, among whom the one that most gratified me, was YOURS! You, probably, scarcely remember a girl with (what in Irish we call) a Cathath head, and a very nimble foot at crossing a ford and dancing an Irish jig, or taking a game of romps out of "little Malby;" but *she* can never forget days so happy and so careless, and which furnished forth the details of the *Wild Irish Girl*, — the progenitress of her own little fame and fortune! Still living on amid all these pleasant impressions, I cannot resist writing you a few lines, not only to recal myself to your memory, but to set at rest all my traditional *shanaos* of the Crofton family. I found my claim on your attention by a fact of which perhaps you are not aware — that I have the distinction of being the grand-daughter of one who had the honour to be a daughter of the house of Crofton! Sydney Crofton Bell, in her time celebrated for her poetical and musi-

cal talents, and bearing the Irish cognomen of *Clasagh
na Valla* — "the Harp of the Valley"; from this
gifted individual has been derived whatever talent
has distinguished her descendants for three genera-
tions. She threw her Irish mantle over us, and though
somewhat the worse for the wear (as Irish mantles
generally are!), it has stood us all in good stead. Your
own amiable and distinguished grandmother, my dear
Lady Crofton, the friend and protectress of my own
early life, and one of the noblest creatures I ever
knew, always acknowledged the Irish cousinship, of
which I am as proud as I am of my relationship with
Oliver Goldsmith, though his illustrations were not
of such genealogical distinction as the descendants of
the *friend* of the Earl of Essex, who founded your
family. If you admit the "propinquity of kin," dear
Sir Malby, I should be much gratified. Now, tell me,
dear Sir Malby, why, in *Burke's Peerage*, they date
your baronetage only from 1838? *Time immemorial*
your grandfather Malby was always titled. I had heard
there was some forfeiture "in the time of the troubles!"
Why, too, was the ancient seat of the family called
Longford? had it not an Irish name? and *what* name?
Is the old chapel standing? or the original Crofton
apple trees, that were brought over to Ireland in the
time of Queen Elizabeth? Well, I will *bother* you no
more with my antiquarian questions, but in conclusion
only say, that if you or any of your family should
come to London, and will try my "tap," at the sign
of the *Irish Harp*, you will meet with "cead mille
falthœ" from, dear Sir Malby,

Yours very sincerely,
SYDNEY MORGAN.

Sir Malby Crofton to Lady Morgan.

LONGFORD HOUSE,
BELTRA COLLOONEY,
March 22, 1858.

MY DEAR LADY MORGAN,

Accept my best thanks for your kind letter, to which various engagements have prevented my giving an earlier reply.

Believe me, it is our house which should be proud of a kinswoman who, having fought her way to fame, as you have, is willing to remember her friends of "long ago," even to the romps with "little Malby," who, for his part recollects well, one whose name has been a household word at Longford. You desire a history of the Crofton's since you were among us; it would be tedious to any one else; should it prove so to you, you must only confess that you provoked it. To begin with the title. It was discovered, some time after my grandfather's death, by the *Herald at Arms*, that we were descended from the *next brother* of the *first* baronet, and not from the first baronet himself, to whose male *issue* that patent limited the title. This was a great trouble to us at Longford, and a surprise to the whole family, among whom there never had been any doubt as to my grandfather's right to the title; but there was no help for it, and after an effort to obtain a revival of the original grant, my father had to put up with a new patent, so that now, although I am the acknowledged head of a family numbering in it one baron, and, including Lord Crofton's baronetcy, three baronets, my title dates later than any of the others. You are too *Irish* to laugh at this trifle being deemed a grievance; but here, by the shores of the

Atlantic, where little questions of precedence still at times arise, it was unpleasant, to say the least, to be obliged to make way for those who ought, as they used, to follow us.

My father died six years ago. I myself have *left* to me three sons and three daughters.

Now for the Longford estates. Longcuth, I believe, is the Irish for it. When this latter passed into Longford, I am unable to discover; but am disposed to think that the first Crofton possessor changed the name — so much for the name. The estate itself is the same as it was, — very large. Since the troubles of 1668, we have not parted with an acre of it, nor are we likely to do so. Thanks to the Encumbered Estate Court, which gave every facility for selling Irish estates when, from the *condition of the country* they were *least valuable; many* an ancient family has been *pressed* out of *home* and *fortune.* One family (some of the members of which you must have known) the Percivals, of Temple House, in this county, must, I fear, transfer to strangers an estate which they acquired by intermarriage with us; but God, who gave us the property (you remember the motto "Dat deus incrementum"), still permits the Croftons of Longford to hold their own. They do little more, however, than hold their own, for the family exchequer has never been full enough to rebuild the house, the scene, dear Lady Morgan, of our romps, which was burned down in my father's time; but though the old house is a ruin, there has grown up beside it, by little and little, a house reasonably large and comfortable. That would be a welcome day to it, and its *inhabitants*, on which you would come and visit us; you would find the chapel as in your youth, and beside it, the home of *Friar* John Crofton "Comitisque flavicomæ," the companion which good-natured people represent to have been a fox — the ill-natured, as a *nymph*, with golden hair.

Time has eaten away the trunks of the Longford pearmain, the original Crofton apple; and it is said, but I don't believe it, that with the decay of the original stocks, the apple has universally degenerated.

If ever I have the opportunity, the "Irish Harp" may rely upon a call; but as I seldom leave home, I will, for this once act, if you will permit me, by deputy. Should my son and his bride be in London in June, as is probable, I promise he shall pay his respects to you, and I trust you may esteem him worthy of the ancient stock. Grateful of your kind recollection of me and mine,

Believe me, dear Lady Morgan,
Very sincerely yours,
M. CROFTON.

Early in February had appeared a volume of Rogers's *Table Talk*, which had set the critics of society at war. The indecency of hurrying into print with anecdotes and sayings which could not fail to offend living persons, even before the hatchments were down, or the table at which the jests had been made, was sold, struck every one. Soon, the voice of protest echoed through the journals. Among those who felt themselves most aggrieved were the daughters and friends of Madame Piozzi. For many weeks, the *Athenæum* contained this sparkling controversy, in which Lady Morgan joined with her usual liveliness. From her private correspondence with the connections of Madame Piozzi on this scandal, the following letters are selected: —

BALSOVER CASTLE, CHESTERFIELD,
June 19, 1836.

DEAR MADAM,

I take the liberty of addressing you on the subject of our common correspondence with the editor or author of Rogers's Table Twaddle.

There never was anything more false than that my dear old friend, Viscountess Keith, and her sister, Miss Thrale, and her late sister, Mrs. Meyrick Hoare, refused to be reconciled to their mother. On the contrary, as soon as Mr. and Mrs. Piozzi returned from their wedding tour of four or five years on the Continent, Lady Keith and her two younger sisters, then fine, handsome girls, fresh from school, made a point of soliciting a renewal of intercourse. And Lady Keith has often related to me their first meeting, which was a very curious one, at Mrs. Piozzi's own house, and after that Lady Keith, who had a very handsome establishment, gave Mr. and Mrs. Piozzi many good dinners, and thereby aggravated Piozzi's gout, — Piozzi, of whom Lady Keith always speaks very kindly.

Long after Miss Thrale's marriage with Lord Keith, Mrs. Piozzi died, and Lady Keith went from Tulliallan, in Scotland, to Bath, to attend her death-bed. It is very unfair to bring such stories forward, which are

calculated to annoy two excellent old ladies — I say
two, because there never was any question of reconciliation with the youngest, Mrs. Mostyn, *who lived with
her mother* until her marriage, which, by-the-way, was
a run-a-way one.   Old Rogers ought to have known
better than to circulate such false trash; for he was at
one time intimate, and was, indeed, an admirer, if not
a suitor, to one of the younger Miss Thrales.

I could have given the editor of the Twaddle a
much more pleasing anecdote of old Rogers than any
of those in his book. About nine years ago, a letter
containing bills which I had signed, amounting to up-
wards of two thousand pounds, was not received by
my steward, to whom I had addressed it. It was
found, a month after, safe at the bottom of the dead-
letter box, in the post-office of Glasgow, having been
oddly mistaken for a valentine. However, for some
weeks I was in great alarm, and I called on Rogers,
with whom I had, for some time, been acquainted, to
ask his advice, as he also, shortly before, had the misfortune to have bills to a very large amount abstracted
from his bank. After very kindly telling me how he
thought I ought to proceed under my supposed loss,
he went on to say (and here his face became quite
beaming with benevolence and satisfaction) that as soon
as *his* loss became known, he received offers of pecuniary aid and credit to any amount, from hosts and
hosts of friends, amongst the highest character, station,
and rank in England — men from whom he little expected such proofs of disinterested regard. He added,
that his opinion of human nature had, from that day,
been immeasurably improved. This is, I think, a more
pleasant anecdote than any contained in the Table

Twaddle, and on that account I beg you to pardon this long letter.

> I have the honour to be,
>> Dear Madam,
>>> Very truly yours,
>>>> JOHN HAMILTON GRAY.

Mrs. Mostyn to Lady Morgan.

SILLWOOD LODGE,
Tuesday.

Would that I were near you, dearest Lady Morgan, to accept your agreeable invitation of a chat between four and six: but there is always a reaction in our society at Brighton. After our winter season is ended, we begin again with fresh friends, who stay till Easter; and I have not the moral courage to leave them to an empty house.

The *Athenæum* confirms one's opinion of the editor of Rogers's *Table Talk*. As far as I am concerned, they are all wrong. Being but a child of nine years old on my mother's return to England, I was taken home to Streatham, and brought up an opposition child, living with her and dear Piozzi until I was married, in 1795.

On that occasion the reconciliation took place, and I then saw my three sisters for the first time; my mother must have been about sixty, and she always called them "the ladies."

These are not important events to bring before the public; and Rogers appears to have talked very little of Streatham, considering he lived there so much in my time; but he never *was* a talker. I have many letters, or had, and now possess his proposal of marriage to me at *thirteen*, with my impertinent caricature of him, and old Murphy calling me a saucy girl.

Excuse an abrupt conclusion to this family gossip, dear Lady Morgan, for I have a long dinner table to-day, and my head full of domestic cares.

Very sincerely yours,

Dear Lady Morgan,

C. M. MOSTYN.

CHAPTER XXIV.

PASSING AWAY.

AN interesting notice of Lady Morgan's old house at Drumcondra occurs in a letter from her brother-in-law, Sir Arthur Clarke.

Sir Arthur Clarke to Lady Morgan.

TUESDAY,
May 19, 1857.

MY DEAREST SYDNEY,

José and I have just returned from taking a sketch of Drumcondra House, and inclose some flowers, out of your old garden, which is in great preservation. The house is now the post office, kept by a Mr. Heith, and his wife remembers two ladies some years ago calling to see the house; — one was Lady Morgan, and the other was Lady Clarke. José will send you the sketch when finished, and it will look beautiful. Tell little Syd. I received her letter this morning, and that I will write to her in a day or two.

I overheard two gentlemen in the United Service Club yesterday talking of your *matinée*. One said, he had often seen the Miss Owensons in Enniskillen, that he knew their father intimately, and that he was a handsome man; had the heart of a gentleman, the looks of a gentleman, and the manners of a gentleman; and that he also knew Dr. Burroughs, the author of *The Night before Larry was Stretched*.

Ever yours affectionately,
A. C. CLARKE.

A letter to Lady Morgan from her niece, Mrs. Inwood Jones, gives a description of the inauguration of Moore's statue, about which Lady Morgan was much interested, and which she had been the first to suggest.

Mrs. Inwood Jones to Lady Morgan.

DUBLIN,
October 17, 1857.

DEAREST LADY MORGAN,

Your last letter was so *beautifully* written, that it put me *quite out*, and I could not read it! It is too bad, after devoting the *best part* of my life to deciphering your dear old hieroglyphics, to be at this time of day treated to a common place, plain hand writing, that *any one* can read. Well, let it pass; and now for my news. The inauguration of Moore's statue was a curious sight; and I believe that in no town in Europe could there have been another like it. Conceive a *mob* of, I should think, six thousand persons, collected, *perfectly* well disposed, and I must say, *far* more *civil* and courteous than an *English* mob, for José and I *passed* through it (being separated from our gentlemen) without the *slightest* annoyance or pressure. We were at last discovered by Papa, who, in his capacity of steward of the committee, marshalled us up, with his long white wand of office, to seats near Lady Charlemont and Lord Carlisle. Conceive all this in the open streets, the gentlemen with their hats off, and the ladies in the most charming of light dresses. The speeches were all spoken from the little circle, of which Lord Carlisle was the centre. Lord Charlemont spoke with feeling and good taste; Lord Carlisle's speech was all poetry and pathos, and was charmingly delivered; his quotations from Moore's beautiful verses were very apposite; and of course he was enthusiastically applauded, for his speech did honour to his *heart* as well as his head, which you know always goes a great way with us in Ireland. But the speaker of the day, out and out *for eloquence* and *extraordinary* oratorical powers (such as I never heard, and could only imagine Grattan's or Curran's to have been) was Mr. O'Hagans's! It was perfectly astounding. Now I understand what is called *Irish eloquence*. The immense flow of *words* of the *best* language, gave one the idea that his *imagination* was *overflowing*. It was extraordinary. I think, with all this, he would have no success in our English house of parliament; and that men would go to sleep on the benches with the word "*bosh*" on their lips, and they would not be altogether wrong.

The Lord Mayor said his *petit mot* with the richest of Irish brogues, and with a simplicity that brought us all down from Moore's pedestal (where the great orators had left us) to the *shop* in *Grafton Street*. He created a deal of merriment amongst the mob, who encouraged him with sundry "Don't be frightened, my

19*

boy," and "spake out like a man." When all this was over, and the statue uncovered, I could not help thinking that it was the least inspiring object I ever saw. It is almost *grotesque*, and might be any one else than little Moore. The crowd dispersed in perfect good humour. The tops of houses, the roofs of the Bank and College, and lamp posts, were all crowded with spectators. It was really a *very* curious scene, and I was glad to witness it. And now good bye, dear, for I am quite tired after the Powerscourt *fête* of *fêtes*, from which we did not get home till five o'clock this morning, of which I shall tell you in my next.

S. L. J.

Lady Morgan sustained a great sorrow in the November of this year. Sir Arthur Clarke, her friend and brother, died in Dublin, of bronchitis, after a very short illness. To the last he was active, alert, and genial. He had taken great interest in the progress of the "Odd Volume," and in the preparation for her Memoirs, which he had hoped to assist in arranging. He had been the best and truest of her friends, and the most ardent of her admirers. His death was a great shock to Lady Morgan, and she never ventured to speak of it. It was a sorrow that seemed to resume in itself all her other griefs, for he was connected with the memories of her early Dublin life, — with her father, with her sister, with her niece, Olivia (so early dead), with her husband; — and when he was taken away, all her ties with the past were broken. Her niece, again a widow, was settled near her; but Lady Morgan's standing point in life was rapidly crumbling away. Of all who had begun their career with her

and who had held friends in common, hardly one
remained.

Lady Morgan's life passed on with an even tenor,
she never allowed grief to appear, but when alone she
was subject to great depression of heart. She endeavoured all the more to find pleasure in the comforts
and society that surrounded her, although her new
friends could not invest themselves with the charms of
old times and early associations. There was nothing
old or infirm about Lady Morgan, nor was there any
decay of faculty or dimness of intelligence; her vitality
seemed unquenchable. The preparation of the *Odd
Volume* was an amusement to her. Early in the year
1858 she had an attack of bronchitis, but she threw it
off. A note from Sir William Napier refers to this
period of sickness: —

Sir William Napier to Lady Morgan.

SCINDE HOUSE,
January 26, 1858.

MY DEAR LADY MORGAN,

Having heard that you were ill, I enquired, not at
your house, but of your friends, and was told that you
had got over the attack. Grieved I am to find from
your note that you still suffer. My only excuse, and it
is a real one, for not having called upon you, is extreme feebleness; not of vitality, but of limb; I can
scarcely get across a room, and pain is constant as
well as severe.

Believe me to be with most sincere wishes for your
immediate restoration to health, your devoted servant
in spirit; in flesh I cannot be any person's servant, —
at least I should be a very unprofitable one, being

only fit for "Worms, brave Percy!" They, indeed, with respect to me, are like the young Irishman who proposed for a lady of fortune; and being asked what *his* fortune was, answered, that he has no actual one, but had *great expectations* — from the lady.

W. NAPIER.

P.S. — As to your "*turning to stone*," if you *ever do*, it will be a pumice stone, covered with magic words.

Later in this year, Lady Morgan had another and more severe attack of bronchitis, which was of longer duration than any of her previous illnesses, and gave rise to serious fears of a fatal termination. But she struggled through it, and recovered, to all appearance, her former health. Nothing could exceed the kindness and attention lavished upon her by her friends, nor the care and skill of Dr. Ferguson and Mr. Hunter. When she recovered sufficiently, she went to Sydenham a short time for change of air, and returned to London as bright as ever.

December 25, 1858, was Lady Morgan's last birthday. She assembled a few of her old friends at dinner, and did the honours with all the *verve* and brilliancy of her brightest days. She told stories and anecdotes with delicate finesse and drollery; and after dinner she sang a comic song, because as she said, being written by a Church dignitary, it could be nothing but good words; so she sang "The Night before Larry was Stretched," in a style that was inimitable. At her age, "many happy returns of the day" could not be looked for; but none of those then with her felt it too sanguine to look forward to at least "*one* cheer more;" but this Christmasday proved to be the very last.

CHAPTER XXV.

THE END.

THE first entry in her diaries for 1859 relates to the *Odd Volume*, which she had prepared for the press with all the enthusiasm of a young author. Her spirits and energy, her power of doing hard work, was undiminished from what it had been in girlhood. After working all the morning, from the moment she awoke to two in the afternoon — her dinner hour — and sending the friend who worked with her, home, completely tired out, Lady Morgan dressed for the day, and seated herself on her small green sofa in the drawing-room, as fresh as a lark, ready to receive visitors, to tell and to hear the newest gossip of the day, and she frequently had a large party in the evening, till she retired at last, declaring "she was dead."

January 1. — This day my *Odd Volume*, probably my last, made its appearance in the world, *l'enfant de ma viellesse.* I lingered over the idea of writing a preface. Starting up one morning, I called to my maid to give me pen and ink, and dashed it off; and so it went uncorrected, and is not the worst morsel I have written. This *esquisse* has a success more universal and cheerful than ever attended any of my works.

A letter to Lady Combermere shows no signs of failing health or strength.

Lady Morgan to Lady Combermere.

DEAREST LADY,

Be all that constitutes a merry Christmas and happy
new year laid at your feet for your gracious acceptance,
if you please to accept such "tag rag, and bob tail,"
the rubbish of times old and monastic. I only wish
I could lay myself on a sofa beside you. That
charming *commérage* which only you know how to
sustain! I will not dwell on the recent melancholy
events of this season of sorrow, carried on in the
midst of storms and fogs, of mists and misery, with
death waylaying the young and beautiful, the loving
and loved, the happy and prosperous; but it is wonderful in calamity! Of the many distinguished men who
gathered round my supposed death-bed *last year*, three
have already gone before me! I am getting so blind
I must stop.

Well; my life-wearing task is done — my book, I
believe; ready for publication; but why not published
I know not; its title is impertinently changed by
Bentley. Miss Jewsbury gone to the bosom of her
family! *chemin faisant*, to the glories of Combermere
Abbey, Mrs. Jones off to hers, and I am (or have been)
"left and abandoned by my velvet friends," to a
degree unexampled in the history of human vicissitudes.
London is a desert,

"Silent, oh Moina, is the roar of thy waters,"

and I am literally left "the last woman," looking out
in vain for the last man! At last he turns up! It is
the Duke of Wellington, on his way from Strathfieldsay
to Windsor; others drop in, and so the sun shines upon

me again; and now I await some occurrence to con-
clude this dull note. Yours, dear Lady Combermere,
with my most respectful regards to the Field-Marshal
de cœur et de corps.

SYDNEY MORGAN.

On the 17th of March, St. Patrick's Day, Lady
Morgan had a musical morning party, — all that was
best and brightest at that time in London were gathered
under her roof. Lady Morgan looked as likely for
life as she had done any time for the last six years,
and no one anticipated that the breaking-up was so
near. One week after this gay celebration of her
patron saint's *fête*, Lady Morgan caught cold. At first,
it did not seem serious.

This letter, dictated by her, and addressed to Lady
Combermere, was the last she wrote: —

Lady Morgan to Lady Combermere.

April 11, 1859.

MY DEAR LADY COMBERMERE,

Your letters are always to me fresher than flowers,
without their fading so soon. I am still confined to
my bedroom and all the tiresome accompaniments of a
sick room. My cough and breathing very troublesome,
yet, upon the whole, Dr. Ferguson and Mr. Hunter say
I am progressing most wonderfully towards health.
As to food and nourishment, I have two *detectives*
(yourself and Lady Braye) continually watching me,
and I must "move on." Nothing is wanting, but the
"*nosebag*," (recommended by Lady Combermere) to
fill up the interval of eating and drinking — a most

capital idea, which nobody but yourself would think of, and worthy of my adoption. I think Ferguson will be rather surprised at finding me *muzzled* in green satin to-day, "by order of Lady Combermere." So much for self, and now for "that fool the public." Yesterday's report of the resignation of ministers I have not yet heard confirmed; but suppose it is true. Mr. Lowe resigns his pretensions to Kidderminster, and seeks a more admiring constituency.

> I am, yours, &c.,
> SYDNEY MORGAN.

Although she was now very ill, neither Dr. Ferguson, who had attended her in all her illnesses, nor Mr. Hunter, her ordinary medical attendant, feared a fatal termination: they had seen her recover from more dangerous attacks. But the scene was drawing to a close. On the morning of the 16th of April she seemed rather better; she called for her desk and papers, and began to write a letter on business; but although her mind was lucid and vigorous, her bodily powers were fading away; and on the entrance of her doctor, she reluctantly gave up her pen. Painful attacks of spasmodic breathing came on, and at the end of a fierce struggle for breath, she said to her niece, who was supporting her, "Sydney, is this death?" She saw and spoke to an old friend who came to see her in the afternoon. She then lay still, speaking occasionally, and with increased difficulty, but with gratitude, for the attention shown to her to the last by those she most loved and valued.

She met her end patiently and with perfect simplicity. She died on the evening of the 16th of April, 1859.

She was interred in the Brompton cemetery, where a tomb, executed by Mr. Sherrard Westmacott, has been erected to her memory, by her niece.

CHAPTER XXVI.

CONCLUSION.

LADY MORGAN'S house was the resort of all who were the best worth knowing in London society, and she had the art of drawing out all the best faculties of those who came to her. She herself had become a name connected with the past — a tradition of times, and manners, and events, which had been historical. Her own conversation was to the last hour brilliant and fascinating as it ever had been, not a shadow had fallen over the sparkling wit and grace of her stories and *bon mots*. The sarcastic severity of tongue, which had made her formidable to friends and foes in early life, softened greatly during the later years of her life. She used to say, that it was only the *young* who were pitiless in their judgment of others, and when she heard any one saying bitter things against another, she would say, "Ah ma chère ne vous chargez pas des haines." At the severest, her sarcasm had been always light and airy — it shared the harmlessness of hard words, in that "it broke no bones," — it glanced off the object, and did not burn into the feelings or rest upon the memory. Lady Morgan was always a true, steady, and zealous friend to those she cared for, and had a singular faculty for attaching her servants to her; she interested herself in their welfare, and treated them with invariable courtesy and respect; during her illness, their affectionate attentions had been those of attached relatives rather than servants; they had all lived many years in her service. She had the courage to tell her friends the truth when it was needful; she was essentially sincere, though not always consistent, for she never troubled herself to reconcile the opinion she might have expressed one year with that which she held another; she said what she thought and felt at the moment, and left discrepancies to take care of themselves. With all her frank vanity she had shrewd good sense, and she valued herself much more on her *industry* than on her genius, because the one she said "she owed to her organisation, but the other was a virtue of her own rearing."

Perhaps no other woman ever received so much flattery, or had such brilliant and tangible success; both as a woman and an author, she seems to have had a larger portion of the good things of this life than generally falls to the lot of the daughters of Eve. Her prosperity was almost unclouded during her long life. The death of her husband, her sister, and her favourite niece, within a short period of each other, was her share of affliction, and she felt it deeply.

She was not afraid of death; but she disliked the idea of dying very much. Often when looking round her pretty room, she would say, "I shall be very sorry to leave all these things and the friends who have been so kind to me — the world has been a good world to me."

Lady Morgan was not a woman to be judged by ordinary rules. She was the last type of a class long passed away; she belonged to another time and mode of thought altogether; she was like the French women of the old *régime* to whom society was the only condition in which they could exist, who would go to a ball or a hunting party when in the last stage of mortal sickness; who would insist on being attired in full dress on the day of their death, and who would not die except surrounded by their circle and doing the honours of a *salon* to the last. Oddly enough, clergymen were very fond of her society, and she used to tell, with great fun a whimsical incident, *à propos* to this. She had written a note to a dignitary of the Church, a very old friend, addressing him as her "dear father confessor," saying, to pique his curiosity, "come to me — I want to have a talk with you." He was from home and the note went to his curate, who took it *au sérieux*, thinking his rector could only be sent for professionally. He went to her house, and gravely said "that as his rector was out of town, he came to see her ladyship, and if she had any thing upon her mind, he would be happy to give her his best advice." Of course he was soon disabused of his mistake; but the drollest part of the story was the indignation of her maid, who, when she was told what had passed, drew herself up and said with scorn, "As if your ladyship had wished to confess, you would open your mind to a *curate!*"

Lady Morgan kept her faculty of enjoyment to the

last; she had as much pleasure in her books, music, and society, as in her youth. She loved the young, and was always charming with them. She said that, "living with the young kept her young."

END OF VOL. III.

INDEX.

20*

* The reader is requested to substitute the correct form of Pückler
for "Pucklen" a mistake which has slipped into our text from the London
edition.

THE END.

PRINTING OFFICE OF THE PUBLISHER.

Tauchnitz Edition.

Latest Volumes:

3199. Hilda Strafford and The Remittance Man. By Beatrice Harraden.

3200/1. Phroso. By Anthony Hope.

3202. A Haunt of Ancient Peace. By Emma Marshall.

3203/4. The Massarenes. By Ouida.

3205. Trooper Peter Halket of Mashonaland. By Olive Schreiner.

3206/7. A Foreigner. By E. Gerard (Madame de Laszowska).

3208. The Money-Spinner, etc. By Henry Seton Merriman & S. G. Tallentyre.

3209. A Child of the Jago. By Arthur Morrison.

3210. Lovice. By Mrs. Hungerford.

3211/12. The Scenery of Switzerland (with Illustrations). By Sir John Lubbock.

3213. The Years that the Locust hath Eaten. By Annie E. Holdsworth.

3214/15. A Modern Corsair. By Richard Henry Savage.

3216. Sketches in Lavender, Blue and Green. By Jerome K. Jerome.

3217/18. A History of our own Times. By Justin McCarthy. Vols. 6 & 7 (supplemental).

3219. A Passing Madness. By Florence Marryat.

3220. A Rose of Yesterday. By F. Marion Crawford.

3221. The Ways of Life. By Mrs. Oliphant.

3222. Uncle Bernac. By A. Conan Doyle.

3223. Dear Faustina. By Rhoda Broughton.

The Tauchnitz Edition is to be had of all Booksellers and Railway Libraries on the Continent, price ℳ 1,60. or 2 francs per volume. A complete Catarue of the Tauchnitz Edition is attached to this work.